SNAKEBITTEN

SHADOWS OF EIRELAND
BOOK THREE

JOANNA MACIEJEWSKA

To futures hopeful and brighter,
may you always come

CHAPTER ONE

S adb cut low and wide, her speed close to unnatural. I leaped backward, with much less nimbleness and with much more desperation than I'd hoped for. I slashed my own weapon rather blindly, not even trying to strike her, only hoping to buy myself some time.

As I landed, I caught a smirk, making it clear I failed to fool her, and all of a sudden, the training room became smaller. Even though I was somewhat in the middle of its open space, I felt like a cornered animal with no way out.

My instincts weren't wrong. Within several quick steps, Sadb was in front of me, her training blade by my neck. All I got to do in that time was blink.

I spread my arms in a surrender gesture, because I was tired enough to make even more mistakes, and I had no doubt that I'd pay for each dearly. Ever since I got serious about training with her, Sadb had stopped beating me up, but bruises still happened. While she always delivered her strikes with immaculate precision, my own moves still resembled jerks of a spider hit with bug spray, so once or twice I put my limbs in the trajectory of her training weapon.

"You came to train on a morning after a dangerous ambush when ceannasaí told us all to rest," she said. "And you haven't used your curses at all."

Suspicion was clear in her words, and I couldn't blame her. Curses, or rather the props we used during training, were the only thing that made it possible for me to land any hits on her. And with my officially joining the team, which took me off the hook when it came to "basic training," Sadb was right to expect me to skip a day, or even a week, of being her punching bag.

She inspected me with narrowed eyes. "Is this about Riagán?" she asked before I could come up with an answer. "Last night, in the showers, you looked comfortable enough, so we left you two alone, but if he did something..."

I shook my head without hesitation. "No, everything's fine."

At least, I hoped it was.

We had plans for that evening that included fulfilling our promises to each other and, if I understood it right, expressing feelings for each other. Showering together, to wash off the memories of the ambush we'd both risked our lives in, was the first step. And then the second step had never happened. Hot water and Riagán's caress took away the immense stress of being bait and worrying for his life, and once they were gone, my body was ready to give up on being alert and awake. I vaguely remembered getting back to Riagán's room and into his bed, but no conversation ever happened.

I could swear he said something before I faded off, but I had no recollection of his words, only his voice, soft and caring... But was there disappointment in it as well? In the morning, I regretted not making an effort to stay awake, even if I had to fight my body every step of the way. But with Riagán still asleep, in that deep slumber exhausted people fall into, it felt better to go about my routine rather than lie awake and speculate.

Something of my thoughts must have reflected on my face, because Sadb said, "And that's why you're here, training, and without curses on top of that, as if you were asking for a beating."

"It's because I realized you were right." I gave her the victory she was due and got an arched eyebrow in response. "I rely on my curses too much, and after each fight I will have to restock or remake at least some of them. If I'm in the field longer, I might run out of them too quickly."

I expected her to at least give me the "I told you so" look, but instead, she was looking at me with a mix of concern and suspicion.

"I can never tell with you whether you're saying what you think I want to hear or if you actually mean it," she said. Her face changed, with a flash of pain twisting it, but she got it under control quickly. "If Laoise was here, I'd send you straight to her. Or Cait. They were both much better at it. But there's only five of us now, and unless you'd rather talk about Riagán with Faolan or our ceannasaí, I'm your only choice."

She took me by surprise. In the past weeks, her attitude toward me had changed, and my being a team player when it came to the ambush we'd set and other situations likely had something to do with it, but I hadn't expected she'd be actually interested in any kind of personal relation.

At loss for words, I said the first thing that came to mind:

"You have a point there, but I could also try Connor…" Outside of the Scáthanna, he was my only friend at the Court, and I was comfortable talking to him.

Sadb snorted. "Taking relationship advice from a mythborn who can't get his own feelings sorted? At least I can say I had a relationship."

The way she said it made it clear it had been a good one, too. And the way she looked at me… She cared, even if only because I was her teammate.

I took a breath.

"We were supposed to talk last night, but I was so tired that I didn't really make an effort to make it happen," I said. "I don't want Riagán to think that I was trying to avoid that conversation. When I woke up, he was still deep asleep, so I came up here."

Her eyebrows shot up in a genuine surprise. "You sleep together."

Since I found no disapproval in her voice, it must have been something normal enough among mythborn. I nodded without getting into explaining that we *just* slept together.

"It's not how the humanborn do it, is it?" she asked with genuine curiosity.

"Humans… We… *They* are all over the place. Some have sex almost immediately, while others wait till marriage." I shrugged. "I suppose figuring out relationships is difficult no matter if you're human, humanborn, myth-touched, or mythborn. But Riagán and I are trying, and we haven't ruined it so far."

Her face softened with a smile. "When Riagán got interested in you, we all thought this wasn't going to end well. You proved us wrong. More than that. It's been a while since a certain humanborn who was playing a myth-touched walked in here." Sadb made a gesture encompassing the room. "Now she's a real myth-touched and a real Shadow. If you still want to train, come in the mornings when you're free, and I'll teach you more. I'll also get Faolan to spar with us. This way, you can learn how to fight alongside your teammates... and maybe finally get a win."

I was quite certain that such a feat would require both Cathal and Riagán to join the sparring match, with all four of us against Sadb, and I still anticipated our loss.

"Now that would be a victory worth celebration," I said more to myself than her.

She cocked her head, attentive and catching that there was more to my remark.

"Yesterday wasn't enough." She didn't make it a question, as if she knew I wouldn't deny it.

That "yesterday" she referred to already felt like a lifetime ago, though the echo of adrenaline still coursed through my veins, and the memories of the ambush I was willing bait in were still fresh. "Yesterday" was when I expressed my disappointment that our efforts brought us nothing but the name of our enemy, something he could easily change, and his description, which also could be altered to a degree. But "yesterday" was also when the Scáthanna recognized me as their member, and it meant a lot to them after all the losses they'd suffered, even if I personally felt like I hardly did anything worth such inclusion.

But the way Sadb said it... It wasn't a question, and it wasn't an accusation either. She was agreeing with me, and knowing enough of her personal past, I understood why. We all wanted revenge for the deaths of Laoise, Cait, and

Lorcan, but even if they were like family to everyone on the team, only Sadb had a lover among them.

"It's not going to be enough until he pays," I said with force.

Sadb gave me a short nod. "He will."

I didn't share her conviction. While I had no doubt that the Court had enough power to chase down a mythborn like Muiredach simply by finding his associates, hideouts, and other resources he relied on, Eireland was big enough and empty enough for him to disappear somewhere in the countryside. He could hide in Wicklow Mountains or even far in the west, staying clear of large cities, and if enough time passed, the Court would be less willing to stay focused on a one-man hunt. Out of sight, out of mind... Or, as Polish people would say, what goes away from your eyesight also goes away from your heart—and the Court's heart would be hardly in it to begin with. This was the Scáthanna's enemy.

Sadb was watching me, and I had a feeling she knew exactly what I was thinking. "*We* will never stop hunting him."

There was power and determination in her words. It said that nobody came after the Scáthanna and got away with it. Muiredach hurt us bad, and we would make sure he paid... even if it meant hunting him forever.

"But that's tomorrow." Sadb gave me a friendly nudge. "Today, you should rest. Spend time with Riagán."

It was kind of her to say so, especially when she was dealing with her own loss, but at the same time, I felt a pang of guilt. It wasn't hard to picture her sitting alone in her room or maybe training to exhaustion, consumed by dark thoughts and overwhelming pain.

I'd been where she was when my sister died by a giant,

and I knew all too well that being alone during such time brewed wrong ideas and even worse actions.

I hesitated, unsure what I could offer her. She'd hardly be interested in hanging out with me and Riagán, being an obvious third wheel, and I couldn't force her to spend time with anyone else. I also didn't have the stamina to insist she trained me more.

"Don't worry about me," she said all of a sudden. "I have a name. I have a target. I'll be fine."

I should have dropped the topic, allowing Sadb her excuse and myself some peace of mind. But just as she cared about me, I did about her, so I asked, "And what happens when the target is no more?"

"After that, I suppose, I could show you how to kill giants."

I gaped, thoughts running through my head like panicked little animals. I hadn't told anyone in the Scáthanna, not even Riagán, about how my sister died. Only a handful of people knew—my old team from the wartime, Albert, possibly Orla...

My thoughts came to a screeching halt. This was enough. I might never talk about Ela's death, but it wasn't a secret, and I didn't see it as one. So it would take as little as someone mentioning it to someone else in passing, perhaps out of care or concern for me, and another person would know. Then another, and another... Then someone else eavesdropping would pass the knowledge further, and there were many information brokers in Dublin, some more interested in secrets and personal details that could be exploited, so it wasn't a surprise that the Scáthanna learned about my past, especially about an event so important to me.

Sadb had already turned away from me, starting a series

of complex strikes and transitioning from training me to practicing on her own.

I took the cue, put my training weapon and curses away, and headed for the door.

Yet her words still rang in my ears. I had never expressed a desire for revenge, and I hadn't even thought about it. At the time my sister died, I was too shocked to feel anything but the overwhelming pain that tore me apart, shattering any clear thought I could have had. I didn't even care to pay attention to the giant who did it. Ela's death was all that mattered at that time. Of course, I hated giants and feared them all the same, but I never attached those feelings to any particular creature. Even now, when perhaps I finally had means to exact some kind of revenge, I didn't feel the need for it. I always perceived giants as mindless beings, so to seek retribution from them would be like seeking retribution from a storm that tore your house's roof.

Sadb was smart, and she clearly knew me well enough to have guessed that. I had no doubt that she wouldn't back out if I decided to take her up on her offer, but I was also certain her remark was meant to be something else. She was reminding me that I experienced a loss as great as hers, and I managed to go on, no matter how much I suffered.

So when she said she would be fine, she meant it. Perhaps she was also suggesting that I shouldn't be butting into her grieving process, whatever it was, especially since it wasn't likely her first loss either. Of course, it didn't mean I shouldn't care or be concerned about her, but until she sought my help, I should stop mommying her.

"Same time tomorrow?" she asked just when I was about to leave.

I sent her a smile. "Sure. If I have nothing better to do."

Her dry laugh was the only response.

I SPENT way too much time in the shower, especially considering that I was in there alone, without any distractions from one handsome and cheeky mythborn archer. Of course, simply thinking of Riagán made me long for his company, especially that we didn't get to talk the previous night.

I had never considered myself overly romantic, and war —along with my tangled relationship with Albert—had washed out any sentiments toward heartfelt expressions of one's feelings, but Riagán's behavior had reignited the spark of wanting something like that in a relationship. I was certain he wouldn't go all mushy with me, but the prospect of having someone looking softly into my eyes and at the same time being ready to have serious conversations instead of a string of constant arguments was an appealing one. It seemed... healthy. Like something a relationship should be.

Sadb was right about spending some time with him, as worry-free as we could manage before we had to risk our lives again.

Then, when I got out of the showers, I saw Cathal leaning against the doorframe. Deep in thought and motionless, he came to life as soon as our eyes met, giving me that sinking feeling I wouldn't get to spend the day carelessly.

Much less relaxed than moments ago, I rushed to put my clothes on. Cathal might not seem in a hurry, but I wanted to know what was going on.

"Riagán said you were training with Sadb," he said when I finally approached him. "And she said you already left. Is there's something else you were planning to do?"

I wanted food, and I wanted Riagán, but I shook my head. Both could wait.

He headed out into the corridor, motioning for me to follow. We walked into his office, and after he closed the door, he pushed his only chair toward me.

"Take a seat."

Before I could object, he sat on top of his desk in a relaxed pose, suggesting we were going to have an informal talk... or at least that I wasn't in trouble. With no other choice, I sat down as well.

"You're going to Trinity," he said. "The lady requested it, and I won't refuse."

"She *requested* it?" I couldn't help my suspicions.

After months of keeping me away from Albert and other Trinitians, Lady Eithne was all of a sudden sending me to Trinity... There had to be more to it, and I could only hope it wasn't Albert doing something stupid out of an ill-conceived care for my wellbeing. There was also the matter of Eithne playing some political game in which she wanted me as her pawn. Just because I answered to Cathal now didn't mean I could ignore her requests, no matter what schemes she weaved.

"We lost contact with Tadgh." Cathal seemed to be reading my mind—not that it was difficult, considering what I thought of Eithne. "Our other sources at Trinity suggest that he might have been imprisoned, but we don't know on what charges. The lady believes you might be the only person who can figure out what happened without putting him in more danger."

I exhaled slowly. Last time I'd met Tadgh, the only myth-born Trinitian, he implied that he had ties with the Court, but to hear about it so openly reminded me once more that no matter how I wanted to look at my current situation, I had switched sides. What was worse, no matter how much I wanted or tried, from now on I'd be forever keeping some things secret from Albert.

I just hoped that the price I was to pay for my choice of joining the Scáthanna wouldn't be too steep.

"I'll do what I can," I said. I didn't have to tell him to not expect miracles.

Cathal nodded. "I'll send Sadb and Faolan with you. You'll be the lady's messenger, and they'll act as your guards. You should receive the Court's emblem and a suiting outfit shortly."

If the mood was lighter, I'd amuse myself by picturing one Kaja doing an impression of one Eithne, complete with trying to move so gracefully that it looked like flowing in the air. Yeah... That wasn't going to happen even if I wanted to try.

"If it's possible, I'd prefer to go in my uniform instead."

I'd surprised him, and he didn't manage to hide it. "That's... unexpected."

Even though I didn't fuss too much about wearing the Scáthanna's outfit in general, he must have suspected I was still uneasy about it at times. I also didn't wear it when we went to visit my alchemist friend, Max, and he likely thought I'd prefer to wear something neutral for a Trinity visit too.

"Albert will learn soon enough, if he hasn't already," I said. "If he catches me lying, I blow any chance I have at helping Tadgh. I assume that the lady's hope of solving this relies on me still having Albert's trust."

"Wearing our uniform isn't going to help with that trust." Cathal was watching me with curiosity.

"No, it won't," I agreed. "But at least I'd have the chip of never having lied to him to play."

"Very well. You're being sent because you know how to best handle Albert, and since the lady decided to leave it up to you, I see no reason to impose anything on you." He sighed. "I would, though, accept both the emblem and the outfit when they are delivered."

"Less hassle this way," I agreed.

The last thing we needed was Eithne overruling my decision and forcing me into an outfit that could be considered deceptive.

"Take your time with this one, Kaja. If you think your success requires you to be friendly with Albert and spend hours talking about the past, or the present, no one will hold it against you. And if you need a private conversation, Sadb and Faolan will know not to insist to be by your side all the time, although it would be good if they were always nearby."

I knew he wasn't suggesting that I was in any real danger from Albert or other Trinitians. Sure, Albert could insist on keeping me there if he decided that the Court was using me against my will, but he wouldn't put me in any real danger.

"Muiredach," I said.

Cathal nodded grimly. "I'm sure he's going to try again. He targeted you once already, even when he suspected we were baiting him, which means he believes you have whatever information he seeks."

I wasn't so sure about it. I'd been with the Scáthanna for such a short time, I barely had access to any secrets, but the fact was that Muiredach didn't seem to care. Unless, of course, I became an unexpected opportunity, and he wanted me for other information I knew. I *did* know many Trinitian secrets, and once he was done extracting those, then he'd resume hunting for what he wanted from the rest of the Scáthanna.

I sighed. I couldn't reassure Cathal that Trinity would be

a safe place. Muiredach clearly had spies at the Court, so we had to assume he had informants among Albert's people as well.

"There's one more thing I want to discuss with you," Cathal broke the silence first. "I won't give you an order. This is something that you have to agree to, because I'd put you in more danger than just being bait in a trap. I'll tell you what I have in mind, but if you agree, you'll mention it to no one, not even Riagán. I trust all of my team, but it would be enough for someone else to eavesdrop on your conversation with others, and Muiredach could learn about it. If it happens, it'll mean your death." He looked me in the eye. "This goes way beyond the orders I give, and if after hearing me out you aren't certain you can do it, you should refuse, and I'll think no less of you. We'll find another way."

I took a slow breath in, then let the air out even slower. The tone of his voice made it clear that whatever he had in mind verged on a suicide mission. Yet if it was within my means to do it, I wouldn't refuse. In the war, I carried out Albert's orders without questioning them or thinking about myself, and I was hardly a Trinitian back then. I couldn't do less for the people who were becoming my family and for whom I was starting to care about deeper than anyone else.

Besides, if we didn't do something to gain the upper hand over our enemy, I could end up dead anyway—along with all other members of the Scáthanna.

"If you think I can do it, I'll do it."

As soon as I changed into my uniform, I knocked on Riagán's door.

Perhaps I should have waited to have my mind clearer

after the conversation with Cathal sent it spinning, but I didn't want any more delays. Even though Eithne's request wasn't urgent enough to force me to drop everything and go immediately, I sensed that neither her nor Cathal would appreciate my sluggishness. After all, Tadgh's life could be on the line.

Riagán's voice came from the inside, the mythborn word that I'd learned to recognize as an invitation to enter, so I opened the door and stepped in. He was sitting at his desk, with his bow in front of him. I didn't know much about bow making, and I knew he wasn't well versed in charms, so it had to be some sort of a regular maintenance.

"Kaja?" He looked at me, surprised. "Ceannasaí came looking for you, so I thought you'd have headed out already."

"Without a goodbye kiss?"

His surprise shifted into a smile. "Now that sounds promising. How much time do you have?"

"Enough," I replied while I closed the door behind me—though, looking at the hunger in his eyes, I couldn't help wondering whether even an eternity would be "enough." It was great to feel wanted that fiercely, and I had to make sure he knew I wanted him too.

He got to me without delay, his embrace as strong as always.

"I'm going to Trinity." As soon as I said it, I felt him stiffen for a heartbeat. "Lady's orders. But I didn't want to go before we talked."

He let go, looking at me with a serious expression. "You don't have to."

"I want to. And it's not about going to Trinity or Albert."

Before he had a chance to say anything, I spun us around and pushed him against the door. Not a feat I could have accomplished if he was on his guard, but thankfully, he didn't see it coming. It got his attention, and he remained silent.

"I like that we're taking things slow and building something that will last, but I wanted you to know that it doesn't mean I'm unsure. Not anymore." I took a deep breath. "I love you."

There, I'd said it. It didn't feel like the right way and the right time, but one thing I'd learned during the war was that if you waited too long, you had already lost your chance. Just yesterday, either of us could have died in the trap the Scáthanna had set, and now Cathal was sending me on a dangerous mission. Even if I couldn't tell Riagán anything about our ceannasaí's true plan, I could at least ensure neither of us would regret waiting should the worst come to pass.

He was looking at me, quiet and calm, his eyes shimmering with silver. Too quiet for his cheeky nature.

Perhaps waiting would have been a better choice...

I broke the silence before it became uncomfortable. "This is not how the mythborn do it, is it?" I might have sounded slightly dismayed—leave it to Kaja to pick the wrong time and the wrong way.

Without any warning, he pulled me closer. His lips beside my ear, he whispered something in mythborn language. It sounded like the words he'd said the previous night, right before I fell asleep. Without my listening skill engaged, which allowed me to understand other languages, I didn't know what exactly they meant, but there was a mesmerizing beauty and softness in their rhythm and sound.

"This is how the mythborn do it," he said softly. "Though circumstances are usually more fitting for the occasion," he added with a hint of amusement. "But the humanborn way... Kaja's way has a certain appeal." He brushed my face, looking at me with sudden gentleness. "I have a feeling there's more to it, and it's not that we didn't get to talk last night."

I hesitated. The last thing I wanted was to avoid the truth with Riagán as if it meant falling into my old relationship patterns with Albert—even if said avoidance came long after we'd split. I couldn't tell him everything, and I was certain that he would be the one to understand. After all, he'd been taking orders from Cathal much longer than I had.

Yet I could still offer him as much truth as possible. "I worry. I talked to Sadb this morning, and it made me realize that I don't want to regret never telling you. Neither of us leads a peaceful life to afford ourselves waiting, perhaps forever, for the right moment. Today, I'm going to Trinity. Tomorrow, ceannasaí might send you to the other side of Eireland. And the day after tomorrow... The day after tomorrow, it might already be too late."

"I understand," Riagán replied.

He didn't try to belittle my fears or argue how unlikely something was to happen in a span of just few days, and that alone made my confession worth it.

"Whatever time we have, we will use it all," he added.

"How about breakfast together, then?" I asked. "I need some food before I head out. I don't think I can deal with Albert on an empty stomach." I wanted more than just a breakfast with him, but as he said, we'd use the time we had.

Familiar, playful sparks appeared in his eyes. "Sharing a meal with a meager mythborn archer and making the commander of Trinity wait even longer than he already has? How could I refuse such an offer?"

I chuckled, enjoying his teasing tone. After all that we'd been through just recently, to have him in a good mood was making my own concerns fade. As I hugged him tight, not caring whether we'd be able to walk down to the day room that way, I clung to those feelings of joy and carelessness, hoping that I would be able to forget for a little while about the suicide mission I had agreed to carry out.

CHAPTER TWO

Faolan, Sadb, and I walked most of the way to Trinity along the river's north bank. An ambush was probable on any route we chose, but with the river to our right, we only had to worry about being attacked from one side.

Sadb also instructed me that if there were too many opponents, I was to make it to any bridge and plead to the bridge dwellers to let me through—or to offer me shelter—promising a reward from the Court. According to her, the dwellers who lived in the bridge communities, were the least likely to actively conspire with the Snake, and even if one of them was a spy, he or she wouldn't do anything open while the whole community was watching.

I didn't like the idea of leaving Sadb and Faolan behind, but it made sense that the two of them would have a much better chance at surviving if they didn't have to worry about protecting me.

The Liffey's black surface looked calm, without a single ripple disturbing it, but my myth-touched senses couldn't ignore the chaotic magic boiling within, like a shoal of piranhas in a feeding frenzy. In a way, it resembled the old me, humanborn on the surface but within consumed by chaos and corruption of the magical affliction I suffered from. If this was how the mythborn saw me, it was no wonder that back then, both Eithne and Tadgh could see how little time I had left.

Wearing our full gear, we startled strolling mythborn and the few humanborn who had business on the north side of Dublin. With Eireland Office still lying in ruins, courtesy of the recent bombings orchestrated by servants of the Snake, the air carried fear of another war, and three battle-ready members of the Scáthanna must have fed those concerns. Unfortunately, we didn't have time to put people at ease, so the best we could do was keep moving to at least reassure them that they weren't our target.

We crossed the O'Connell Bridge, and the bridge dwellers let us through without demanding any toll, throwing uneasy glances at our weapons. I doubted the three of us could take them all down, but we clearly looked the part. Many bulging eyes followed our passage from behind the curtains that hung at the entrances to their primitive shacks. Even if in the war the dwellers kept to themselves, ignoring most of the fighting, they still worried. War meant that commerce would die first, and people would have fewer reasons to go across the river. Not to mention that at any time their homes, the bridges, could become a target for destructive curses if the humanborn or the mythborn tried to prevent each other from crossing.

As we stepped onto the south side, we drew even more attention, though most of the humanborn didn't stare. One glance at our uniforms and weapons, and they would carry on whatever they were doing in such a devoted manner that it was clear they didn't want to stir any trouble. Or, perhaps, they were counting on the Trinitians to take the brunt of any confrontation, and there was wisdom in that approach.

Only now and then did some tourists, funny with their cheap protection charms attached to their electronic devices, shamelessly snap a photo or two of us. None had the courage to ask to have a picture taken *with* us.

I tried to imagine how it was out there, away from Eireland, in the world that was magic-free. Those who could afford a visit must be excited to experience Dublin first-hand. It always had seemed magical to the newcomers, but ever since the Magiclysm, it was much more than just the city's atmosphere. They got to tour magic-altered places, observe cruel rituals of the bridge dwellers, and witness the workings of amulets and charms while still experiencing all the best that Eireland had to offer—its famous stout, whiskeys, beautiful countryside, and many monuments.

I sighed. If the country got back on its feet, we'd make a lot of money on tourism, magic research, and maybe even pop culture if some mythborn were willing to star in movies and so on. Undoubtedly, they'd love the attention and the crowds' awe... Instead, the heavy cloud of brewing conflict seemed to endlessly hang over the island, competing with actual clouds, which at least had the decency to clear up every now and then, even if hardly anyone noticed those flashes of good weather.

"Not looking forward to seeing your friends?" Sadb asked.

She must have misread my sigh, but she wasn't wrong, and her question swapped one kind of concern for another.

"It'd be easier if I was actually going there to see them, not for other reasons."

"The closer we get to Trinity, the more humanborn you

sound." Faolan didn't hide his discontent. "You could at least pretend you're one of us now."

"That would make me useless to the lady, wouldn't it?" I fired back. "The only reason I'm going is that I'm as human-born as you can get without having to trust an actual humanborn."

"Or you could tell us where they usually hold their prisoners, and we'd have Tadgh out before you were even done saying hi to Albert," he replied with worrying cheerfulness.

Sadb chuckled and nudged Faolan, and I just gave them a side-eye, because we were about to approach Trinity's gate. I'd rather not have a Trinitian overhear any breakout plans, no matter how jokingly they were put.

The guards tensed at our sight, so we approached slowly, and I raised my hand, presenting the Court ring I got from Eithne. Fancy but heavy silverwork of entangled Celtic weave with the Court's emblem carved into an emerald bigger than necessary if it was there for decorative purposes. This piece of jewelry was likely valuable enough to ensure a four-member family's survival for a year. And much, much longer if they sold it outside of Eireland.

Sadb and Faolan kept half a step away, following Cathal's order to act as my guards. Neither of them complained about it, even though both were my seniors and better fighters. Obeying Cathal's every word aside, the Scáthanna cared little about made-up ranks and much more about who was the right person for the job. They also knew that if it came to fighting, I'd follow their commands in turn.

"What business do you have in Trinity?" A middle-aged woman with a burn scar covering part of her forehead at least tried to sound neutral, but the glare she gave us made it clear she recognized the Scáthanna's emblems.

In a way, I now understood the role my team had in the

war. Though they weren't any worse than any other myth-born and definitely didn't do anything that everyone else, humanborn and mythborn, wasn't doing, they were the best and most efficient, and their uniforms and emblems made them instantly recognizable, so instead of hating some face-less mythborn, Trinitians had a much less abstract object for their loathing.

"I need to speak with the commander." I scanned their faces, but none looked familiar. Not that, I realized belat-edly, it would have helped me if they did... After all, I doubted anyone would recognize Kaja in me, and claiming my old name could be seen as deception—though it would certainly get Albert's attention. "On behalf of the Court."

If all else failed, I had my old Eireland ID at the ready, and they would have to report to the higher-ups that the Scáthanna had brought a humanborn document. Most of the officers knew my name, and the message would eventu-ally reach Albert.

Yet it seemed that Eithne's ring had enough metaphor-ical weight to add to its actual weight to instill some trust. The woman cringed but whistled, and a messenger girl came running from the inner yard. They exchanged several hushed words to the side, unaware that I could hear them perfectly, and then the kid saluted and took off. I shook my head slightly, looking at Sadb and Faolan to let them know that the Trinitians weren't planning to ambush us... at least not yet.

"You may enter the yard." The tone of the woman's voice suggested she'd rather refuse us. "You will wait there until someone comes to collect you."

They let us in without a scan—what a relief! We all wore all of our gear, which meant plenty of protective amulets and offensive curses. Reasonably, the Trinitians would have to have expected we wouldn't enter the grounds unarmed, but they could still argue against letting us in unless we surrendered all the offensive gear... which was not going to happen. And then, when we refused, I could see how the situation could escalate, potentially all the way up to physical violence, which would not help my mission in particular and maintaining peace in general. Wars had been started over smaller things.

We walked into the yard, drawing glares and stirring whispers of both concern and hate. There was bitter amusement in my realization that they knew of their most loathed enemies so little, they didn't even recognize a newcomer in me. Any mythborn could wear our uniform and receive the same treatment.

Not that I was any better before I met the Scáthanna for the first time. I knew of Riagán, though only because of his signature arrows, and when it came to the rest of the team, they were people one avoided in the war.

While we stood in the yard, I engaged my listening skill, making sure nobody was trying to set up an attack, so I heard Orla's firm orders to stop gawking and get back to work as soon as she got to the yard. I turned right in time to meet her as she approached from the side.

She looked me up and down, ignoring the two others, and I had no doubt she recognized me.

"Your fashion choices have become worse since the last time I saw you," she said dryly, and between the lines, I read her disapproval.

"Then you'll be delighted to hear my radiant personality didn't change at all," I offered in return.

That earned me an amused smile. "One could have hoped for the opposite..." Her voice warmed up. "Do we get to talk to you in private, or do we have to invite your... companions?"

The look she gave them was hardly friendly, but on the other hand, it was Orla. "Friendly" wasn't how one would describe her behavior even on her best days.

I hesitated, keeping Cathal's words, *all* of his words, in mind. Yes, they were supposed to be my guards and should stay nearby, but if we wanted Muiredach to try something, we had to take risks. Outside of the Court, Trinity was the only place where it would be justifiable for me to be relatively alone.

Faolan glanced at me, likely reading my hesitation all wrong, and he grinned at Orla as if unmoved by the cold reception. "Do you have somewhere comfortable for us to wait? Or are we supposed to remain on display until Kaja's done?"

Sadb was watching at me with an unspoken question in her eyes. I gave her a cautious nod—yes, I knew what I was doing.

Orla waved, and the same messenger girl approached us. "Rita will take you to one of our guest rooms."

"This way, please!" The girl straightened her back, and her brown ponytail bobbed as she pointed toward one of the side doors. With that serious expression on her youthful face, I couldn't help but wonder whether she was trying to imitate Orla.

I doubted anyone else could tell, but I knew Sadb and Faolan well enough to see they were uneasy about leaving me alone, even on Trinity's grounds... Or perhaps *especially* on Trinity's grounds? I might be a myth-touched and a member of the Scáthanna now, but I still felt safe and comfortable within the old college's walls, while to them it was nothing more than the enemy's stronghold. In a way, I felt uneasy about losing them from my sight too. Without me around, they were perfect targets for subterfuge or provocation, and they couldn't rely on their knowledge to tell foul play apart from general but harmless unfriendliness.

"Now I understand why your letters were so brief," Orla said once we were alone.

She led me inside and through the familiar corridors. In the past, I would walk that route alone, unless some overzealous officer decided to assign an escort to me, but I didn't look like myself anymore. With my new physique and my uniform, I looked like an enemy, if officially a former one, and no one in their right mind would let a person like that wander alone through their safe haven.

In a way, I was lucky that it was Orla who came to collect us from the yard, because she knew me and wouldn't insist on an even bigger escort, though it also meant I had to put up with her disapproval and remarks.

I'd be lying if I said her behavior toward me, colder than usual, didn't sting, but there was a price to pay for every-thing, and I'd made my choices. Shortly after the whole mess with Muiredach started, Cathal had given me an opportunity to leave, but I decided to stay. I didn't regret it. I was part of a team again, and it was one that—contrary to Trinity—made me feel like I belonged. They were worth enduring mean glares and Orla's remarks.

We walked up the stairs, passing several Trinitians who eyed us with curiosity and caution. Undoubtedly, word would spread about the unusual guests, but I hoped Orla and Albert wouldn't go about telling everyone who I was. Eithne had said nothing about keeping the existence of the myth-touched secret, and she had to know that sending me to Trinity was bound to make some people aware of it. I just didn't want to deal with it, not yet. Not when I had to figure out what happened to Tadgh, and not with Muiredach still out there, posing an unknown threat.

"So what happened that you finally decided to visit us?" Orla asked.

I couldn't answer that question, so I went for correcting her assumption instead. "If it was *my* decision, I'd have been here the very moment I came to after the ritual. But Eithne had her own ideas, and then things got complicated."

I didn't feel bad about badmouthing Eithne. After all, my lack of visits was mostly on her. And if she hadn't kept me contained at the Court, instead giving me back my freedom, I'd have never ended up in the Scáthanna...

No. I immediately realized that it wasn't true. With Laoise's death, Cathal still would have made me an offer, and even if I wouldn't have been desperate to take it in order to gain any freedom from Eithne, I had a feeling I would have agreed anyway. I never forgot how they'd saved my life back when I wasn't even one of them and, for all they knew, I was about to turn into a monster.

"And that's why you're walking around wearing the enemy's uniform?" Orla asked.

It didn't escape me that her tone held an extra layer of hostility compared to how she'd treated me in the past.

I didn't take the bait. I could tell her that the only other choice I had was death, or that the mythborn weren't enemies anymore, but I knew Orla well enough. She didn't forget all that had happened in the war, and though she kept her feelings to herself, she didn't trust the mythborn much. In a way, I understood her. To see me in that uniform likely felt like betrayal to her, and even if I wasn't going to let her drag us into argument, ignoring her question was not an option.

Within a heartbeat, I moved in front of her, my eyes locked on hers. "Your understanding is the last thing I need. You never liked me anyway, so how I look or what I wear changes little."

If my speed surprised her, she didn't show it. "You got a point there," she replied without the previous animosity, as if my behavior reminded her that no matter what I looked like, I was still Kaja. "But you know, it's not going to be easy, and what you wear isn't helping," she added like a peace offering.

"I'm not expecting it to be, but I never lied to either of you, no matter how difficult the truth was." Sure, we both knew sometimes I walked a very fine line, but she would remember that more often than not I was upfront about things... even if it meant admitting I couldn't share some information with them. "I might have changed sides, as you see it, but I didn't become a liar."

She didn't have to believe me. If she thought my changing sides meant adapting to mythborn ways, she could be convinced this was exactly what a liar would say, banking on the long years of trust the humanborn Kaja had built. I couldn't do anything about it. All I had was the truth and a somewhat clean record of always being trustworthy, even if sometimes I wasn't entirely open about things.

We stopped at the door to Albert's office. Orla stood quiet, looking at me in thought, and I knew she hadn't decided outright that I was a liar, but she was uncertain if she could still trust me as much as she had in the past. I took it as a win.

The corner of her lips curled ever so slightly, as if she knew I knew. After all, we had enough of the past in common to make it hard to deceive each other.

"Good luck," she said, and walked away.

I stood in the corridor alone, her words making me realize that, indeed, what she thought of me was not important. The real test awaited me behind the door in front of me.

Before fear could get the better of me, I knocked.

ALBERT WAS WRITING at his desk when I entered. He looked as he always did, his hair cropped short, his square jaw cleanly shaved, and his battle slacks in perfect condition. As he lifted his head to check who his guest was, he froze, and we stared at each other for a painfully long moment.

"Kaja." The tone of his voice suggested he wanted me to deny it.

I could read suffering in his eyes, the expression reserved for the nearest and dearest who ended up badly scarred or maimed in an accident.

"I wanted to come sooner, but they wouldn't let me," I offered as an apology.

It felt wrong to simplify the complicated situation at the Court to one sentence, but it wasn't the time for lengthy explanations.

He grimaced. "It's quite a coincidence, then, that you get to visit right after I caught Eithne's spy." He sighed and gestured for me to sit down. "Tea? Or something else?"

Oh, Albert, always courteous and polite, no matter the circumstances.

"Tea's fine." It seemed that I couldn't even count on a bit of a catch-up between friends before we got to business, but perhaps there was no friendship between us anymore. "And indeed, quite a coincidence that you find a so-called spy right when someone is trying really hard to lure me out of the Court."

Albert went to turn the kettle on, another grimace flashing on his face. "Do you really think I'd have my own people accused and imprisoned just to see you? And that Eithne would care about it if she didn't actually have a spy here?"

"Not you. But the mythborn are being hunted, and I'm likely next on the list." I leaned back in my chair, twisting my head to keep him in view. "And the spy you caught is, of course, the only mythborn in Trinity, because it's easier to accuse him than make you believe one of your fellow humanborn could be working for the enemy."

He served us tea, and to my surprise, I found no milk in mine. After years of not paying attention to my beverage preferences and absent-mindedly adding milk to both cups, he'd finally remembered. It was a bittersweet victory, seeing as it came after my transformation most likely had shattered our friendship. I tried to hide my feelings. Yes, I looked different, but I was still the same person, and I hoped for at least some willingness to look past my new physique.

"Yet you're here, proving that Tadgh is not as innocent as he's supposed to be. Eithne must be a fool if she thought I wouldn't connect the dots," he said.

His remark gave me pause. Eithne was anything but stupid. I thought of her emerald eyes, staring intensely as if nothing escaped them, and about all those times she'd played me with ease. She must have known Albert wouldn't ignore facts just because I finally showed up at Trinity, yet she insisted on sending me. She was expecting something— something only I could make happen.

I smiled when the puzzle pieces fell into place. "I think

she counted on me being open with you, and that you would listen."

Before we left, Cathal made it clear that I was to handle the matter how I saw fit. He never mentioned any secrets that I should keep away from Trinitians, and he didn't even caution me about revealing too much even when I shared my plans to be truthful with Albert. I might be wrong, but if I wanted to make sure Tadgh didn't end up as a dead traitor, honesty seemed the best way to go.

"Yes, Tadgh has ties to the Court," I continued, "but as far as I know, he's not here to spy, and he never did anything to harm Trinity or people here." I lifted my hand as Albert opened his mouth, likely to protest. "He's been here since the war. Back then security was tighter, and he was watched closely and hardly trusted. Doesn't it seem odd to you that after all those years his foot slips all of a sudden? He's been here for years, and he isn't stupid enough to allow himself to be off guard, no matter how lax Trinity's security might be."

Albert took a sip of tea, and I could almost sense the battle he was waging with himself. He'd rather not admit that I had a point, but after my honest display, he seemed uneasy about discarding it. "You said someone's after you."

Normally, I'd curse him for changing the topic to a more personal one, but in this case, the question was actually related. "We don't know much. He's a mythborn who goes by the name of Muiredach, and so far he's been targeting the Scáthanna. He has spies at the Court, and some human-born work for him. I wouldn't discard the idea that he has someone here too."

"The Snake again?" Albert asked.

I wasn't ready to share my suspicions that servants of the Snake, a malicious otherworldly being threatening the peace, seemed to be involved in all the turmoil across

Dublin, and perhaps even all of Eireland. He'd likely discard them as paranoia, so I shrugged.

"Maybe. I don't know. If he serves the Snake, it's something more than a sentient Afflicted distributing pamphlets and explosives. This mythborn is cunning. He sets up traps, and so far we've found no solid trace of him."

"But you know his name." Albert arched his eyebrow.

We also knew his voice, but that was another thing I wasn't about to mention to Albert. Honesty was one thing—not talking about things that could give up the only advantage the Scáthanna had over our enemy was another.

"We got some of his henchmen alive, and they decided they valued their lives more than loyalty."

I knew better than to mention we'd set up a trap in which I was bait. Even though it would likely take us in a familiar direction about my willingness to put myself in danger and his overprotectiveness, it was a path that ultimately led nowhere. I wanted to know that some of our friendship was still there, but not for the price of bringing back everything that was also wrong about it.

Albert rubbed his temples. "So you don't know anything more, and that mythborn might be executing some personal vendetta using anyone and everyone. And this uniform is the only thing that puts you in danger." He pointed at me.

"They saved my life when I found Emma." To me, the uneven fight with an Afflicted, a person who succumbed to a chaotic magic, transforming into a monster, felt like a lifetime ago, but I knew Albert would remember. It was the very event that caused me to become what I was now, a myth-touched. "Besides, Cathal offered me a way out when things went south."

"But you didn't take it," he said with clear accusation but

then offered me a bitter smile. "You know, up until now, I hoped that you'd come back to us."

I shook my head, letting sadness show on my face. "I didn't fit in here even before the change. But I did think I'd be able to go back to my old life. I was wrong."

He leaned forward, his eyes narrowing as always when he caught onto something I said. "They forced you to stay, didn't they? No matter what you were writing in your letters. Was it the ritual? Did Eithne threaten you?"

One "yes" and Albert would spring to action, maybe keeping me in Trinity, maybe making demands to Eithne and Cathal. But instead of giving him the excuse he was searching for, I shook my head.

"I stayed because it only seemed fair after they saved me from the affliction. The ritual..." I cringed at the memory of the excruciating pain that I experienced for what had turned out to be four long days. "It was difficult and painful, but it changed only my body."

He didn't conceal his inspection of the very body I mentioned, and I didn't mind, because it felt like for the first time since I entered, he was looking past his concept of a mythborn that he must have subconsciously applied.

"Quite a price to pay," he said in a neutral tone, though his face revealed mixed feelings.

I could only guess he didn't necessarily dislike the way I looked, but at the same time, not only was I not the Kaja that used to be his lover anymore, but I also looked like an enemy. Putting his reaction against the memory of Riagán's fascinated gaze was enough to smother any traces of regret I might have had about how things turned out.

"I haven't changed that much."

"The Kaja I knew wouldn't join the enemy." It was clear he regretted the words as soon as he spoke them. "I'm sorry. I'm not being fair. I told you to take Eithne's offer myself."

"Neither of us knew what would happen. But hey, I'm alive, and I'm still myself. And... I still consider you my friend, even if, as the commander, you can't trust me anymore." I added the last part to give him a way out. Contrary to what his letters, so inviting and full of concern for me, had suggested, Albert wasn't ready to face the myth-touched me. I hoped giving him time would help. "Will you tell me what happened with Tadgh?" I steered the topic back to business.

"Someone I trust shared their suspicions with me, and we caught Tadgh red-handed dealing with a mythborn who has strong ties to the Court."

I almost smirked at his attempt to hide the identity of his informant. He must have expected that I'd argue over that person's credibility. I took another route. "Could that person have been misled? Manipulated?" I suggested with caution. "It might have been Muiredach's plot to influence someone you would trust."

Albert spread his hands. "Even if it was, Tadgh still got caught, and there were witnesses. Assuming that I wanted to entertain Eithne's unspoken request and let it slide, I can't release a mythborn everyone considers a spy."

"But you could release him to the Court." I had no doubt that Tadgh wouldn't like it, but it seemed a better option than being tried for treason. Peace treaty or not, the penalty was death, and with such a sentence, Eithne would have a hard time saving Tadgh if she really cared about him instead of just considering him an asset. "I'm sure they would find some sort of a suitable compensation."

Albert shook his head with a sigh. "Trinity has enough of its own resources."

I huffed. It seemed that I'd overestimated his fondness of Tadgh, or maybe he had already judged the mythborn as guilty, therefore not worthy of caring for. "Then ask for something other than resources. Ask for humanborn craftsmen to be sent to the Court as apprentices. Ask for their healing charms or knowledge on how to make them."

That got his interest. "Would Eithne agree?"

"I'd say you have the upper hand on this one. Unless it turns out she doesn't care about him enough." I cringed, as I could picture Eithne refusing to yield in the name of mythborn pride or politics. "Then you'll have your spy, and you'll be able to make a show of sentencing him to death for treason."

"You sound bitter," he said, displeased. "Back in the war, you didn't have such sentiments for spies."

Back in the war, acting on a heart's whim, I'd saved a mythborn warrior from a giant's path, but that wasn't something I'd ever mentioned to Albert, and I wasn't about to do so now. I had no need for an argument about me having kept such secrets from him.

"I just know how he must be feeling right now. Alone among his former enemies, trying to make it work." I leaned forward. "This could have been me, at the Court. I was almost as close to being branded a traitor. But I was lucky, because Cathal decided to show me some goodwill."

"I doubt your potential charges were as severe as being caught spying for the enemy."

I didn't miss the challenge in his voice, so I gave him the truth he couldn't have expected. "I withheld crucial information, and because of that, a mythborn died. And trust me, it wasn't a pretty death." To my surprise, the mere mention of Cait brought all the guilt back, and I looked away as my voice broke on the last words. At least Tadgh didn't get anyone killed.

"I'm sorry," Albert whispered with a sudden softness. "I didn't even ask how you were getting on there."

He reached out and touched my hand gently, as if unsure whether such familiarity would be welcome now. Before I realized I should have warned him, he skimmed past my skin and withdrew quickly, drawing a sharp breath.

"I should have told you. It's mythborn magic." He must be reacting to me the way all the humanborn reacted to the mythborn, and our mutual, very intimate past wasn't helping. After so much time at the Court, I'd forgotten about it. "I don't have the antidote with me, but if you drink a bit of whiskey, it should ease the symptoms."

"I'll be fine. It's not like I didn't feel that way before you changed." He waved me off with a smile. "I'll see what I can do about Tadgh," he offered. "There's no easy way out of this situation, but if Eithne's willing to pay some sort of a compensation that would look reasonable, I won't make it difficult."

I was about to thank him when a sudden idea struck me. "What if this was all staged? Tadgh could have been helping you uncover the real spy. You might have been working with the Court all the time to catch the remainder of the terrorists." The Snake's agents, always lurking in the dark, made perfect scapegoats. Whenever we needed an excuse, we could claim there was a bigger plot beyond the one just uncovered, so if we couldn't get rid of their menacing, we could use them to our advantage. "That would also explain the Scáthanna's presence here. Of course, I'll still make sure you get something of value for it."

He gave me a rather skeptical glare. "It's far-fetched, but we've worked with the Court before."

"It'd be a nice reassurance that neither side is preparing for another war," I added. "Working together to uncover more terrorist plots will look good in the eyes of the public."

It'd been long months since Trinity and the Court announced the results of their joint operations to eliminate the threat and prevent more bombings, so it would be nice to show that this cooperation didn't end back then. Anything that helped stabilize the volatile city was worth the effort, in my opinion, and as a bonus, we not only got to clear Tadgh of the charges, but he could also stay in Trinity. A trusted mythborn working with Albert would have a much better life than a suspected spy, even if he was proven innocent.

Albert must have come to similar conclusions, because he stood up. "Let's talk to Tadgh, then."

CHAPTER THREE

Not everyone knew, but Trinity had two prisons. One was smaller, consisting of several rooms repurposed into holding cells, and served as a temporary confinement for those accused but not convicted and for anyone who stirred up trouble in Trinity—big enough to catch Albert's attention, but nothing serious enough to treat like a crime. The second prison was bigger, better guarded, and over time it had been reinforced with powerful wards. This was where Trinity kept people considered hard-boiled criminals.

On one hand, I agreed that holding them in the heart of a humanborn fortress that boasted a lot of additional security was a good idea, making it harder for any foul play to occur. On the other, I couldn't help picturing those menaces of society breaking out one day and wreaking havoc across Trinity. Albert, of course, dismissed my concerns, confident in his people and protections, but I still thought about it every now and then—I just didn't voice my doubts anymore. We had enough topics for arguments as it was.

They kept Tadgh in the smaller prison. It looked much like a normal corridor with doors on each sides, leading maybe to former classrooms or something similar, but the reinforced doorframes and doors made it much less inviting than regular Trinity spaces.

The guard, usually posted at the entrance, accompanied us all the way to the cell, his distrustful glare focused on me as if I was going to jump his commander at any moment. Albert's unconcerned stride did nothing to ease that man's suspicions.

I expected him to insist on accompanying us inside as well, but Albert waved him off, and he left as we entered the small cell.

Tadgh was sitting motionless, his back straight and his gaze fixed on the wall in front of him. He didn't seem to have eaten anything recently—a bowl of food was still full on the table—but considering he'd been accused of treason, he wasn't looking too bad.

"I have nothing to say." He didn't even turn his head toward us.

"I didn't expect you to," Albert replied dryly. "But I'm not here to question you. I already know what I need to know."

Tadgh finally looked at us, his surprise revealed only in the slight arch of his eyebrows. "Commander. And..." He inspected me with narrowed eyes. "You seem familiar, but I don't recall your name. You haven't been with the Scáthanna long, have you? Never mind that. If it's worth anything, I'd prefer that you left. This is Trinity's matter."

"The lady seems to think otherwise," I replied.

His eyes widened. "Kaja." In a heartbeat, Tadgh was in front of me. Albert jerked in alarm, but I held my hand up to stop him. The mythborn scientist deserved a look.

"I didn't expect the ritual to be so... thorough. Had you not spoken, I'd never have guessed."

I half expected him to inspect me more closely, but Tadgh just stood near, his expression focused as he took in my new physique, though the fascination on his face had nothing to do with how attractive he considered me now, and everything to do with being able to see a unique specimen up close. I didn't blame him. Stuck at Trinity, he couldn't have had a chance to see a myth-touched before.

I offered him a smile. "To the lady's disappointment, my personality didn't change."

"The lady shouldn't concern herself with that, since you seem to be taking orders from Ceannasaí Cathal." He glanced at Albert, then at me again, as if ensuring he wasn't spilling secrets. "But what are you doing here?"

"The lady's request, but ceannasaí obliged."

Tadgh cringed. "You came to give the Court's secrets away."

"It couldn't have made your situation worse," Albert said, "and with her reassurances that your ties to the Court are... harmless, I've decided to overlook this whole situation. She also came up with a way to clear you of your charges without making anyone suspicious, so if I were in your place, I'd consider myself lucky."

There was a warning in his voice, as if he was reminding his prisoner that forgiveness didn't mean forgetting Tadgh *did* have ties with Trinity's enemy. I couldn't help thinking that Albert still felt uneasy about letting the mythborn off the hook and allowing him to continue on as if nothing happened. I suspected that after this matter was resolved, the two of them would have to have a serious conversation to rebuild at least *some* trust.

Tadgh took a step back, his disbelief clear as he looked

back and forth between me and Albert. "You would… Even though you know the truth…"

It must have been the first time I'd seen him at a loss for words. Unceasingly composed and analytical in his behavior, Tadgh always seemed to me more a scientist than a mythborn, so to witness him in an emotional moment felt like seeing a unicorn.

"Can you tell me what happened?" I asked. I hoped that with his future brighter, he'd be willing to give me some details that would help link this whole matter to Muiredach. "I find it hard to believe that you were… compromised after so many years."

Tadgh hesitated, and he glanced toward Albert, telling me the mythborn wasn't comfortable discussing the matter in front of Trinity's commander. "I believe there's a spy in Trinity, serving… a power other than the Court."

"The Snake," I said. "Albert knows." Things were so much easier when no secrecy was involved.

Tadgh nodded, but whatever he meant to say next, I never got to hear it.

The door to the cell opened, but instead of a guard walking in, a small item rolled across the floor. Both Albert and I reacted instinctively, leaping backward, but Tadgh didn't have war-bred reflexes. As the explosive curse went off, he got caught in the blast.

I dashed toward Albert, and my new, enhanced amulets activated, shielding him as well, but the power of the blast still threw me against him. He stood firmly in place, catching me before I made us both collapse.

My choice was an instinctive one, but even in afterthought, it was the right one. No matter how much I cared about Tadgh's wellbeing, Albert was more important, even if I put my personal sentiment aside. If he died, we'd have war, because no one else in Trinity was so willing to cooperate with the mythborn and aware that we wouldn't be able to win any more than we did the last time.

As soon as the flames died out, Albert headed for the door, with determination in his gait. Even if I wanted to, I wouldn't be able to stop him, and I only hoped that there wasn't another curse coming in.

"Catch!" I called out, and as soon as he looked at me, I tossed my blade to him. It wasn't much, but at least he wouldn't be running out defenseless. In the heart of Trinity, the safest haven of the humanborn places, he didn't carry anything himself.

He caught it with nimbleness which suggested that no matter how much time he spent behind the desk, he did not neglect physical training, and he was off.

I didn't follow him. Tadgh was alive but badly wounded. My healing charms could keep him breathing for a little longer, but he'd need a miracle to pull through. A miracle, or...

I knelt beside him and pulled out my charms. Perhaps there was a way to save him.

"Gone." Albert reentered, his face twisted with anger, though I was certain he wasn't letting emotions get the better of him. If anything, they fueled his determination, and whoever was responsible would soon learn of his meticulousness and persistence. "Tadgh?" His expression shifted to concern.

"He doesn't have long unless we get him to the Court." The magic of the healing charm was losing the battle against the mythborn's wounds, but, mindful of a lesson that Lorcan gave me before he died, I wasn't trying to heal Tadgh, only keep him alive, so I limited its flow of magic.

"Please. He knows something important if our enemies risked trying to kill him like that."

"What if you were the target and not him?"

The last thing I wanted was to explain to Albert that Muiredach wanted to capture me alive. I could clearly picture his reaction at the news that the Scáthanna's enemy intended to interrogate and torture me, and it wasn't the kind of response that would help Tadgh in any way.

"We can argue about it for the next hour and let him die, or you can allow the Scáthanna to get him to the Court," I replied. "I know this wasn't what we agreed to, but I promise I'll ensure Eithne makes it worth your while. And if she doesn't, all mythborn be damned, I'll move back in here, if you consider it a compensation good enough: a myth-touched for a mythborn."

Albert arched an eyebrow, but the smile creeping in the corner of his mouth told me that he liked what I'd said. I didn't want to spoil his good mood by remarking that if I gave Eithne a choice—either she handsomely compensated Trinity or I became a Trinitian—she'd definitely choose the former, no matter how much it would cost her. I'd already learned too many of the Court's secrets for her to risk I'd share them with Trinitians.

And if it turned out that after all she didn't care what kind of knowledge I had, I was sure that Cathal would make his own arrangements, because he hadn't invested a month of training me and making me part of the Scáthanna only to lose me to Albert and Trinity.

"Deal." He handed my weapon back to me and headed out again, his voice echoing in the corridor. "I need a medic! And somebody get the other mythborn here. Tell them I need to see them urgently, and bring them up here without delays. And for fuck's sake, be polite about it. They're guests, after all!"

I snickered at the last remark, but Albert was right to make it. I didn't want to guess how Sadb and Faolan would react to demands or general rudeness.

Tadgh opened his eyes. "Kaja..." His blistered lips moved, but hardly any sound left them. "Albert's..." He passed out before he could say anything else, and I squeezed the remaining magic out of the charm binding his fleeting life to his injured body for a little longer. The Trinitian medic better get to us quickly, because I caught the urgency in Tadgh's voice.

I activated my second charm, trying not to think about how I only had one more left.

THE MEDIC ARRIVED when my third charm was dying. A young woman, who at this age before the war would have been a high school student, wore a band identifying her as fully trained. Lack of civilization had definitely sped up education. She gave Tadgh one glance and spread her arms in a telling gesture, and I couldn't help wondering whether her quick surrender had anything to do with her seeing a mythborn—or even two, since she likely considered me to be one of them. At least she still knelt beside me. The healing charm she took out was weak and almost magic-less compared to what I had at my disposal, and I made a mental note to tell Albert about it later. If he wanted a good deal from Eithne, he wanted the charms.

"I can ease his pain and keep him alive a little longer," she offered in a soft voice that carried a trace of French accent. So young, she must have been a child when the

Magiclysm hit. I didn't want to wonder what happened to her family. What mattered was that she had a family among Trinitians now. "If you need to say your goodbyes, now would be the time."

I needed Tadgh to talk, but we definitely wouldn't indulge in farewells. Information was more important. I had no doubt that he was attacked because he'd discovered the Snake's spy, and it had to be someone close to Albert, otherwise they wouldn't have risked such an open assault.

The medic had already activated her charm, pouring its meager magic into him, and I felt the time slipping away from me. I doubted she could even keep him stable for long, let alone make him wake up.

Sadb and Faolan stormed into the cell, their expressions showing readiness for a battle. They relaxed when they saw I was unharmed and tensed again at the sight of Tadgh. The medic scurried away, but she seemed too intimidated to walk past them and leave.

"There was an attack, likely by Muiredach's henchmen. Can you get him to the Court in time to save his life?" I looked at Faolan. "He has information we need."

"I could, but I'd need Sadb to cover me." He was already on his knees beside Tadgh, using his healing charm, and I could swear there was compassion on his face. "And that would leave you vulnerable."

"I'll stay here," I offered. "I'm sure the commander won't mind taking care of me for a while."

It wasn't perfect, but I'd only slow them down if I tried to accompany them. Not to mention that it might have been a ruse to set up an ambush when we were at a disadvantage. Besides, there was one other thing—that order Cathal hadn't given me, but I had chosen to follow anyway. It could convince Sadb and Faolan to go along with my plan... if only I would tell them. I knew I couldn't.

Faolan cringed, but Sadb nodded. "Your call," she said. "I don't like it either, but if you say Tadgh might have a lead..."

"Or we gain nothing taking unnecessary risk," Faolan snapped back.

I was glad that Albert wasn't here for the discussion. Though perhaps, this once, he'd actually take my side instead of arguing.

"This is Trinity. No mythborn will be able to sneak up on me unnoticed, not to mention attacking me or dragging me away." Of course, humanborn could as well do the deed for Muiredach, but I wasn't about to undermine my own argument. I pointed at Tadgh. "Do you think he can wait while we discuss the best approach?" Faolan's first charm's magic was already dying, and they'd need all they had for the return trip.

"She has a point," Sadb said. "And she's the one making the decision anyway."

To my surprise, Faolan didn't argue anymore, as if reminding him that Cathal gave me the lead on this one was enough. He lifted Tadgh, and his swift move startled the medic. She shuffled away, her back now against the cell's charred wall. Still, her eyes remained on the healing charm he held that kept emanating magic. I could read longing on her face, and I could relate. In her position, a charm like that would be my dream too.

Sadb nodded to me, and they rushed out without wasting time on farewells.

I walked out of the cell, and the medic scurried past me as if making sure I wasn't about to ask her to stay. Albert wasn't around, but I didn't expect him to be. Trinity was just attacked, and he had to take all the necessary steps to ensure everyone knew it wasn't the Scáthanna. I also assumed he'd try to run an investigation—the guard who'd accompanied us through the corridor should have seen someone entering, unless he had something to do with it himself... or was another victim of the attacker who tossed the curse.

I engaged my listening skill. Perhaps someone around would be discussing the failed attempt or the next steps, giving me a lead. The cacophony of voices was annoying at first, and I had to focus to separate them, especially as I didn't know which conversations could turn out important. I could probably ignore the cook giving orders to his assistants, but what about the officer making a routine check of the outside posts? There was nothing to it... until a culprit tried to get out.

I shook my head. Following them all would only put a strain on me, so I let my instinct guide me through the voices. It was going to be a stroke of luck either way.

My thoughts wandered around what had transpired. I avoided trying to estimate how quickly Sadb and Faolan could make it back to the Court and pondering whether Tadgh had that much time. His last words bothered me. It couldn't have been a simple "Albert's in danger," because Tadgh was not one to waste words, so perhaps he meant one of Albert's officers. This made sense. Albert had discovered Tadgh's connection through "a person he trusted," so it couldn't have been someone random. But knowing that he had a spy amongst the closest companions gave me chills, and I fought the urge to find him. Without any solid evidence, Albert was likely to dismiss my warning—because, well, he trusted his people.

"Hello, Kaja."

I froze at the familiar voice speaking in a casual manner. Fear was stronger than reason, and even though I knew Muiredach couldn't be close by, I still looked around. But it also meant... Adrenaline rushed in my veins as I realized he knew of my skill. The Scáthanna had kept it secret, so —how?!

"I know you can hear me," he continued. I wished I could tell him he just got lucky, but if he learned about my skill, he must have assumed I'd be using it in a situation like this. "If you try to warn anybody, I'll have more curses detonated across Trinity."

I wanted to ignore his threat, but he'd somehow gotten to Tadgh. Not only had he exposed him to Albert, but he also managed to have him assaulted in his cell. If he could do that, he likely had means to push Trinity into chaos.

"Be so kind and come over to the entrance yard," Muiredach said. "I'm sure you're as curious to meet me face to face as I am to speak with you in person."

I made my way through Trinity's grounds, followed by the curious glances of passing Trinitians, but no one stopped me or questioned my presence, which meant the word of the Scáthanna's visit had spread. I could still see their uneasiness about a mythborn—they didn't know better and saw me us such—wandering freely through the humanborn stronghold. I didn't blame them. Quite to the contrary. Not so long ago, I'd have also been the one tracking every single move of any unfamiliar mythborn.

Thinking about them made it easier to forget about the fear that made my own blood pulse in my ears, and I managed to keep straight face making my way to the main gate.

Muiredach was cunning enough that he'd likely anticipated the turn of events: my conversation with Albert and going to see to Tadgh. The explosion, though likely intended to make sure the mythborn scientist didn't reveal anything he might have discovered, was also meant to force our hand. I had no idea whether he'd foreseen that I would volunteer to stay in Trinity, but I wouldn't put it past him. He knew enough about me to know I felt safe within its walls.

All that meant that whatever came next was also part of his plan, and I was going to become his prisoner one way or another. I tried hard to push images of Cait away, but they lurked at the back of my mind, feeding my fear.

Trinity's entrance yard looked normal, and I could only hope the main gate was the place Muiredach had in mind.

I leaned against a nearby wall, making an effort to look relaxed enough to not draw any attention. If Orla walked by, she'd figure out something was wrong, but with the attack on Tadgh, she was likely occupied elsewhere.

I didn't wait long. A mythborn wearing the Scáthanna's uniform approached. He was tall and rather skinny, on the verge of being sickly, with sharp features that made his pure amber eyes stand out even more from his ecru-hued skin that resembled a polished stone. He kept his hair, gold like fields of wheat back in Poland, at ear length, and its straight strands danced in the breeze.

As he got closer, he opened his palm, revealing a small and smooth object between his fingers—undoubtedly a curse.

"Please, let's not make a mess." He stopped beside me, just far enough away to ensure I couldn't grab him without lunging, and matched my relaxed pose. To any Trinitian, we probably looked like two mythborn waiting... No one knew the Scáthanna well enough to recognize an impostor in

Muiredach. "Trying to take me down would only result in our deaths."

"Aren't you concerned that I'd pay the price?"

He sent me a smile, and there was something enchanting in the way his mouth creased. If I was to make bets, I had just discovered how Muiredach found his followers and henchmen, and why so many were willing to die for him. If a simple arch of his lips could stir fascination, I had no doubt that he had even better tricks up his sleeve.

"I know you value your life, and you're too wise to attempt something that could look like a mythborn attack on Trinity."

I swallowed. Sure, I liked the idea of surviving and not making sacrifices for any greater good, but the prospect of taking him down had a lot of appeal. Yet he had a point. If an explosion tore through the yard, originating from two mythborn wearing the Scáthanna's outfits, there would be no way to avoid war. No matter how much Albert tried to preserve peace, others wouldn't listen in the light of such a blatant attack on their home.

He kept smiling as if he had a way to follow my thoughts. "The curse I'm holding is powerful enough to level this whole yard and maybe affect some of the buildings as well. I'll give it to you if you walk outside Trinity's grounds without raising alarm. If you refuse... a lot of humanborn will die today."

I shifted. If I could get my hands on it before he activated it, he'd lose his bargaining chip, but he must have prepared for me to try something. "Once I'm outside, you'll have no reason to keep your word." This was the problem with all hostage situations—and I was definitely in one right now.

"Mythborn tend to keep their word, Kaja, even if we sometimes try to interpret the promises the way it serves us better. It's something you should learn if you truly want to become one of us." He moved his hand away, caging the curse under his bent fingers. "So in the spirit of truthfulness, I'll admit that I won't give you the curse, as it's a rather valuable thing. But for the same reason, I won't use it unless you force me to do so." He glanced at the building. "And if you're waiting for your humanborn friends to arrive, don't bother. I ensured that they're busy chasing the leads of the most recent attack."

That was actually good news. I didn't want Albert and Orla anywhere near the yard, not only because it could become the target of Muiredach's curse. Albert knew me too well. If he saw me with Muiredach, he wouldn't believe that I was fine, and he'd come to my rescue, while Orla saw the faces of the two mythborn who had accompanied me and would get suspicious of a stranger wearing our uniform... So if either of them were around, nothing would end well.

"And what happens if I walk outside with you?" I asked, my voice almost steady.

"Trinity, including your dear Albert, will remain untouched, and you... You don't have to worry, Kaja." His smile could be comforting if I didn't know who he was and what he did. "What happened to poor Cait was unfortunate, and it was truly a waste of life. I've learned my lesson. I hope that you and I can approach our conversation from a more reasonable angle and strike a bargain that would satisfy us both."

I gave him the best of my dubious stares.

"If at any point you find my company unbearable, you can make use of your new tattoo." He looked me in the eye. "But you're a survivor, Kaja. You'll take your chances with me, because it's a better option than dying here and not only taking a lot of others with you but also being the reason for the next war. So let's start walking before some unforeseen circumstances make the choice for you."

He made an inviting gesture but didn't move, and I involuntarily smiled. Despite his confidence, he wasn't sure whether I'd try to take him down if he turned his back on me.

I started walking. He didn't have to know that I had other reasons to try staying alive. He didn't have to know that while he'd woven his complex plans to lure me out of the Court and capture me, Cathal was not a fool. Our ceannasaí had anticipated that Muiredach would make a move, and came up with his own plan. So I wasn't about to throw away my life in an explosion in the middle of Trinity if I could, instead, risk it in a near-suicide mission. The latter had at least a minuscule chance of success.

"This way, please," Muiredach said politely, but still kept half a step away.

If he thought this distance was making him safe, he had no idea what kind of training Sadb had put me through. I resisted the urge to test my combat skills as he moved the curse to the hand that was further away from me. His concern, no matter how subtle under his mask of confidence, was lessening my fear of him, but I still wanted him to believe he had the upper hand. This was where he would slip for the first and final time. All had to do was to be patient.

He didn't lead me toward the main gate, picking a side entrance instead. None of the guards questioned us, and we made it outside.

"I knew you would be reasonable." Muiredach turned to me. "But I won't take chances."

A quiet whiz warned me of an incoming arrow, and both my training and instincts kicked in, but Muiredach lunged and grabbed my wrist before I could leap backward. The arrow hit the ground by our feet.

The last thing I saw was Muiredach dropping along with me when a powerful sleep curse secured in the arrow's shaft activated between us.

CHAPTER FOUR

I woke up tucked in a bed, in an unfamiliar room. Before the war, it might have been a bedroom in a residential building, but the wards that covered the boarded-up window told me I wasn't in a random apartment. As I shifted under the heavy duvet, it brushed against my bare skin.

"I apologize for that." Muiredach walked in as if on cue, and I entertained myself with the thought that he'd been standing in the corridor, waiting for the right moment to make an entrance.

He wasn't in our uniform anymore, wearing an olive-shaded tunic and leather pants that looked like a myth-born's failed attempt at skinny jeans. Subtle jewelry showed his status, but it wasn't as flashy as some of the pieces I saw worn at the Court.

His changed clothes also meant that I'd been kept asleep longer than he was, but I doubted it was more than overnight. It served me well. By now, Cathal and the others already knew I was gone and were looking for me, while I had been relatively safe and unharmed.

"I didn't know how many curses you had on you, so I asked Lisa, one of my associates, to remove your uniform and other belongings," Muiredach continued almost apologetically. "I can assure you that she was alone with you and instructed to be respectful." He laid simple mythborn clothes on the chair. "I brought you something else to wear."

I didn't move, staring at him in hopes he'd take the hint. After all those reassurances, he surely didn't expect me to parade naked in front of him.

"Once you get dressed, I'd like you to join me." He walked back to the door. "I won't have you bound, but nevertheless, you *are* my prisoner. If you abuse my hospitality, you'll find yourself in a much less comfortable setting."

I arched my eyebrow at such a display of civility. Not what I had expected of him, especially after what he did to Cait, but at the same time, it didn't surprise me. Muiredach seemed like someone who thrived on games and manipulation, and he must have figured out this was the only way to get whatever he wanted from me.

"You could simply tell me what you want," I said before he left. "I would refuse, and we could move onto the next point of your master plan." The one that had torture, or at least threats of it.

He smiled, and his charm filled the room like the scent of cologne—a particularly unpleasant one, I should add. "Unfortunately, I can't have you refuse. So get dressed, please. We'll talk over breakfast."

I inspected the clothes—a tunic and pants in neutral blues but made of good-quality fabric, along with a set of human lingerie roughly my size, because the faceless Lisa was apparently thorough and considered my own underwear to pose unknown dangers. I'd like to see myself defeating Muiredach and his hordes of his henchmen with the use of nothing but my old bra. Now that would be a feat that even Sadb couldn't one-up!

With no other choices or any cunning plan, I put the outfit on and headed through the only doorway available. The door was sturdy, and it had latches and bolts on the outside that made it much like a prison cell, but the narrow corridor past it looked a lot like an apartment hallway, complete with a reproduction of a random art piece and two holes where a coat hanger might have been.

The corridor connected to another one through a doorless opening, and the ugly off-white paint on the walls and equally ugly gray tiles under my feet confirmed that we were in a residential building. Not that it helped me narrow down my location...

I engaged my skill, but even though I heard voices of people around, they all seemed close by, as if my hearing's reach had become limited. I grimaced. Back when we were looking for Cait, we assumed she was being held behind powerful wards that made it difficult to pinpoint her location. I was likely in the same place, and magic barred me from hearing anything outside the building.

Muiredach was waiting nearby, and he led me into another apartment.

Before the war, the room we entered must have been a living room, but its impersonal furnishing suggested it was now a place for rent, likely short term. In the years preceding the Magiclysm, it had become somewhat of a plague in Dublin. Instead of renting apartments to working professionals, property owners offered it as a hotel alternative to tourists or worldwide corporations that wanted a place for their visiting employees to stay, cashing in more money but devastating an already strained housing market.

Then the Magiclysm came, and it devastated everything else.

We approached the table in the corner of the room, as impersonal as everything else, and the meal was already waiting for us. Muiredach's choice of breakfast reminded me of humanborn food: toasted bread, eggs, and some meat that could pass for local sausages.

"You have to forgive me for not matching the Court's meals," he said as we sat down. "I prefer to use my resources for more meaningful purposes."

I really, *really* wanted to ask him how kidnapping and torturing people was meaningful, but as much as I'd love to give him a piece of my mind adorned with a wreath of suitable insults, antagonizing him would accomplish nothing. Except for feeling good about myself, of course.

"It's not poisoned; you needn't worry." He offered another of his smiles along with a gesture inviting me to eat. "Please, enjoy it."

The tableware was of humanborn make, a mismatched collection of cheap plates, mugs, and cutlery scavenged from abandoned stores. After the war, with the population decimated, there was no shortage of non-perishable products, and the only challenge anyone faced was finding undamaged goods. Having a full matching set was a secondary issue, at least for most humanborn, and it seemed that, contrary to the Court's mythborn, Muiredach cared little about aesthetics. In some other circumstances, perhaps we could even get along.

I poured myself something that resembled tea, throwing glances around and not being very discreet about it. There was no point in my pretending that I didn't want to know my surroundings. Staring at plain beige walls—standard color in many rental apartments—couldn't reveal any escape routes anyway.

"How did you know of my skill?" If I was bound to have a conversation with him, I might as well make it a useful one. He could have learned my name and many other facts about me easily enough, but only the Scáthanna knew I could hear conversations taking places far from me.

I didn't expect any answer, but to my surprise, he gave me the smile of a satisfied cat. His reaction confirmed that he was a mythborn convinced of his own genius, and one who liked to flaunt it too. I could learn a lot if I was strategic with my questions.

"Torture isn't the only way to make people talk," he replied. "I can be very persuasive."

The way he said it struck a memory.

"Lorcan," I said in an instant.

We'd assumed he killed himself before Muiredach could get to him. We were wrong.

Muiredach gave me a nod of approval, as if he'd expected I'd put it together. "He was very cooperative when he learned I'd become a host to his mate and daughter. Sending an invitation to him was risky, and you almost caught one of my pawns, but ultimately it paid off."

I stared at him dumbfounded. Cathal claimed that the Scáthanna kept no secrets from each other, but if what Muiredach said was true, I wasn't the only one on the team with trust issues, because if Cathal knew of Lorcan's family, he'd have ensured their safety. At least now some events from the past made sense—the servant I spotted in our quarters who ran from me was the one to deliver the message, and Lorcan left the Court without a word to make sure no one learned of what he was about to do.

Muiredach leaned forward, his amber eyes staring with inhuman intensity. "They're both alive and well, safe away from any strife, and I would have allowed Lorcan to join them, but he was quite adamant on paying the price for what he considered betrayal." He shrugged. "A foolish decision, if you ask me."

I disagreed. I could relate to the struggles of Lorcan, who was torn between two families and made a choice that I'd have made if my loved ones were in immediate danger. And like him, I wouldn't be able to bear the thought of living with guilt of betrayal.

"So if he told you all you wanted to know, why am I here?" I asked. I didn't add the "instead of being dead" part. No point in putting ideas in his head.

"You'll make a curse for me," he stated it as if I had already agreed. "The one that can kill a Léanmhar."

After the revelations about Lorcan, I wasn't surprised he knew of that as well. Back when I was a humanborn suffering from magic affliction, I made a curse that would kill me the moment I turned into a monster. All the Scáthanna knew about it, because I used it to save Laoise's life.

Sudden anger rose within me. Thinking about her reminded me the bastard on the other side of the table was responsible for her death too.

"Why would you need it?" I asked to give my emotions time to settle. I had to be levelheaded if I wanted to survive. "I saw the curse that wounded Aengus." I still remembered the blue lava crawling across the mythborn commander's chest, and I never got a chance to ask Cathal or Connor about it.

"This wasn't a curse. Larbharóin are a gift from the Snake, but breeding them can be quite troublesome," he replied. "Not only is your curse easier to produce, but it also has many more uses."

I played with the eggs on my plate. They were already cold when I sat down, so entirely inedible by my standards. "And what will you do when I say no?"

"I'll make you change your mind." His voice overflowed with confidence. "Normally, I'd give you a taste of pain, but I've heard enough about how loyal you are to consider that you're more likely to kill yourself than submit." He made a dismissive gesture, as if the concept wasn't even worth discussing, though I had no way of telling whether he meant the topic of torturing me or one of my loyalty. "But I'm sure I'll find another way. Everyone can be persuaded if the incentive is strong enough."

I couldn't disagree, so I remained silent. If he threatened any of my friends, I'd meet many of his demands immediately. Oh yes, I understood Lorcan's choices all too well.

Muiredach put his cutlery away. "If you're finished with your meal, let's go."

I'd have loved to stall, but the food had lost all of its already dubious appeal, so I stood up.

In silence, he led me through a maze of corridors. I got to peek into some of the apartments, with walls knocked down and repurposed for storage and other uses. Several mythborn and humanborn passed us by, each moving with intent and throwing anxious glances at us. Their body language suggested they got punished for idleness or even dawdling... Or perhaps for anything Muiredach wanted to punish them for at the time.

Two stories up, and we entered a room larger than any other, guarded by two bulky mythborn who followed us inside but stayed behind our backs. In the middle, a human-born woman hung by her wrists. She didn't lift her head at our approach, and Muiredach ignored her, leading me to a long table. The stench of old blood and urine hit me as we passed her by. The woman looked unharmed, but it wasn't hard to guess there had been many victims here before her. I knew one of them...

I cringed as I eyed blades and other devices of torture. My vivid imagination instantly painted pictures of Caitríona's torment at Muiredach's hand.

It didn't help that Cait's suffering was on me. I couldn't forget that it was my mistrust that had led to her capture... or at least limited our chances of preventing it. It was guilt that I would forever carry with me, but I directed my negative feelings toward the mythborn who truly deserved them. If Muiredach wasn't after her, what I did or didn't do wouldn't matter, and just like I shouldered the burden of guilt, he had to pay for what *he* did. And I could make him pay.

The urge to kill rose within, but I fought hard to stifle it. As confident as he was, I doubted he was careless. The guards lingering behind us suggested that he must be considering that I'd try killing him. If I made an attempt, I'd fail, and taking Cait's place was not going to help anyone—her, me, or the rest the team.

I knew it all. I *still* wanted to try.

He kept watching me as if he knew of the inner battle I was waging, and that made my bloodlust die. I wasn't Sadb or a trained assassin. If I wanted a chance, I had to wait and strike when he wasn't prepared.

"First, we'll test the strength of your compassion," Muiredach said.

At his sign, two mythborn grabbed me. I didn't resist and let them drag me to a chair and force me to sit down.

Muiredach slapped the other woman awake. "Ann, this

is Kaja," he said in a gentle tone. "She's the one who can make the pain stop, so be sure to call her name whenever you feel uncomfortable."

Ann's wide eyes froze at me, a silent plea clear on her face. She was young, though her face bore the marks of a harsh life. She likely had someone out there—friends or family...

I looked away.

"I won't force you to watch this time." Muiredach approached me. "You'll hear everything, and that's enough for now. And in case you're more of a martyr than I expected, your death won't save Ann from torture—only your compliance will. If you kill yourself, she'll pay tenfold, and I'll send one of my servants back to Trinity with the curse I showed you."

I braved a glance as he walked away, but as soon as he picked up the knife, I shut my eyes. I couldn't do the same with my ears, so moments later the first of Ann's many screams tore through the room... and through me, each shrill reverberating deep in my bones.

I SHIFTED IN BED, awake all too soon. It had taken four days for Ann's body to succumb to the torture, and during that time, I got to hear *everything*. Muiredach kept his word and didn't make me watch, but each evening, as his guards led me away, I got to see his handiwork. The sickening shining in his eyes made it clear he enjoyed the process so much that the goal of persuading me was almost secondary. He actually looked disappointed when Ann died—as if he had expected more of her.

I felt guilty all the same. She'd suffered for days because

I kept saying no to Muiredach. Ann's suffering did move me, even more so when I imagined Cait in her place, but I wasn't going to give in. I had my orders, and when I agreed to Cathal's plans, I'd known I'd have to make sacrifices. Not that it made it easier—Ann's death was on me, and I had no doubt that there would be another victim waiting for me after the torment of eating breakfast with Muiredach, which he kept insisting on, as if we were acquaintances sharing a casual meal.

Whenever he addressed me, he was sickening in his fake courtesy, and that, combined with Ann's torture, pushed me to the verge of snapping. So many times I wanted to take my chances, to choke the life out of him...

I kept reminding myself that it wasn't the time. I wouldn't save anyone by failing to kill him.

As I got up, fresh, plain clothes waiting for me on the chair, I couldn't resist eavesdropping. It had become a morning ritual of mine. Even if my skill wasn't strong enough to get through the heavily warded walls and windows—I was almost certain this building was Muiredach's stronghold of sorts—I could fish for information inside. Muiredach knew what I could do, so it was unlikely he would say anything that would compromise his plans, but his henchmen... Even if he cautioned them about discussing anything sensitive, people blabbed to other people, especially when they thought they were alone, and I doubted he'd shared the knowledge of my skill with anyone else. I had a chance at learning something of worth, so I listened as I got dressed.

"This isn't what you promised me!" The female's voice sounded familiar, especially with that ring of pure Irish accent, but I couldn't quite place it.

"I promised you I would remove Kaja from the picture,

and I did." Muiredach's reply was so calm that it left no doubt how little he cared about the accusation.

"But now everyone's searching for her, and Albert's worried sick!" The female didn't give up. "She should have turned up dead by now, so he can mourn, and I can comfort him."

My eyes widened as I finally recognized her and reeled with disgust. Jemma was Muiredach's spy! And judging by her accusatory and demanding tone, she was a traitor by her own choice, not a poor victim coerced into cooperating.

I clenched my fists. How long had she been playing Albert and betraying Trinity? At that, my heart almost stopped. Albert would be shattered if he learned that the woman he slept with, perhaps even considered something more, was using him.

"I need Kaja alive," Muiredach responded with the same composure. "But let's make Albert worry about you instead. Stay here for a while, so he can miss your presence. Later, we'll stage your rescue, and I'm sure you can convince him that you've suffered so much by my hand that he'll forget all about Kaja."

"Suffered?"

She let out a murmur of pleasure, and I had no trouble imagining what was going on. After all, she was a human-born, and Muiredach could play her with as little as his touch. One kiss would get her addicted, and if he kept his smile on, she'd be his without even realizing it.

I wanted to question her feelings for Albert, but with the way jealousy jarred her words, they must be at least some-what genuine. Yet she was betraying him in so many ways. I thought a woman in love would do much more to stay true to the man she had feelings for, but perhaps Jemma had different standards of what was allowed en route to her happily ever after.

"I'll make you beg," Muiredach whispered.

My stomach churned, and I stormed out of my room. The mythborn guard who was waiting to escort me stayed behind, dumbfounded at my unexpected rush. Indeed, never before had I been so eager to meet with Muiredach.

With every step I took, Jemma's murmurs of pleasure were becoming more and more unnerving, and in a moment of doubt I pondered whether I wanted to walk onto whatever they might be doing. I didn't stop. I had to look her in the eye... to see whether she had any remorse at all.

When I walked into the room in which I usually had breakfast with Muiredach, she stood in his embrace, docile and obedient, and he caressed her with his eyes narrowed. The calculating expression on his face told me what I'd suspected: he had no affection toward Jemma.

"Go. I'll be right there," he whispered, and she obeyed.

As she passed me, her absent eyes only skimmed past me without any emotion or recognition. Whatever Muiredach had done to her, it robbed her of any will.

"I thought you'd be listening." He approached me. "Did you come so fast because you were jealous of my attention?" The mocking tone indicated he didn't treat his question seriously. "You know, she *is* happier this way, receiving what she needs rather than scrambling for the attention of a man who doesn't love her."

"And you using her as a spy has nothing to do with it." I couldn't resist.

He gave me the confident smile of a man who wasn't ashamed of his deeds. "I could make you happy too." His voice changed, lower and huskier, carrying magic and promises of pleasure within.

As he approached, his presence became close to overbearing, but at the same time, it didn't dim my wits, and it definitely didn't make me want fall into his embrace. Compared to Riagán's magnetic magic, Muiredach's was repulsive. Then I remembered what Lorcan had told me about how magic worked between mythborn—because I was a myth-touched and not a human anymore, without some connection or attraction between us, Muiredach could use it for years and never get anywhere.

This realization came with overwhelming relief. To know that he couldn't make me into a copy of Jemma, addicted to him and compliant, took a serious concern off my ever-growing list of things to worry about.

"That's a lousy attempt," I said as he reached out to touch my cheek. "You should try harder looking like you're interested in me."

He immediately took a step back, dropping the mask of lust. "It was worth a try," he replied in his normal tone. "Things would be so much easier this way, don't you think?"

I didn't grace that remark with a response, and as I sat down at the table, determined to enjoy the food no matter what, Muiredach headed for the door.

"Since I have other... obligations, I'll leave you alone today," he said. "I'm sure you'll pass the time quickly trying to figure out how to get your newly acquired piece of information to Albert." He sent me a smile. "I'd be glad to inform him myself, if you decide to cooperate. If not... That's one more reason to stay alive, isn't it?"

I huffed. Of course he wouldn't have let Jemma flap her tongue if he didn't *want* me to learn that she worked for him. Even though he acted as if he knew me well, he still must feel uncertain enough if he was trying to give me reasons to stay alive rather than kill myself. Letting Albert know he had the Snake's spy in Trinity was indeed a compelling reason to suffer Muiredach's company for as long as I had to. Dead Kaja couldn't warn anyone.

Not that it made me feel better. I'd been here long enough to know my chances of escaping were close to none, so all my knowledge, no matter how precious, was useless.

Muiredach was right, though. I'd gladly spend the day figuring out how I could win against him.

CHAPTER FIVE

T he next morning, as we sat down to eat breakfast, Muiredach was in a good mood. Yet something sinister lingered in his smile, as if his joy wasn't that of a mythborn who got laid. Considering that he was uninterested in Jemma, spending a day with her—his "other obligations," as he put it—might have indeed been nothing more than a chore.

"I have a surprise for you," he said in a tone a man would use to tease an expensive gift for his lover.

As if on cue, my innards twisted, making me sick. Nothing good could come from such a statement, and since he was so excited about it, he must believe he could break me with it. I gave him a blank stare as I bit into a piece of toast, hoping I wouldn't throw it up later, and I could swear he looked somewhat disappointed.

I congratulated myself for my stone expression and focused on eating. Muiredach looked so eager to share his "gift" that he could cut breakfast short, and I had a feeling I'd need strength to get through whatever he'd prepared for me.

We spent the rest of the meal in silence, but his amber eyes shone with such excitement and anticipation that I knew this would be my last somewhat peaceful moment for the day, if not longer.

Then, no surprises, he led me to the torture room, and I braced myself, anticipating another victim... or actually becoming one, seeing as two guards had joined us on the way up. Anxious didn't even begin to describe how I felt, no matter how much I tried to not give in.

I chased all the thoughts out of my head and focused on maintaining steady breathing. Cathal believed I could do it. I had to stay strong.

We entered the torture room.

I thought I was prepared for whatever Muiredach would throw at me, but when Riagán's silver eyes fixed on me, I almost collapsed.

He hung from the same chains that used to hold Ann, and he was gagged, probably so that he couldn't kill himself. His legs were also tied and fixed to a metal hook in the floor that I hadn't noticed before—Ann was not a threat, while I could see how Muiredach would rather not take chances with Riagán.

His crumpled uniform bore marks of blood, suggesting he'd put up quite a fight, but to my relief, he looked unharmed. Not that it mattered, given the circumstances.

My blood was already rushing, and so were my thoughts, slowly changing into a chaotic noise in my head. I could feel panic encroaching like a monster devouring everything in its way, and I wanted to run. I had to stay clearheaded!

Easier said than done, of course.

"It was a real challenge to capture him." Muiredach almost burst with satisfaction, watching me closely.

I wasn't certain how much of how I felt was reflected in my face or posture. Any other time, I'd pull myself together and snicker at the thought that he must have been figuratively dying to reveal his big surprise, at the same time regretting that said dying couldn't have been more literal. Maybe I'd even share the thought with him, to burst his little bubble of conceited celebration.

Any other time, I would. But this was Riagán.

I had only enough strength to keep myself from collapsing and to keep my breaths coming in and out, in and out, in and out...

My mind felt blank, as if a sudden barrier separated me from my own thoughts, and even though I could hear them screaming at me, filled with panic and desperation, I couldn't grasp any of them except for one.

Muiredach had Riagán.

All my clever remarks, cautious plans, and cunning plots were gone, shattered by that one realization. Until now, I'd thought I had a chance, but with Riagán here, I couldn't protect us both.

"The warrioress, Sadb, cut through my pawns quicker than I expected." Muiredach's voice, still smug, tore through my stupor.

His comment brought an image of Sabd, who could plow through enemies as if they were glass figurines, and it made me wonder just how many people Muiredach had lost to keep her away. Undoubtedly, whatever the number was, he considered it a reasonable price to pay.

But Sadb... She likely thought that number wasn't enough. I could easily picture her blaming herself for Riagán's capture, adding this on top of the guilt I suspected she felt because of her lover's death, even if realistically she couldn't have done anything to save

Laoise, and I was certain she'd done everything to save Riagán.

Sometimes, it just wasn't enough. *We* weren't enough.

"Now, shall we start?" Muiredach said with anticipation.

The sickening smile on his face was a promise that Riagán would suffer as much, and more, as Ann had. This time, without a doubt, I would be made to watch.

That thought made me snap out of misery and hopelessness, desperation fueling my thoughts. No matter what, I *would* be enough. I would save Riagán.

And there was only one way I could do it.

"No," I said firmly. "I'll do what you want."

Riagán, who had so far motionlessly watched our exchange, jerked in his binds. His eyes locked on me, and his expression became insistent. The Scáthanna, his stare was reminding me, didn't make deals with the Snake.

I looked away. It wasn't the time for arguing about what was right and what wasn't, even if we actually could, and I wasn't going to ask Muiredach to allow us a conversation. I knew Riagán would kill himself only to make sure I didn't have a reason to betray the others, and I couldn't let that happen. I had to believe that there was a way for both of us to survive. I had to trust Cathal's plan, and I had to hope that Riagán would trust me.

"That quick?" Muiredach arched his eyebrows as if surprised, but with an unconcealed pleasure. After days of refusal, he'd finally gotten what he wanted. "I expected you to be stronger than that. Until now, you were doing so well..." His eyes shot toward the table where he kept his torture tools.

"You've already shown me what you're capable of, and we both know that I'd give up eventually. No point in making him suffer," I said quickly, before he made a decision I couldn't change. "You'll get what you want. I'll make the curse that kills the Afflicted." As I spoke, I kept my eyes on Riagán, ignoring the expression of betrayal on his face. I couldn't pass on the information, but he could. "But Riagán goes free."

Muiredach regarded me with narrowed eyes. "You're asking a lot for someone who has no bargaining power." With a few steps, he was at the table, picking up a small knife. "Perhaps a little demonstration will make you less demanding."

I shot toward him before that screeching "No!" even left my lips. The guard behind me, as expected, grabbed my arm and yanked me backward with a force that suggested I was a real threat he was stopping, not a desperate myth-touched with no power or weapons.

I didn't fight back, letting him hold me in place, and looked at Muiredach. "If you refuse, no deal. If you torture him, I'll kill myself."

My reaction gave him pause, and even though the pleasure of watching my helplessness was still on his face, caution sneaked into his expression, as if he wasn't sure how determined I was to carry out my threat.

"If I let him go, you'll have no reason to be compliant," he said.

"I'll give you my word. You wanted me to trust yours, and I did, so now it's your turn," I replied with a hint of challenge. "Here are my terms. You'll let Riagán go, and I'll make a blood-bound charm, so that I can be certain you didn't kill him when I wasn't watching anymore." I sent him a nasty smile, because trust only went so far. "Then I'll make the curse for you. Even better, I'll make two identical curses, so you can test one and make sure I didn't deceive you."

"And what if your lover decides to end his own life?"

Muiredach asked. His tone suggested it was exactly what he expected Riagán to do. "I'd be the one to blame, and you won't keep your part of the deal."

"He won't kill himself. I'll make sure of that. May I?" I gestured toward Riagán.

Muiredach nodded, so I knelt beside Riagán. I brushed my hand against his face, and he turned it away, pain replaced by flickers of anger. I couldn't blame him for considering me a traitor, but I had neither the time nor the privacy to explain. I wanted to tell him to trust me, but I couldn't risk that Muiredach would suspect that there were other reasons behind my agreeing to make a curse for him.

"Ree," I said softly, but loud enough for Muiredach to hear, "you have to live no matter what you think of me. Think of our promises." Riagán finally looked into my eyes, his expression still one of anger, and I dropped my voice to a whisper. "Lorcan talked. Jemma spies for the Sna—"

I knew Muiredach would catch on soon enough, but the speed he got to us still took me by surprise.

I had enough time to raise my hands in defense before he delivered a vicious kick, and then I flew to the side, my poor arms taking the brunt of his anger. As I landed on the floor, I prepared for another hit but didn't move otherwise. I'd rather not reveal to Muiredach how proficient I was at fighting, and I didn't want him to think I was a threat.

He didn't attack me again, watching me instead with a displeased expression that brought about an unexpected feeling of satisfaction. It would be the first time I'd managed to shake my captor's composure.

"I gave him a reason to live," I said. Riagán would survive long enough to get information to Cathal, and then I hoped that our ceannasaí would explain everything to him.

Muiredach grimaced but nodded. "Clever." He evaluated

me with narrowed eyes, as if he'd only just realized that I could be dangerous. "I'll agree to your deal unless you spill any other secrets of mine."

"Fair enough." I nodded as I got back on my feet—slowly, to make it clear I wasn't about to lunge at him. "I'll need curse-crafting tools, and it's going to take me at least several weeks to make those curses," I said. "I only made one before, and I didn't take notes during the process."

He didn't like it, and he didn't hide it. "I'll give you two weeks." He waved at one of the guards. "Get someone to bring me a blood-bound charm."

We stood in silence, waiting, and Muiredach regarded us both. Riagán still wasn't looking at me, and I didn't try to get closer to him, unwilling to risk the deal I'd just struck.

"He doesn't seem very grateful for what you did," Muiredach remarked casually. "So typical of the Court mythborn. Stuck in their blind pride, they don't appreciate any sacrifice other than giving one's life for a pointless cause."

"I didn't do it for him to be grateful," I replied in a colder voice than I intended, but I was walking on thin ice and didn't want to give Muiredach reasons to become suspicious. "I had a life debt, so it seemed suitable that this time I repaid it with something more than a lousy brooch."

It was risky to make the last remark, but I had to know if Muiredach would react to it in any way. So far, he'd made no indication that he knew that the Scáthanna had means to find me, and I clung to the hope that perhaps Lorcan hadn't told him about it. As Muiredach said himself, mythborn tended to keep their word, but they also tried to interpret the promises made in the way that suited them best. Perhaps it wasn't something Lorcan was obliged to reveal, or maybe Muiredach didn't ask the right question to learn about it.

Riagán lifted his head, and when he fixed his eyes on me, I was desperate to believe that his expression had softened a bit. My mention of the brooch must have reminded him that I knew they were looking for me and I was playing for time.

"Life debt?" Muiredach arched his eyebrows, his expression stuck between curiosity and suspicion. "For when you killed my poor Emma?"

"No, that would be the third time he saved my life, and I still owe him for the second one."

That was a lie, but a relatively safe one. Muiredach was aware that I cared about Riagán and was now discovering how much, but it was unlikely he knew all the details of how our relationship became what it was, because even the Scáthanna had little clue about that part. I knew because both Sadb and Lorcan had asked questions about it. Therefore, I risked the lie so that I could mention the brooch.

"It seems that Lorcan hadn't told you *everything*," I added with a smug smile.

I chanced a glance at Riagán. Muiredach would likely take it as a jab, but Riagán would figure out that Lorcan might have not told Muiredach about locating charms.

The first one was something I'd made to track down a terrorist threatening Dublin in the times that felt like a lifetime ago. Then Riagán copied the idea, with the help of a skilled mythborn craftsman, Connor, and made a better one to find me. Since then, we'd used one to search for Cait when Muiredach took her. We'd never gotten to make one to search for Lorcan, who took all his personal belongings with him when he left the Scáthanna, and I suspected he did that so we wouldn't be able to find him... and not because he intended to tell Muiredach about it.

The more I thought about it, the more certain I was that Lorcan hadn't revealed something that gave us an advantage. At the same time, he *had* revealed my skill to Muiredach...

But it didn't matter now what kind of deal he struck. Muiredach wouldn't tell me everything that he knew, and by asking questions, I could reveal something or lead him to believe there were still secrets to extract.

Riagán closed his eyes slowly. I took it as a yes and a good sign. He was starting to understand there could be more at play in my making a deal. That was all I needed for now.

Muiredach, on the other hand, gave me a cold glare. "Perhaps Lorcan didn't know. Someone in the Scáthanna has been quite secretive about his deeds and real feelings, hasn't he?" He walked over to Riagán and held his chin, forcing him to look up. "I wonder... If the roles were to swap, would you be as eager to save Kaja's life, or would you watch her suffer?" Muiredach smiled when Riagán didn't react, giving only a blank stare. "I'm almost tempted to check."

I gritted my teeth, resisting the urge to remind Muiredach he'd made a deal with me. With his obsession with torture, he could decide the curse wasn't worth as much as inflicting pain upon both Riagán and me. Things already weren't going in the direction I'd have liked them to go, and I didn't want them to lead us both to our deaths.

The guard's return brought unexpected relief, focusing Muiredach's attention back on the deal. To my surprise, as soon as Muiredach received the charm, he threw it to me.

"Play nice, Kaja." I caught the clear warning. "I don't

think you have much more information to reveal, but if you speak even a word to him..."

"Then why don't you activate the charm yourself?"

The corner of his lip lifted ever so slightly in a mocking smile. "So that you don't get to claim I hurt him and call off the deal."

I huffed. "For someone who's advocating for trust, you seem quite distrustful yourself."

"You've spent too much time among the Court myth-born, and they are deceitful, conniving bunch." He threw Riagán a glare full of disgust. "I'd like to believe you're different, but I won't risk blind faith in your honesty. This agreement is already stretching the trust I'm willing to bestow on you."

It was stretching mine too, but neither of us had a choice. That was why I always hated hostage situations. They usually occurred between people who had no reason to trust each other but no choice other than to do so.

From the array of the tools on the table, I picked a simple knife, the one that looked the cleanest of them all. Again, the urge to lunge at Muiredach fought with the voice of reason for control over my body and actions. Riagán shifted, and I could swear he shook his head, advising against an assault, but the motion was so limited, I couldn't be certain. Either way, I had to get him out of this place before I entertained my own options. He wasn't a part of my plan.

I cut a shallow line on his forearm and let his dripping blood wash over the charm before I activated it. Then I brushed his cheek with a reassuring smile, taking comfort that this time he didn't turn his face away, and I stepped back before Muiredach could complain.

"Done."

"Very well." Muiredach gestured at the guard. "Take her to the workshop."

As I left the room, I threw Riagán one last glance. Insisting that I wanted to see him leave was pointless. Muiredach would never allow me anywhere near an exit, so I couldn't be certain he would keep his part of the deal. He could have Riagán taken elsewhere, hold him captive there or even torture him, and I wouldn't know, but I had to take that risk, just like I had to agree to making those curses for him even though this could be my undoing.

I was treading on very thin ice, and below it, horrors awaited.

My hands were shaking when I walked down the steps. The adrenaline that I didn't realize had been powering my body through the whole conversation with Muiredach was waning, and in its place, fear flooded my thoughts.

I'd struck a deal with Muiredach, and there was no backing out, but I couldn't be sure he was going to keep his word and release Riagán. Perhaps all of this was for nothing...

I closed my hand on the blood-bound charm so hard it felt like I could crush it.

Part of me wanted to run back, to attack Muiredach with my bare hands—to do anything that felt like I was actually saving Riagán. I stifled that desire. I'd chosen my path, the path I thought could save us both, and to lash out like this would endanger the agreement I'd made. For my plan to succeed, I had to make Muiredach think I trusted him, so he would trust me in return—as limited as it would be, given our circumstances—and that meant I had to show I believed he'd keep his part of the deal.

Yet as soon as I left the room, I engaged my listening skill, even though Muiredach knew about it, which meant whatever he said could be calculated to ease my concerns and make me complacent. But I couldn't help it. I needed to know what happened next.

At first few steps down the stairs, it was quiet, but then Muiredach spoke.

"Quite a sacrifice, don't you think? She threw away everything, her whole life and hopes, to keep you alive and unharmed."

Riagán, of course, couldn't reply, but I would have expected him to remain silent even if he was able to speak.

Muiredach laughed all of a sudden. "Oh, don't you worry. I *will* let you go. Kaja's cooperation is worth to me more than you, so I'll keep my part of the agreement. Besides, even though I agreed to not harm you, this is a perfect way to make you suffer. You'll be back at the Court, alone"—his voice became full of vicious satisfaction, and I could imagine how he leaned closer to Riagán as he spoke —"and knowing that Kaja's in my hands, safe and unharmed but doing my bidding now. And because of that, even if you keep searching for her, even if you ever manage to find her, as unlikely as it is, you'll never be able to save her. You'll rescue her only so that your treasured ceannasaí can run his sword through her."

The guard and I were already at the bottom of the first flight of steps, and I wanted to turn around, run back, and tell Riagán not to listen to him. To once more look at Riagán and reassure him that everything was going to be fine. I wanted to make sure he knew he could still trust me.

Instead, I just clenched my jaw. Going down the stairwell was like descending into hell.

At the same time, I found reassurance in what Muiredach said. Even if he'd lied about letting Riagán go, my archer was safe for now, because he'd be kept somewhere else, out of Muiredach's immediate reach, and that was the best I could do. Everything else hinged on the plan I was putting together. If it failed, both Riagán and I would end up dead anyway.

I almost laughed at the thought that this was the only comfort I could offer to myself. Yet it made me all the more determined to succeed.

There was only one path to make it happen, and all I could do was go forward.

CHAPTER SIX

The workshop was a vast space one level above my assigned room. Filled with tables, various items, and tools, it was a true playground for any tinkerer, and about a dozen mythborn and humanborn were currently taking advantage of what it had to offer. Yet it didn't escape me that the two groups kept mostly to themselves. The humanborn worked on mechanical contraptions like traps and projectile weapons, while the mythborn crafted their amulets, charms, and curses. It seemed that even under the Snake's banner, the two groups weren't fully ready to forget their animosities, but at the same time, the atmosphere inside seemed friendly rather than hostile. In the relative silence of the workshop, I caught quiet conversations and even a short burst of laughter.

When I entered, a molekind mythborn stood up from his workstation and approached me.

"Kaja, yes?" He evaluated me with his beady brown eyes as the humanborn guard who accompanied me nodded and left. "Welcome to our workshop. I've been told you'll need curse-crafting tools." He waved at me to follow him, and we walked over to a table on the mythborn side of the room. "You can work here, and if you have any questions or you need anything, Brendan will be happy to help." He pointed at the dark-skinned mythborn sitting on the opposite side.

I gave the workshop a quick scan. "I'd prefer to work over there." I pointed at the far corner of the room, where there were only several tables loaded with what looked like junk. No one seemed to be working there. "Unless I can take what I need back to my room."

The mythborn shifted and threw me an uneasy glance. "It'd be better if you stay here. Muiredach... He'd insist you do. He believes in sharing knowledge."

"Of course he does." I didn't bother to ask whether that information sharing was encouraged via threats and torture when people weren't eager enough. "But my knowledge is what keeps me alive. I share it with you or anyone else, and he doesn't need me anymore."

His eyes widened, and his expression froze with his mouth half-open, making him look like a frightened rat. "I... understand," he said more quietly. "Of course you can take the corner. I'll get someone to help you make some space, and I'll find a set of tools for you to use."

"Thank you." I grabbed a free chair, an old one, but still looking like it belonged in a luxury office or in a gaming den rather than a makeshift workshop, and headed toward my chosen spot, ignoring the whispers of other craftsmen. Their uncertain expressions made it clear that Muiredach didn't bother to let them know I wasn't a voluntary addition to their team.

Uninvited, the mythborn followed me. I should have been blunter instead of just suggesting everyone should leave me alone. I forgot that the mythborn were adept at not taking the hint when it suited them. I considered this and their lack of respect for personal space to be their biggest personality issues.

"Name's Gobán." He stretched his arm out.

I looked at him. "That's a human gesture."

He gave me an apprehensive smile and rubbed his hand against his leg in a nervous manner that suggested I might just have passed for a mythborn.

"I apologize. I got used to it with so many humanborn around." It was his turn to stare at me. "Your name isn't mythborn, though."

I couldn't pass up that opportunity. "I apologize. I got used to it."

To my surprise, Gobán grinned. Then, with a skill suggesting he'd done it countless times, he pulled himself up onto the table and sat on it, kicking his legs in the air. "So what's your story, Kaja?" Before I could open my mouth, he lifted his hand. "I suggest you skip the part where you make it clear that we aren't friends. I know everyone here, and you'll be no exception."

I huffed and shook my head with a smile. "I appreciate what you're doing, but I can't afford indulging in small talk. I've got a job to do and way too little time to do it."

He leaned toward me, his smile sly all of a sudden. "Oh, but you can. I keep pestering you, you complain to Muiredach you can't work fast with all the distractions, and before you realize, you'll have many more days to finish your task. Because that's what you want, isn't it? More time to figure out how to escape."

I had quite a few sarcastic responses lined up in an instant, so I could pick and choose, but Gobán must have reasons to suggest he'd go against Muiredach, and snark wouldn't help me get answers, so instead I went with a less confrontational option. "I find it hard to believe you'd risk his anger for me."

"Why would he be angry? I'm just fishing for information while making you feel comfortable." He gave an innocent shrug. "You have knowledge Muiredach wants. If I'm guessing correctly, you won't freely give it to him, but maybe you'd share it with someone friendlier, right?" He glanced at the door, then at the others in the room. "But if you happen to escape before you do... If you don't serve willingly, you're a threat to all of us and to the Snake's cause, so you're better gone." He whispered the last words, and his voice made it clear: he wasn't my friend any more than I was his, but he had reasons to aid me. "Come, let's get you the tools you need," he said louder as he jumped off the table.

Mythborn and their games! I followed him, grinding my teeth in frustration. He was either being honest or he was playing me to get information. I wouldn't put it past him to do both at the same time, and that made me think of Muiredach. Yet I had to step up to the challenge if I wanted to survive and learn anything, so I plodded along as he headed back to the other tables.

"So, what do you make around here?" I offered in as amiable manner as possible. "Curses?"

As he shot me a glance over his shoulder, his yellow teeth flashed in a grin. "So, you decided to play nice with us?"

"Might as well join the game, right?"

Gobán beamed. "There ya go, lass! I was beginning to think there was something wrong with you."

He had no idea, but I wasn't about to inform him. Muiredach knew I was myth-touched, but a controlling player like him wouldn't part with that or any other information if he didn't deem it necessary, and nobody in the workshop had need for such knowledge.

"So, what will you need?" he asked.

I scrutinized the sets laid out on the table, each consisting of fine mythborn tools slotted into strips of soft leather for easy use and transport. Connor had shown me similar ones before, and Muiredach's lackeys had more or less the same range of etchers, embossers, and cutters. I could make the curse with as few as one or two of them, since when I first made it, I had no idea about how various tools affected the outcome.

Before I voiced that thought, another one struck me. I bit my tongue and took my time inspecting the sets to finally pick one of the expanded ones. "That'll do."

Without a doubt, Muiredach would be trying to gain insights into my process, maybe through Gobán, maybe through other means, and if I wanted to keep the curses' secret from him, I had to make their creation seem as complex as possible. Even if it meant I'd be wasting time poking random holes in them and adding meaningless squiggles—anything to throw his craftsmen off would be worth the delays.

"And what kind of base materials do you need?"

I shrugged. "Some inconspicuous items. Pieces of wood or metal, or even plastic."

I hid my smirk when he cringed at the last word. Mythborn stayed away from the industrially made material, claiming that it didn't work well with magic, but I had enough experience with their craft to call it what it was: bullshit born of pride. "And two items that would be small and easy to throw, like balls."

Gobán scratched his head, his nose moving in a way a sniffing rodent's would. "I'll see what I can about the orbs.

The other materials should be over there." He pointed at another table, its wooden surface almost sinking under the weight of assorted items any sane person would call by their name—junk.

"You still owe me a story," he threw out, and walked away.

Making promises I didn't intend to keep wasn't my style, so I remained silent, but I didn't think he expected any reply, as he was already checking on other workers' progress. I couldn't be the first person coerced by Muiredach that Gobán had to deal with, and he must have known to tread lightly. I didn't envy his position, balancing his superior's demands with his coworkers' good relations, but I didn't allow myself any compassion.

After all, no matter how friendly he might be, Gobán had admitted that he was working for the Snake willingly, and I wouldn't be surprised if Muiredach had picked him for the supervisor role because of his personality. A jovial molekind could befriend unsuspecting captives and gain their trust much quicker than his vile master.

I rummaged through the junk pile, though it made little difference which objects I'd pick. I'd entertained the thought of choosing something big and unwieldy, rendering the curses impossible to use in any meaningful way, but Gobán and others would study and replicate them soon enough. I was going to stick to my original plan, and I would play nice until I made my move.

CHAPTER SEVEN

Four days in, and I had the bare bones of the curse's structure laid out—much faster than the first time I made it, but back then, I wasn't a myth-touched who got to study the craft with Connor, and I only had a vague idea of what I was trying to accomplish. As much as I had hated memorizing mythborn runes that Connor had insisted on before I swapped his tutelage for a place in the Scáthanna, it broadened my understanding of how they could be weaved together.

If I ever got out of here alive, I'd be sure to thank him for his persistence. I could imagine how he'd be amused that his lessons were what helped me survive, as if he'd taught me a deadly combat skill. That thought made me miss his presence and sunny demeanor.

The mythborn working in the workshop made attempts to befriend me, reassuring me that Muiredach would keep his word if I did what he requested, so I didn't have to worry, but no matter their words, I didn't let them take a look at my creations. I also wasn't fool enough to leave them around for the night. My own survival depending on that knowledge aside, I had to be certain I left Muiredach's servants no latching points. Someone as crafty as Gobán could use them to figure the curse out.

I was staring at the four items I'd been working on when the sounds of footsteps accompanied by the quietness that befell the workshop made me swing around in my chair.

"I've been told you aren't friendly with anyone here," Muiredach said.

"I don't need distractions," I replied with just a hint of attitude to remind him that I hadn't volunteered to make the curses, "and I certainly don't need someone looking over my shoulder taking notes."

He hissed in disapproval. "You know that once you give me those curses, I'll have others study them. You might have quite a unique style, given... your past, but it's not going to be impossible to copy. Trying to keep it secret is pointless, and it makes me wonder whether you're truly working on them as you promised."

I slid my chair to the side, the old wheels squeaking on the worn wooden floor. "I'm working." I pointed at the pieces. "But I didn't say I'm going to make it easy for you to copy anything."

"Four of them?" Muiredach narrowed his eyes, suspicious again.

I almost snickered at the thought that to get what he desired, he had no choice but to trust me. This lack of absolute control must be killing him, even if he wasn't going to admit it. The perfect manipulator like him, always pushing his pawns across the board and playing others, must be suffering through every moment of the uncertainty.

Of course, I didn't pity him. We both had our own pains, because just as much as he wasn't sure whether I was doing what he requested, I had no way of knowing whether he'd released Riagán as promised. But at least in my case, it didn't matter. Even if Muiredach didn't keep his word and moved him to another place, all I cared about was that Riagán wasn't in immediate danger. My plan could still work as long as Muiredach couldn't threaten killing Riagán to keep me in check.

Yet if I wanted for things to go smoothly for me, I couldn't torment Muiredach too much, no matter how much pleasure I found in it.

"Two sets, to be precise," I replied in a casual tone, as if I were explaining my work to a friend. "The curse I designed can indeed kill anyone who has magic within, but it only activates on its own when a certain threshold is broken. Without it, the curse is dormant." I allowed myself a smile. "I'm guessing you haven't asked me to make these to prevent some humanborn from becoming an Afflicted, but to kill. That's why I'm preparing catalysts as well." I pointed at the sets. "They should be easy enough to throw from a safe distance, so there's no need to get too close, and they only emanate strong magic, so there's no risk for anyone else being hurt if you don't want it." Unless there was someone in the last stages of the affliction around, but that was beside the point.

"And what if I did?"

I chuckled. "Then you wouldn't have made a deal with me. You would have just used something from your vast arsenal." I threw my hand to the side, encompassing the room we were in.

He gave me an appreciative nod, and suspicion eased off his face. "You truly are an asset, Kaja. You should consider abandoning your foolish attachment to those who won't appreciate you."

"And what? Work for you instead?" I couldn't resist.

His cringe looked forced, as if he wasn't truly displeased —as if he'd expected my response. "That sarcasm isn't necessary. The Court mythborn care only for themselves, and to them, you'll always be a lowly being. Someone to be used but never regarded as an equal. I'm sure you know it yourself. Eithne's manipulations... Even your own team, your family, as Cathal would love to put it, doesn't fully trust you." He took a step closer, his eyes fixed on me. "The Snake cares only about the value you bring, not where you come from. You could be someone here, and you could make a difference. You could change the future of this bleak land. Working here, you could make Eireland into a place where it doesn't matter whether you're a humanborn or a mythborn."

He sounded quite convincing, and on a better day, some time in the past, I might have fallen for his arguments or at least considered his perspective. But that would have to have been before I witnessed him relishing in torture, before Laoise and Cait died, before he threatened Lorcan's family, forcing him to become a traitor, and before the bombings orchestrated by his agent almost tore Dublin apart. Not to mention his eagerness to mutilate the mythborn I was emotionally invested in, if I really wanted to go the personal route.

There was also something familiar about his rhetoric, about everyone living happily together under the Snake's rule... The future that was undivided, the future where mythborn and humanborn lived together, might be a bright one, but only for as long as one didn't remember that the Snake required obedience—no, the Snake *demanded* obedience through people like Muiredach. It wouldn't matter if you were a humanborn or a mythborn if you disagreed with the Snake—you would die or be forced to cooperate.

I knew those patterns well from human history, from the history of my own country. Only fools believed the propaganda, no matter how many honeyed words flowed from Muiredach's mouth.

"There are many wondrous things you could explore away from the Court's controlling hand. I'd give you freedom you don't have with Eithne and Cathal, because I want your brilliance to shine," he continued like a salesman who'd read my silence as hesitation. "Safe, away from the strife... And I'd make sure Riagán joined you soon enough."

"Chained to the wall, so that he doesn't escape?" I didn't hide my sarcasm.

It was one thing to assume I could be lured by his promises and entirely another to suggest that a longtime member of the Scáthanna would serve the Snake willingly. Lorcan's decision was dictated by fear for his family, and it wouldn't work on Riagán, because he knew I wasn't in danger. I clearly remembered that look of feeling betrayed that he gave me when we last saw each other. I might have done it all to get him out of Muiredach's hand, but I doubted it mattered from his perspective.

That thought hurt, but I was hoping that once Riagán talked to Cathal, he would understand and at least forgive me.

"Do you really think we'd need that?" Muiredach looked at me with curiosity. "He'd come to you if I promised I wouldn't make him betray his comrades. You might see him as unyielding, but eventually, everyone gets tired of fighting an endless and pointless war. My offer would be a safe haven from it, and you are what he considers his future."

It all sounded awfully nice. Like something he thought I wanted to hear: safety and stability alongside the companion I chose, doing work that wouldn't make me feel like I was betraying anyone if all he ever wanted me to do was to invent new curses. He made the offer alluring enough for me to agree to it.

At the same time, had Muiredach missed an important point, and it showed that he might have learned a lot about the Scáthanna, but it was unlikely that he *truly* knew any of us. Neither Riagán nor I were the "settle down" types. I didn't think quiet life was ever meant for either of us, and I doubted Riagán wanted it any more than I did. Being together? Yes, sure, but it meant doing our jobs together, not running away.

Of course, I wasn't about to point it out to my captor. Two could play the manipulation game, so I returned the favor and gave him what he wanted to see. I pretended to hesitate and consider his words.

"I don't think he'd ever agree," I whispered as if only to myself, adding a hint of sadness to my voice. "I saw it in his eyes. He felt betrayed by what I did." I allowed the real hurt I felt at the memory to sneak into my voice, adding a ring of truth to what I said.

Oh, the glint in Muiredach's eye! My performance was testing the limits of my acting skills, but clearly, it sufficed. He was certain he had me, and it was only a matter of time before I could be persuaded, no matter how much I kept resisting and refusing.

"It's because he was trained to think that way. With time, reflection will come. He'll remember that you did it only to save his life. He'll miss you and will want a chance to talk to you about your motives, to understand. And then he'll realize that even if the Scáthanna ever manage to find you, you'll be imprisoned or even sentenced to death. Do you think this is what he wants for you?"

I gave him a cunning glare. "You're telling me what I

want to hear." If it looked like I fell for his deception too easy, my own wouldn't work.

"Maybe. But it doesn't mean that it isn't true or couldn't become true. After I released him, Riagán got imprisoned under the suspicion of serving the Snake. And it was only because he didn't turn up dead and made it back to the Court on his own. He's been released now—you needn't worry." Muiredach smiled at me. "Cathal wanted his golden bow boy back badly enough, but that wasn't a surprise. After all, he's desperate for any knowledge, and your little scraps made Riagán all the more valuable."

I arched my eyebrow. "You released him."

"You heard that I would..." he started, surprised, but the emotion vanished as he pretended that an understanding had dawned on him. "Oh, but yes, you were right to have doubts. After all, I'm the Court's enemy. Eithne's lying and manipulating retinue is quick to see everyone as like them."

He wasn't exactly the Court's enemy. Eithne aside, hardly anyone there was aware of his existence, and knowing those noble pricks, even if they had an idea, they'd likely consider Muiredach to be a minor nuisance or a common thug.

He was the Scáthanna's enemy, but I kept it to myself. All I did was give him a reluctant nod, as if I wanted to acknowledge that he had kept his part of the deal. I still wasn't sure whether he truly did—words were cheap when one could spin them without worrying about any proof—but it served me better if Muiredach thought I believed him.

Visibly satisfied by my reaction, Muiredach continued, "I'm sure that by now, Riagán has realized that *you* could never be released. He might feel you betrayed him, but if you give him time, he'll rationalize what you did. He'll see mythborn laws as unjust, and my offer will be a way out."

"You've done that before, haven't you?" I couldn't play too dumb. Besides, I'd already given him enough to make him believe that he could sway me. It was time to give him the impression that I had recovered from my temporary emotional weakness and was ready to oppose him again.

"Haven't you? How many times have you gotten information by giving people what they really desired rather than appealing to their sense of honor or some other abstract concept? I'm not doing anything else."

I kept my face straight, though I itched to remark that our methods were actually quite different. At least, I didn't recall myself torturing and murdering people when they *didn't* give me what I wanted.

"Think about it, Kaja," he said with a gentleness I could have fallen for if I didn't already know what kind of myth-born he was. "We still have some time until I have to decide what comes next. For now, I'll leave you to your thoughts and your work. I trust there won't be any delays."

I shrugged. "I should be done on time. I told you that it's not something I've done enough times to be certain." I wanted to ask for more days, but I couldn't risk stretching his patience too thin, so for now, making him aware that there was a possibility of a delay had to suffice.

As he left, the quietness of the workshop died away, conversations sparking again at various tables, as if the evil had left the land of the living, allowing joy and carelessness to return.

~

THE NEXT MORNING, I ate breakfast alone, which was a pleasant change even if the food wasn't all that good. I munched on toast, made from the same square bread slices

I remembered from before the war. Back then, it was a shock to go from freshly baked Polish bread, with its crust dark brown and properly crunchy and its core chewy and firm enough across the intricate structure of a well-risen dough full of small air pockets, to the tasteless mush that you could easily squish into a ball. Later, I found that some supermarkets were offering freshly baked breads, of the German and Polish kind, and I happily swapped, even it if meant going shopping further away from home, but the memory of the mush squares stayed with me. And now Muiredach's dubious hospitality was bringing it back.

I listened to every conversation around me, finding nothing but the usual exchanges and no clue of where Muiredach might have gone. Unless he was still around, keeping silent, since he knew that I could eavesdrop on him. I hoped this was the case, because otherwise, concerns crept up. According to his own words, he'd released Riagán, but nothing in our agreement prevented Muiredach from going after him again.

The very thought made me want to glance at the blood-bound charm again, finding comfort in its steady light... except that I knew how Muiredach loved torture. There were many ways to inflict pain while keeping someone alive enough for the charm to never show me the difference. Magic, after all, wasn't all-knowing.

Then I caught something interesting. Someone in the building was crying, in that unstoppable, desperate sobbing kind of way. Usually I wasn't one to get interested in any drama, but anything out of the ordinary in Muiredach's household was worth investigating. Several other voices comforted the crying woman, and their words, though suitable for the situation, offered no suggestions as to what had happened.

Disappointed, I finished my food and headed for the workshop, accompanied, as always, by a single guard. I entertained the thought that if Sadb was in my place, she'd have taken him down barehanded, or maybe with a fork, in between the bites of cold scrambled eggs.

As soon as I entered, it became clear that the workshop was the source of the crying. A woman, barely in her thirties, if I guessed right, was sitting on the chair, her eyes red from tears, and her dark blond hair was a mess. Everyone, even Gobán, stood nearby, and their faces expressed compassion.

Yet when I walked in and the woman saw me, she jumped to her feet and lunged.

"It's all your fault!" she half screamed, half cried. "You Court mythborn have to ruin everything!"

She was trying to hit me, but it was an attack of someone blinded by pain and trying to get it out rather than anything that could truly hurt me. I knew the feeling, so I waited patiently and silently as her friends pulled her off me, whispering soothing words.

"Get her somewhere where she can rest for a while," Gobán said.

I didn't wait to see what happened next, heading for my workspace. The only drama that I would be invested in was when someone lashed out enough to try to kill Muiredach... or at least wanted to help me against him.

I hadn't even finished setting up when Gobán approached my table. "I apologize. Her lover, a mythborn, was captured last night when the Scáthanna raided one of our... places. She's desperate to blame someone, and you're the only Court mythborn around."

"I understand," I said.

He looked at me with sudden curiosity. "But do you?"

I shrugged. "She's in pain. I understand being in pain." My reply was harsher than I intended, but I hated being dragged into this. The woman had her scapegoat, someone to hate, and I wasn't going to complain about it. That should be enough for them.

Gobán shifted his weight from one leg to another as if he wanted to add something. "She'll never see him again," he said somberly.

"I understand that too," I replied, my voice quiet enough to not drag others into the discussion. "But it will be hard for me to find any compassion for her or anyone else when Muiredach killed and tortured my friends."

It struck me then. As devious as he was, Muiredach could have arranged everything, because one captured mythborn and one grieving humanborn were a small price to pay if he could convince me of his perspective. Not that I considered myself so valuable, but converting me meant he had his shot at Riagán, and I could imagine converting not one but two of Cathal's team would stroke his ego.

The pieces all fit: a woman, a humanborn I could relate to, would never see her lover again, because of the harsh Court's rules. I was to read the hidden message: similarly, I'd never see Riagán again. Maybe this was the point when I was supposed to remember that Muiredach was willing to help me and become more cooperative, seeing him in a better light. Or maybe he was building up to something bigger.

Gobán didn't hide his sadness. "We aren't all like him. We're just people who believe the Snake can make this world better. And we pay the price, sometimes a high one, like..." He moved his head to look at the door, but the woman wasn't within sight anymore.

"But you report to him. If this is the kind of leaders the Snake chooses... How can anyone believe in what you say?"

To that, he didn't have an answer. He gave me a small nod and walked away, leaving me to my work.

With all that had happened in the morning, I wanted to take a break and be anywhere but the workshop. Well, almost anywhere. The prospect of being stuck in the torture room again, watching Muiredach torment another human-born or mythborn, made me grateful I was here, where the worst that could happen was the tantrum of a woman who'd lost her lover.

But, in a way, perhaps it was worse. With Muiredach, the lines were clear. Everything he did fell into the pure evil category, so I knew where I stood. With Gobán and others... They weren't evil. They were, as Gobán had put it himself, just people who believed in their cause. It was easy to forget that they supported the Snake, who through his agents killed both humanborn and mythborn, most of them inno-cent civilians. In a way, I had to be more on my guard in the workshop than around Muiredach.

I leaned over my work, feeling the glares of others on my back. I hoped they feared their boss enough to leave me alone.

CHAPTER EIGHT

The next morning, Muiredach still wasn't around, and his absence made my captivity a much more pleasant experience, if such an experience could be had, given my circumstances. When I entered the workshop, everybody looked up from their work but quickly returned to it, and I made it through the room undisturbed. The woman whose lover was captured wasn't there, which hopefully meant the day would be drama free.

I made it to my table and settled into work, taking my time etching symbols. Connor would have laughed if he saw me being so precise with them. Back when I was a new myth-touched and his unofficial apprentice, he always remarked about how my runes looked subpar in comparison to mythborn craft, though he was never malicious about it, because we both knew that making the runes look pretty did nothing in terms of the functionality and magic flow. I always thought he just liked giving me a hard time about something, and I appreciated it. Outside of the Scáthanna, who were more like teammates or even a family, he was the only friend I had at the Court, and one of the few mythborn I genuinely liked.

I tried to clear my mind. Thinking about people dear to me that were likely worried sick did nothing to improve my situation, and my time was running short. I doubted Muiredach would have me killed or tortured immediately after I finished the curses. More likely, he'd try to convince me to join his cause. If I agreed, he'd have me moved somewhere away from Dublin, under the guise of his promised "safe haven away from strife," or however he liked to put it.

On the other hand, Muiredach had to realize that he could never be sure whether I'd truly agreed to his offer or was simply looking for an opening to get away... or kill him. He could never trust me fully, and once he realized it, I'd likely be dead. Even if he believed me, I'd have to watch my every step and do things that would convince him of my loyalty. I preferred not to think what kind of tests his cruel mind would conjure.

I preferred not to, but my mind, nevertheless, was willing to oblige, creating darker and darker scenarios, and I was becoming desperate for any kind of distraction from, well, myself.

Normally, I wouldn't bother with any commotion behind me, but this time, I immediately started paying attention. Even some more drama would be better than my own thoughts.

"Muiredach's not here?" someone asked, and his voice sounded familiar.

"No, he has business to attend elsewhere." Gobán approached. "But I can get you what you need."

I still couldn't place the voice, so I turned around. A mythborn stood in the door, so large that he could barely fit into the frame, but he wasn't one of the bridge dwellers. It took me a moment to recognize who he was, but once I did, I couldn't help staring.

Donovan, one of the local leaders of the Mythborn Protection Force, a quasi-guerrilla organization that fought for mythborn rights, who officially denied any contacts with the Snake, was making deals with Gobán in a place that had to be Muiredach's main hideout, judging by the building's size.

Then our eyes met.

I knew I shouldn't have stared, but it wasn't often that one found clear proof of the MPF's involvement with the Snake... Proof that I could do nothing with.

Donovan looked at me with curiosity, and his eyes slightly narrowed, but I couldn't tell whether he'd recognized me without my uniform, so I looked away, like anyone caught staring would.

He waved at Gobán, and they both left the room.

I hid my smile. Neither of them knew that walking away would not save them from being eavesdropped on. Pretending I was focused on my work again, I tuned in to their voices.

"The one at the far table... You know who she is?" Donovan asked.

"She's making some special curses for Muiredach," Gobán replied. "Just a Court mythborn he managed to force to do his bidding. Her name is Kaja."

"If that's her name, she's more than that." Donovan's voice sounded gravely. "She's one of Cathal's and a myth-touched."

"You're kidding, right? Myth-touched don't look like mythborn. I heard they're all twisted at least a bit. Sometimes almost like a Léanmhar. She looks like us, walks like us... Talks a little bit different, sure, but I thought she was one of those who try to sound more humanborn, especially with that odd name she chose."

"The Court got better at making myth-touched," Donovan replied. "And I've seen her once before. Definitely one of Cathal's."

I could imagine Gobán shaking his head as he said, "Are you sure? Muiredach's too cunning to bring someone like that in here."

"Muiredach's obsessed with the Scáthanna. He'd been hunting them for a while now. Took down a few, so there's that. But to keep one alive and make her work for him... That puts all of us in danger."

"She knows you?" Gobán asked, concerned.

"Oh, she does." The way Donovan said it, it sounded like he was smiling. "I had a run-in with Cathal's team not so long ago, and it would be very hard to forget me."

"Well, it's not like Muiredach's going to let her go. You don't have to worry that she'll reveal your ties to us."

"I don't worry about that. It would be her word against mine at the Court. I could have it easily dismissed. And Cathal having his suspicions means little to me," Donovan said with confidence. "What I worry about is that she's still alive. Muiredach should know better. Cathal's looking for her, and he already knows about our operations here more than he should. Muiredach's stupid obsession puts all this in danger."

"Nothing we can do about it," Gobán replied.

"But maybe she can." Donovan's sly tone was a surprise. "She's observant and smart. Likely more dangerous than Muiredach thinks."

I arched an eyebrow at Donovan's unknowing compliment, though he'd somewhat overestimated how much of a threat I was.

"She made a deal, and she looks like the type to keep her word."

"So she'll keep it," Donovan said dismissively, as if it didn't matter. "All I'm saying is that when she makes her move, you should be prepared to run. Because she will make one. Cathal doesn't pick dimwits for his team." There was a pause, as if he was considering something. "It makes one wonder whether she's truly Muiredach's prisoner. Perhaps she's exactly where Cathal wants her to be..."

I swallowed, feeling the sudden urge to storm out and kill Donovan. Not that I had any means to do so, and the damage had already been done. This mythborn was way too smart for his own good. Of course I was preparing to make a move, but my whole plan hinged on making sure nobody saw it coming. Now Gobán was aware I might be plotting something, and he could warn Muiredach...

It was just my bad luck that the MPF leader happened to do business with the Scáthanna's worst enemy. Not that he was much lower on the list himself. A match made in hell!

The problem was that I didn't have enough time to come up with a new plan to outsmart everyone. The only thing I could do was to proceed as I was and hope they did not see through my deception.

The commotion at the door made me look up again. There was no harm in it, since I knew Donovan had recognized me anyway. He looked straight at me and gave me a short nod, one that could be given in passing to an acquaintance.

I could swear there was respect in his eyes.

∾

IN A WAY, being Muiredach's prisoner resembled working for a corporation in a pre-Magiclysm Dublin. You'd get up, go to work, and come back home, having little time for yourself before you had to go to bed and get up again the next morning. Even some personalities fitted: Muiredach could be the great evil boss, and Gobán could play the role of a friendly team leader from the lower management who, with a sad and apologetic smile, carried out his superior's unpleasant directives.

And the workshop even had a lunch break of sorts.

Back in the old days, "lunch" was a mandatory hour of unpaid time the law required everybody to take, with very little flexibility. Mostly because if the break was shorter, it fell into the two fifteen-minute breaks the law required employers to give for every four hours worked, which were to be included in the paid work time.

But if, instead, you gave your employees a one-hour lunch exactly in the middle, it meant they had two four-hour shifts instead of one eight hours long, and no additional breaks were necessary. Thirty minutes of paid time per day saved... With such enormous savings, who cared about making the employees' day more difficult and causing the work day to effectively last nine hours plus commute, which often added another hour, if not more?

At Muiredach's place, there weren't set work hours and no obligatory lunch break, but at a certain point of the day, almost everyone in the workshop took a break and ate something together. Surprisingly, both humanborn and mythborn vacated the room, which made me think that the humanborn just followed their old, prewar habits, and the mythborn adapted to that rhythm of the day without questioning its origin.

I had neither reason nor desire to socialize with them,

and I sensed that, despite Muiredach's insistence on everyone playing nice, they didn't like me much, especially not after that woman's dramatic outburst, so I habitually skipped the midday meal, enjoying the relative solitude. Of course, there were always a few of Gobán's team staying behind, likely to keep an eye on me, but it was better than nothing.

I leaned over my work, pondering my next steps.

Donovan's comments worried me, especially if he or Gobán decided to share those thoughts with Muiredach, but I also had a bigger problem. The closer I got to the completion of my curses, the harder it became to conceal what I was doing and how. At this stage, anyone well versed in runes would likely be able to tell how I constructed the curse and perhaps even finish it on their own. That meant a serious threat to my secrets... and possibly my life as well.

"I'll be here for a while"—Gobán's voice came unexpectedly—"so you can take a break, lads. Go and have a bite."

It would be hard to pretend I didn't hear him in the workshop's dead silence, so I turned my chair just enough to acknowledge his approach. He held out a plate with a sandwich like a peace offering.

I took it and placed it to the side while he propped himself up to sit on the table instead of pulling another chair closer. He did that often with others as well, and I wondered whether he liked the informality or simply preferred to be at the eye level with people.

"Muiredach says I'm not checking on you enough," he said, "so here I am."

"He's back, isn't he?"

It didn't surprise me, even if I couldn't hear him around. He could have returned while I was still sleeping, or had important conversations someplace I couldn't hear him. The whole building was so heavily warded that my skill couldn't penetrate its protections, so it made sense that Muiredach would put even more effort into shielding a place that was his office or a meeting room, *especially* as he knew I'd do my best to eavesdrop on him.

"Earlier today." Gobán nodded. "Not happy, either. Whatever he was busy with, it didn't go how he wished it to go."

"So you're here to check if I'm still keeping my word and making the curses." I put my hand over them in a clear sign I wouldn't let him inspect said curses.

To my surprise, Gobán smiled. "With his suspicious nature, no amount of your reassurances would suffice."

"If he takes these curses away from me," I said coldly, "I'll refuse to finish them."

Gobán narrowed his eyes, his smile becoming slyer. "And what happens when he doesn't need you to finish them anymore? The closer to the end you get, the easier it will be to figure it out."

I remained silent as he voiced my own concerns.

"If I were you, I'd focus on diverting his suspicions," Gobán said. "Give him something else to worry about."

"That's quite the friendly advice." I stared him in the eye.

He gave a small shrug. "I've been thinking about what you said. About how... some people make it hard to put us all in good light." He leaned closer, his voice becoming quieter. "I know what and who you are. That means you have something in mind, and I think you deserve a shot. But if you don't do anything, Muiredach will grow more and more suspicious, and he'll act to stop whatever plots he suspects."

That was something I did not expect. Though, if one thought for a moment, it made sense. They might be on the same side, but it was clear that Muiredach was a thorn in Gobán's side. While the friendly molekind seemed to genuinely believe in whatever ideals had brought him into the Snake's service, his superior was someone obsessed with power and dishing out cruelty, which I would bet jeopardized any recruitment efforts.

Gobán himself wouldn't do anything against Muiredach, even if he had the means to do so, but I could... Having the Scáthanna member do the dirty work for him would be perfect, seeing as it was Muiredach himself who had brought me here. If I killed him—or better yet, if we killed each other—no one would think even for a moment that Gobán was to blame.

"Donovan thinks you're smart," he continued. "But Muiredach... He doesn't consider you all that smart, because he managed to outwit you. You could convince him you aren't that smart. An escape attempt could make him think you don't have a more cunning plan."

"Or make him furious."

Gobán shrugged, unmoved. "It's a risk. You'll have to decide for yourself whether you're willing to take it or hope that he doesn't catch on to whatever you're truly planning. Who knows? Maybe you even make it outside. Truly escape."

I huffed. Without my equipment nor knowing my way around the building, I'd be lucky if I made it one level down. "I hardly have resources for a convincing escape attempt."

He nodded and slid a small item across the table, stopping his hand behind the plate he'd brought me. Anyone walking in would fail to see anything out of the ordinary. "I suppose one misplaced stun curse won't spark too many questions."

One stun curse... Enough to incapacitate the guard who

always escorted me back to my room and locked the door. Or enough to throw it at Muiredach and take my chance before he recovered...

No. I knew he was always on his guard when around me. And he knew that Sadb had trained me and that I *could* have enough skill to kill him. If I wanted to succeed, I had to stick to my original plan.

I still could take Gobán's advice on diverting Muiredach's attention. I swiped the curse off the table. "That's a risk for you too," I said.

If my escape attempt enraged Muiredach enough for him to torture me, I might not be able to keep Gobán's involvement secret—if I was willing to do so in the first place. Given he was my enemy, no matter how helpful, he had to assume I'd expose him in an instant if my own life was threatened.

"I suppose I can't expect you to take risks that would be of benefit to me if I don't take some myself," he said. "I like you, Kaja. I think we could use more people like you here and fewer people like him." He hesitated. "Once all is done, consider sticking around. Get to truly know us. You might think ill of the Snake, but we provide for those who stay with us. On your own, forever hunted by the Court... What kind of life is that?"

I didn't reply. After all, they were also forever hunted, and the only comfort they had was companionship in shared misery. "If there was a chance for a normal life... away from all that... would you take it?" I asked instead.

Gobán gave me a sour smile. "There's never going to be a chance. It's been like that for centuries, and the Court is unyielding. Yes, they could make a promise, but in the end, it would be a lie. It's just prison or death. The Snake's bite is for life, whether you like it or not." He looked me in the eye.

"And now you've made a deal yourself. I hope whatever Muiredach promised you was worth it, because even if you manage to do whatever you're planning to do, there's no return for you."

I swallowed. I'd talked to Cathal about it before we agreed to the plan, and I knew the risks. But because of that, I had hope stemming from the trust I put in my ceannasaí. They had nothing. I couldn't help wondering how many of them stayed because they had no other choice. First they were coerced into doing something for Muiredach or another vicious servant of the Snake, and then they were left with no other options if they wanted to live.

For the first time, I felt sorry for the people in the workshop. I was certain that the pleasant atmosphere around was only due to Gobán's effort to make it feel less like a prison. Sure, some of them served the Snake willingly, but they had no way out if they ever changed their mind.

"Let's see how it all unfolds," I said in a noncommittal manner. "For all I know, I might be dead tomorrow." Or dying, tortured by a psychopathic mythborn.

He gave me a nod. "And how much of those curses can you allow me to see?"

"Nothing," I replied firmly. "I won't risk you figuring it out."

He laughed, shook his head, and jumped off the table. "Right. Well, everyone should be back soon, so I'll leave you to your thoughts. And you better have some food. Heroic acts rarely work out on an empty stomach." He walked away to another workstation, leaving me alone.

I gave an amused huff, painfully aware that it was so easy and comfortable to fall for Gobán's jovial demeanor. Before I even realized, we could become fast friends, and I'd be sharing secrets not meant for him. It was easy to fall blind like that, if I allowed myself to forget that we were enemies bound by nothing more than a common goal.

Watching the door to make sure no one was about to enter, I leaned to the side and slid the stun curse into my shoe. It wasn't the best hiding spot, but I just needed to keep it out of sight for the rest of the day.

CHAPTER NINE

By the time I left the workshop, the stun curse was again in my hand. The guard didn't notice, because I always carried my regular curses back to my room, following the short inspection by Gobán to ensure I hadn't taken anything else with me. Needless to say, he wasn't very thorough this time around. I demonstrated my open palms with the four curses I'd been working on, while the stun curse was riskily wedged between my fingers, its small disc sticking out mostly on the other side.

As I walked down the corridor, the guard behind my back, I pondered my options. It was an early evening, too early for everyone to retire for the night, but I couldn't wait, unless I wanted to try escaping in the morning. If Muiredach decided to have a breakfast with me, which was likely, he'd know too soon that something was wrong, making my chances even slimmer than they already were.

I regretted not staying longer in the workshop with an excuse of needing more time to finish my work, but anything out of the ordinary would have been reported to Muiredach. Taking a few days to get everyone used to my new work times was also risky. At any moment, Muiredach's suspicions could get the better of him, and he'd have me and my room searched.

This evening was my best bet, and it aligned with Muiredach's recent absence too. It would look like I used those days of lax supervision to plot my escape.

We went one level down, and as I approached the door to my room, a familiar adrenaline rush flowed through my body.

I walked inside, just enough to clear the door, and immediately spun in place. As always, the guard was already leaning to reach for the handle to close the door and lock me in for the night, and he wasn't prepared for my abrupt movement. While he froze with an expression that seemed to be saying, "Processing, please wait," I activated the stun curse and flicked it toward him.

It hit him square in the face.

We were close to each other, so I got hit by some of the magic too, but unlike him, I was prepared. He dropped to the ground while I only stumbled backward, fighting the curse's effect, and as soon as I regained my footing, I was by his side.

Dragging his body into the room took more time than I liked. He was a large man, likely chosen for his bulkiness so that he could overpower me easily if needed. I closed the door and searched him, finding nothing I could use as a weapon. Clearly Muiredach didn't want to take risks, relying solely on the man's physical build to control me.

I wasn't surprised. Back when I was a human, I hardly looked like someone who would put up any fight, and my physique didn't change much when I became myth-touched. Training with Sadb focused on precision and skill rather than sheer strength, so I didn't have impressive muscles to show for it, even if I had become somewhat stronger. It was easy to take me for someone weaker.

Stun curses didn't last long, so I pondered my options. Killing him would be the best, but with no blades it would take time I didn't have, and if he came to, I'd be at a serious disadvantage. Besides, murdering an incapacitated man didn't sit well with me. He wasn't a threat anymore.

On the other hand, he was an enemy, and I had no doubt that, were our roles swapped, he wouldn't bother with such dilemmas. I discarded that argument. To give in to such thinking meant stooping to his level. In the war, I'd done questionable things—we all did—but it didn't mean I couldn't try to be better than Muiredach and the like.

That name cleared my head, and I stood up. I didn't have time to ponder ethics, and I didn't have time to kill, either. The guard would soon regain consciousness, and I'd lose my chance.

I glanced around the room. Without any weapons or curses, I would be useless in combat, so I had to count on people taking me for yet another worker in the building sent on an errand. My plain clothes would work in my favor, and I could pick up the duvet from my bed, bundling it. It would conceal my face, but it would get in the way of me seeing anything. I didn't know the building well enough to pretend I knew where I was going.

So in the end, I didn't waste any more time. My chances of escaping were slim anyway. I just had to make it look like I'd tried, making Muiredach think I wasn't capable of coming up with a better plan.

I made my way down the corridor, back to the stairs. I hoped that Muiredach hadn't done any serious work to the place's structure, and like in every residential building, the stairs ran all the way down to the ground floor... or the "first floor," as Americans would have it.

My instincts screamed against walking so openly, and I had to fight the urge to try to sneak or find hiding spots in case someone entered the corridor. In this one instance, acting like I belonged here could get me further.

I made it to the stairwell and peeked over the railing. I could see the ground floor, and it felt like a promise of freedom, but people were going up and down, and I took a step back. The exit would probably be heavily guarded. Perhaps it would be better to find a secluded room and search for any weapons or tools...

I almost snickered. I was taking this whole escape thing way too seriously, considering the real purpose of staging it and the chances I'd had to slip away from Muiredach.

At the sound of footsteps behind me, my instincts took over, even though they shouldn't have if I wanted to maintain my cover of being just another worker going about her business.

"I was waiting for you to try something." Muiredach approached, though he still kept a few steps away, as if unsure whether I was going to lunge at him. "What I didn't expect is such a lousy escape attempt."

He looked composed, but I would bet he'd had at least a moment of panic when he discovered my empty room with the unconscious guard inside.

"I figured you were, and I hated the thought I'd disappoint you by not trying anything," I replied.

His narrowed eyes suggested he didn't like my response. "We had an agreement. I kept my part of it."

I grimaced. The reminder that I'd had to make that deal in the first place didn't put me in an agreeable mood. "I'm making the curses for you, as promised. Not trying to escape was never part of our agreement." I shrugged. "Besides, if I *didn't* try to escape, you'd just grow more suspicious and paranoid and, as a result, even more insufferable. Now we got it out of the way. I tried, I failed, and you can sleep better."

His face twisted in anger as he sneered. "You're forgetting the part where I punish you."

No, I definitely hadn't forgotten that part. I'd spent my whole afternoon deciding whether staging an escape attempt was worth the risk. I still mustered a smile. "I was hoping you'd be benevolent enough to forgive me."

He lunged, and I let him believe I didn't see the attack coming in time. I knew he had never witnessed me fight, so a little deception couldn't hurt. Yet I still had trouble not bursting out in laughter when he slammed me against the wall. Muiredach might be a skilled player, but he was only about as strong as I, so somewhere between pitiful and unimpressive. No wonder he needed an army of henchmen for any attack on us, because one on one he wouldn't stand a chance with a single member of the Scáthanna.

I pushed against him as I looked him in the eye with challenge. "If you aren't done, you better get someone to help you."

He let me go, composed again. "No. The lesson will be more valuable if I teach you myself."

Muiredach leaped backward with more agility I'd given him credit for and flung a small object toward me. It looked much like the curse I got from Gobán, so I had a pretty good idea what was coming. Standing against the wall in a rather narrow corridor, I had little chance of dodging. Besides, if I proved too difficult, I could enrage Muiredach more, ruining my chances at light punishment and survival. It was time to make him feel in power again.

I swatted at the curse, making it look like an instinctive reaction rather than a trained one, and as it activated, a wave of paralyzing pain traveled through my body. *Ugh!* I hated stun curses, especially direct hits. My limbs stiffened in an instant, refusing to obey, and even though I fought the curse's effect, I collapsed within a few heartbeats.

Yet this time I didn't lose consciousness like the few times back when I was a humanborn, as if the magic in my body protected me. This was something I had to keep in mind and perhaps ask Sadb about, because I'd rather not face a mythborn one day only to discover he or she was immune to half of my arsenal.

Muiredach stood above me as if cherishing his great victory. Then he grabbed me by my ankles. Without a word, he dragged me across the floor, and even the thought that he was likely sweating performing this athletic feat couldn't ease the feeling of the floor brushing against my back, cold and hard. My paralyzed arm caught on the railing of the stairs as Muiredach maneuvered through the narrow space, but he didn't even look back as he started his ascent, and a sharp pain traveled up my limb before it broke free of the obstacle.

Then, after the third or fourth stair over which he ruthlessly dragged me, I lost consciousness.

WAKING up to the familiar smell of old blood and urine was hardly a surprise. Hanging by my hands and gagged, I expected Muiredach to be waiting for me to regain consciousness like a giddy little girl, but the torture room was empty. Perhaps he wanted me to stew for a while, trying to anticipate what he was about to do to me. I had enough images stuck in my head from when he'd tortured poor Ann to speculate on how he'd proceed with me, but I didn't bother. Either he'd decided he was done with me, and then it didn't matter what he did, because I'd be dead in the end, or he was indeed only teaching me a lesson, and I'd survive.

I tried not to think that, in order to make curses for him, I didn't need *all* my limbs... And even if he left me in one piece, an ocean of pain stretched between that point and my current, somewhat untouched state.

If my arms could sigh with relief, they would when I got back on my feet. Muiredach must have left me hanging like that overnight. I moved my head carefully, waiting for some sharp pain to announce a serious injury, but I felt fine, so I might have gotten away with only a nasty bump.

"I don't understand why we need to discuss it again." Gobán's voice came from the outside, and then he walked in along with Muiredach. The molekind mythborn froze as soon as his eyes fixed on me. "I want no part in this."

I almost arched my eyebrow at the clear challenge in his voice. Gobán wasn't foolish enough to risk antagonizing Muiredach for someone like me—someone who was an ally of convenience at best, and a serious threat at worst. After all, just because I wanted Muiredach dead, it didn't necessarily mean I didn't want Gobán dead as well.

I watched their interaction with curiosity. It could be the mother of all clichés, the "good cop, bad cop" routine. Or maybe Gobán felt a pang of guilt, as he was the very reason for my current situation.

"And you won't, don't worry." Contrary to his reassurance, Muiredach led Gobán to the bloodied table with all the tools laid out. "I want you to have a look at these."

When he displayed my Afflicted-destroying curses, my

blood turned cold. If Gobán figured out what I was doing and how, I was dead.

"She finished them?" He leaned forward with genuine curiosity.

"You tell me," Muiredach replied, at the same time watching me with narrowed eyes. I gave him no reaction, painfully conscious that Gobán's judgment would save me or bury me.

Gobán snatched up my curses without further encouragement. "The runes are very crude, sometimes hard to read," he mumbled as he turned the objects in his hands. "And the structure is odd... but not random. Makes sense."

Muiredach arched his eyebrow in surprise. He clearly wasn't expecting me to have been actually working on them. "Can you finish it?"

"Maybe. Maybe not. The structure is cleverly laid out. Good base, but still missing enough to make it a guessing game. Somebody might figure it out, but when?" He shrugged. "If we're lucky, it could be days. If we're not, years. There's too many possibilities."

I watched Gobán for any clue that he actually knew what I was doing, but he had a good poker face. No wonder, considering with whom he had to work on a daily basis.

"I see." Muiredach took the curses back. I could swear he sounded less suspicious now.

"So, she coming back to work, or you want us to take chances?" Gobán stared at him.

I had to admire the pint-sized mythborn. He might be working for Muiredach, but he sure didn't cower in his presence. Unless, of course, this was also part of my captor's deception. He knew I'd never trust him, but Gobán came across likable. I wanted to believe it wasn't Muiredach's plot, but even my escape attempt, given how quickly he'd found me, could have been all his doing. In a place like this, surrounded by enemies, my paranoia had fertile grounds to grow, but at the same time, it could be the one thing that would help me avoid any pitfalls.

"Let me worry about it." Muiredach waved off the other mythborn in a clear dismissal.

Gobán shot me a glance that could have been compassionate or apologetic, but he moved his head away too quickly for me to tell. Then he darted out at a speed that made it clear he wasn't comfortable in the torture room. I couldn't blame him. If he was as genuine and caring as he seemed, to witness someone else's torment would be unbearable, especially as it was his suggestion that put me here.

"I thought about what you told me last night about meeting my expectations." Muiredach walked over to me, but his hands were empty. "You play a very dangerous game, Kaja. One that is more likely to get you killed than if you simply met my wishes." He removed my gag. "Instead of doing foolish things to ease my suspicions, just finish the curses you promised me. Yes, I forced Lorcan to betray the Court, but I kept my word when he gave me what I needed. His wife and daughter are safe, and I didn't kill him. I'm even less inclined to kill you, because I *know* you can see reason." He cocked his head, inspecting me. "Unless, of course, you insist on doing things that test my patience."

Of all the witty responses I had at the ready, I chose none. If Muiredach had something right, it was that I trod a thin line indeed. Until Cathal and the others found me, I had to stay alive, and being tortured because I couldn't keep my mouth shut didn't align with that goal.

Muiredach gave me a nod, as if he appreciated my silence. "I'll give you the curses back and allow you to keep their secret until you're done. But since you still need punishment, I'll keep your blood-bound charm."

I clenched my fists. But as much as I'd grown used to finding comfort in the charm's subtle magic reassuring me that Riagán was still alive, I didn't *need* it. The charm didn't prevent Muiredach from going after him again and keeping him captive in another place. But showing emotion would reassure Muiredach that he had leverage over me, so I did my best. After my escape attempt, this would be a subtle way to convince him that he was still in control and that I wouldn't be able to outsmart him.

He unlocked my shackles and headed for the table as if knowing he could turn his back on me, at least this once. I took some time to test the extent of my muscles' soreness with some cautious stretches.

"Let's make a trade, then." Muiredach held up the blood-bound charm. "I'll let you keep it if you answer honestly. How long do you really need until the curses are ready?"

I cringed. My honest answer wouldn't be the one he was expecting. "I'll need all the time I have left. Maybe more. When I told you 'weeks,' I was stretching it already." I added a bitter smile to my words. "I was somewhat desperate to make you agree to the deal, so I might have oversold my capabilities."

Muiredach held out the charm to me. "It wasn't that hard, was it?"

I grabbed it quickly, like a person who feared he'd change his mind. It might have been a bit overdone, but his satisfied expression suggested that he savored the power he thought to have over me.

"It's different to betraying my friends," I said begrudgingly.

He rolled his eyes. "Don't be stubborn. I won't ask you to butcher Cathal in his sleep or reveal Albert's secrets."

"It's not that simple," I snapped. I kept to myself the thought that he *would* ask me to do those things once he ensured I truly had no other choice.

"It is. You don't have to fight, and you don't have to kill. You could be away from those pointless tussles, working on something you care about. And I promise I'll do anything in my power to make sure Riagán sees reason as well. You know that I do keep my word."

I brushed past him, muttering, "I know," and hoping that I sounded upset enough about it. I took the curses from the table. "Now, if you're done, I'll go and make sure I keep mine."

He didn't stop me as I headed for the door. I kept my face neutral, with just a tinge of frustration, like someone who wasn't ready to admit that she was wrong. Deep within, I savored the look on his face. Muiredach's smug expression told me that my escape gamble had paid off. My little show had convinced him once more that he had a chance of swaying me to the slithering side, and that, in turn, ensured my survival.

It didn't escape me that Muiredach didn't assign a guard to accompany me to the workshop, as if he wanted to show goodwill and trust. When he couldn't see me anymore, I smiled, certain that we were both lying about trusting the other. That served me well. From now on, until I was ready, I would play a compliant prisoner.

I SHOULD HAVE KNOWN BETTER than to hope for a quiet day, but then, I shouldn't have tried to eavesdrop on Muiredach.

Shortly after I left the torture room, he had another victim brought in. I swallowed hard when he launched into a long lecture about the consequences of letting important prisoners escape, because I had a good idea of who his victim was. The poor guard I'd left unconscious was going to pay for my "escape" with his own blood, and I doubted Muiredach was going to let him off easy.

I tried to not feel sorry for someone who'd likely carried out all sorts of Muiredach's orders in the past, many of them likely violent or lethal, but nobody deserved to be tortured like that, and for nothing more than one sadistic mythborn's pleasure and the dubious purpose of teaching others a lesson, seeing as the guard wasn't likely to survive—so, enemy or not, I felt some compassion. And the feeling of guilt that accompanied me for the whole morning stemmed from the thought that I could have spared this man his plight if only I took a moment to kill him before escaping.

At the same time, I was grateful that Muiredach didn't make me watch. I could tune out my listening skill and focus on my work, trying to forget what was happening just one floor above us, and I did. Thankfully, everyone in the workshop left me alone.

Around midday, I heard shuffling behind my back. When I looked around, the few mythborn and humanborn who usually stayed behind while others went to lunch were leaving the workshop, and Gobán was approaching my table, carrying a plate with two sandwiches. He wore a wide smile.

"You're coming to tell me that I owe you, aren't you?" I asked once we were alone.

He shook his head. "Nay. I suppose we're even." He set the plate and climbed up onto the table beside it.

My surprise at his response vanished when the pieces

fell into place. "You told him I was planning something," I said accusingly. No wonder Muiredach got to me so quickly... He was likely waiting around the corner, waiting for me to make a move.

Gobán didn't look too apologetic when he said, "You actually escaping wasn't really in my best interest."

"I bet it wasn't." I sounded sour, but I deserved it for allowing myself to trust Gobán.

He became serious and lowered his voice as he said, "Now even more so. Muiredach can't get his hands on these curses."

I understood the message: since I was going to keep my word and make them, I was to ensure Muiredach didn't live long enough to ever use them. Then the other meaning of the words dawned on me. "You could finish them."

"Possibly." Gobán shrugged. "I saw enough to have an idea what you're trying to do, and if I'm right, this is not something that should fall in the wrong hands... perhaps any hands." He eyed me with curiosity. "Since he went through the trouble of getting to you instead of stealing them, I take it you made none for the Court?"

"No one at the Court even knows they can be made," I replied. "The Scáthanna kept it secret at my request, and I have never made any except for the first one, which is now gone."

He gave me a slow nod. "We already have enough ways to defend ourselves, so we have no need for a curse like that."

I grimaced. "You can't pretend that the Snake's supporters aren't already using what you create to sow chaos in the city, bringing us back to the brink of war."

Gobán waved a finger at me, and his expression wasn't playful. "No, lass, you aren't going to bring all your politics in here. We're just a bunch of mythborn and humanborn who are trying to survive the Court's relentless pursuit. You focus on the one who uses such tactics."

I wanted to tell him that turning a blind eye to what Muiredach and others—since I had no doubt there were more like him out there—were doing not only failed to solve his problems but also created more, and in the end, he had to resort to using the enemies, namely me, to solve them, but I bit my tongue. He was right when he said that once the Snake bit you, you had no other choice... Sure, you could try to cut ties, live with your head low, and desperately hope no one recognized you for what you were, because if they did, it was death or imprisonment.

"I will," I promised. "Thanks for today." I grabbed one of the sandwiches from the plate.

"You know... If that plan of yours fails but doesn't get you killed, consider making another deal with him. I know, I know." He waved his hand in a dismissive manner. "Bad Snake and all that. But Muiredach wants something else from you, something that is more important than those curses, and that means you get to live and plan again."

His words gave me pause. The only thing I had that would be of any worth was knowledge—not even that of the Scáthanna, as he'd probably gotten everything he wanted from Lorcan, but that of Trinity and Albert, perhaps some things that Jemma, being just a researcher there, didn't know. That made me wonder how much Muiredach really knew about me and whether he realized that I'd sooner die that put Albert in any danger—he couldn't threaten Albert's death to make me cooperate, and he couldn't make me reveal anything that could lead to Albert's dying, either.

In a situation like this, no deal was possible, yet I said,

"I'll keep it in mind." This wasn't Gobán's problem, and his advice was sound.

He smiled. "Well, I better go, then. After all, it's not like we're friends who share secrets and advice." He jumped off the table, grabbed his sandwich, and headed to his own workstation.

I smiled. He was good. The goal we had in common aside, he was playing me well in that careful approach between forcing me out of my comfort zone and giving me enough space that I didn't feel threatened—as if he was taming a wild animal. I could almost like him. Almost.

If I didn't remember that he, too, was an enemy.

CHAPTER TEN

I finished the curses the day before the deadline Muiredach had given me.

After my staged escape attempt, we'd both played nicely. He didn't bother me with any suspicions, though a guard—this time a mythborn, but equally bulky—still accompanied me to and from the workshop, and I worked without making any fuss or trying anything underhanded.

With each passing day, the feeling that the Scáthanna would not find me in time became stronger and stronger, but I couldn't risk asking for even a few more days. Gobán had already figured out my curses, and if Muiredach lost his patience, he could decide to hand them over to him or anyone else in the workshop.

My time had run out, and I had no choice but to proceed with my risky plan, so to avoid more suspicions, I finished the curses earlier. I needed Muiredach excited, not second-guessing me. Knowing his distrusting nature, he'd still be cautious no matter what I did, so maybe the surprise of me not trying to drag it out would do the trick well enough.

When I stood up from my table, shortly before every-one's informal lunchtime, several heads turned, but nobody stared for long. Only Gobán watched my passage through the workshop with a serious expression. I couldn't read his face, but even if he guessed that I was about to make my move, I doubted he'd reveal anything that could harm him in the future should I fail.

The guard was waiting by the door, and as soon as I got his attention, I pointed up. "I need to see Muiredach."

I didn't bother explaining how I knew he was in the torture room. I'd heard him a while ago, instructing someone to remove the body of his latest victim. The poor man—one of his own lackeys, from what little I'd eaves-dropped on—hadn't survived the night, though I thought that Muiredach wasn't expecting him to. In the time I'd spent as his captive, I'd learned he had two types of victims: those he wanted to last and torture endlessly for whatever wicked reason, and those who were a mere pastime, serving as entertainment or an experiment.

The latter sickened me in particular. While I could reluctantly understand—even if I couldn't sympathize with it—one's need to endlessly torment an enemy either for information or out of revenge, using torture for one's own pleasure or research showed the true depths of Muiredach's twisted nature.

The guard nodded but didn't move, waiting for me to go first. Muiredach must have instructed him to avoid turning his back on me.

We made it through the corridor and up the stairs undis-turbed. It was so early in the day that everyone was busy with their tasks in various parts of the building, so the only passersby were the few mythborn and humanborn who had reasons to move around, delivering things and instructions.

And none would be heading where we did, unless they had no other choice. Even the guard, who accompanied me all the way to the door, didn't enter with me.

The stench of blood and urine was strong in the torture room, and I fought nausea. Muiredach, on the other hand, seemed unaffected. He stood by his tool table, cleaning one of the thinner blades. He smiled when I approached.

My hands in front of me, palms open, I presented my work. "Two of them, like I promised. And two catalysts to activate them."

Still holding the blade, Muiredach stepped to the side, indicating the table. I obeyed the unspoken request and set them there. He still expected that I'd try something, maybe as a last resort.

"Would you like to test one?" I moved away, spreading my arms.

I'd surprised him—he didn't manage to hide it. "You're offering yourself as the test subject?"

"The first one I ever made was for myself. I'm quite curious about how it feels." I looked him in the eye. "And it would be a fitting conclusion to our agreement, don't you think?"

After all, back when I promised to make the curses for him, I'd never bargained for my life or freedom. He wouldn't have forgotten that, so my current offer was nothing but a way to ensure he didn't think back and wonder why.

He cringed. "I'd say it would be a foolish one. After years of thinking you were going to die, you just got your life back, even if only the little Eithne and Cathal allow, and now you want to throw it away?" He shook his head. "If you truly want to die, go ahead and kill yourself. You have the means, and I wouldn't be able to stop you."

I stood motionless, because indeed, I wasn't ready to die

quite yet. It was a risky distraction intended to put Muiredach off guard for my real trap, but hopefully, he'd just think I had doubts about sacrificing myself. After all, I wasn't a mythborn like Lorcan, and I hadn't been a member of the Scáthanna long enough to be unwavering, especially as I had already made a deal with the Snake's servant and made him believe he could sway me even more.

I looked at him with what I hoped was a stubborn expression. I needed him focused on me and on the curses, on the prospect of actually testing them. If he decided to hand them over to Gobán and his team, all would be lost.

He laughed, and I let him enjoy that little victory he believed to have over me. "I thought so. You would risk your life if needed, but you'd never give up if there's still hope." He flicked a hand at me. "Be so kind, then, to step to the side. I have someone else to test this curse, and she should be here any moment now."

As he finished speaking, a guard walked in dragging a woman. My eyes widened when I recognized Jemma, gagged and with her hands tied but still fighting to break free.

Over the last week, I'd allowed myself to forget about her presence in the building, because I wasn't too keen on eavesdropping on Muiredach's nighttime activities. The only thing they ever talked about was her asking when he was going to kill me and send her back to Albert, and the rest of the time...

I felt disgusted even at the memory of what filled the rest of the time.

"I grew tired of her. Humanborn seem so repetitive in their squawks, and since your beloved exposed her as my spy, she's lost any value as well," Muiredach said in such a casual manner, he could have as well been discussing a change of his taste in fashion or music, not someone's life. "I had other plans for her, but with the curses ready, she's going to be of use one more time." His voice was emotionless, confirming that she'd always been only a tool to him, and sleeping with her was a means to an end, nothing more. He glanced at me. "You, on the other hand, have a promise."

"Forget it," I barked. "I made the curses for you, and our deal is done, so we can stop pretending that I'd ever agree to work for you of my own free will."

"I expected such an answer."

He didn't seem upset about it, either. Those few conversations we'd had in the past weeks must have truly convinced him I was only clinging to my past convictions out of habit, and persuading me was just a matter of time and well-chosen arguments. Besides, I couldn't forget what Gobán had said—that Muiredach wanted something more from me.

"You will, nevertheless, remain my guest for a bit longer, and we'll take our time discussing... possibilities." The smile he sent me was sickening. "But for now, let's conclude the deal we already made. Tell me how the curse works."

I welcomed the change of topic. Discussing how I wasn't going to serve the Snake got us nowhere, while talking about the curses could get us places... Places I was desperate to get to. Yet, instead of a smug smile, I offered him a disgruntled glare and a grimace, as if I preferred not to tell him.

"Put the curse on a person you want to kill." I couldn't bring myself to say Jemma's name. "It doesn't have to touch the skin. Clothes or a pocket are close enough. Then you take the catalyst and activate it like any other curse. Once it starts working, you have to place it on the target. I recommend throwing."

"What happens if I don't throw it?" His eyes narrowed.

I shrugged. "I honestly don't know, but you could get caught within the curse's reach. Once it's activated, it'll consume any direct source of magic, much like your little critters. Then it'll self-destruct."

Muiredach picked up one of the small wooden disks and inspected it with curiosity, but he couldn't fool me. He wasn't a craftsman, so he could neither appreciate the intricacy of the work nor cringe at my still-beyond-crappy scribbles that I insisted were my interpretation of the elegant mythborn runes. Gobán, on the other hand, would see too much. Once more a wave of fear washed over me. If Muiredach called for him, my plan would fail, so before he could think about it, I gave him an encouraging gesture.

He regarded me with a smile of satisfaction, but his eyes remained narrow, as if he were still figuring out what kind of game I was playing. Then he walked over to Jemma and, almost caringly, slid the curse across her cleavage and underneath her shirt.

She jerked in her binds and made whining sounds through the gag, her eyes pleading.

He paid no attention to her, but kept glancing at me as if making sure I wasn't about to make a move.

"You don't seem moved by poor Jemma's plight," he remarked.

"She's a traitor. She deserves every little bit of what's coming, and then some." I added some reluctance to my voice and avoided looking at her, as it suited the Kaja I wanted Muiredach to believe in. The one who couldn't bring herself to be ruthless and who, perhaps, saw the Court's ways to be wrong but refused to admit it yet.

"I thought this was more... personal."

I ignored the jab, and Muiredach wasn't interested in digging deeper. I would bet that the second object he was turning in his hand had a lot to do with it. As he played with it, he finally focused on Jemma. He licked his lips, and his eyes shone in that sickening way as he fed off her fear.

I remained silent, letting him treasure that moment of cruelty, hoping it would be his last.

Then he lifted his arm for a throw, and I could tell the exact moment he activated the catalyst, because he froze, staring at his hand. And when his gaze shifted to me, I couldn't resist a wide smile.

"The curse seems to be working just fine."

With so many things having not gone according to plan, I sure enjoyed the moment in which everything went right. Outsmarting Muiredach in the process only added to my satisfaction. He really shouldn't have assumed which object was the curse and which was the catalyst, or that it had a high magic activation threshold like my old curse. Not that the supposed catalysts were safer—I'd made them into explosive curses. After all, he'd wanted me to make the curses, and as much as I was determined to keep my word, any personal additions outside of the deal were fair game, and "a curse that can kill an Afflicted" was a much broader concept than "an exact replica of the curse that can kill an Afflicted I made for myself." Even before the Magiclysm, an exact wording in a contract was the most important thing.

He must have finally put things together, because his eyes first went wide with the shock of realization, then squinted in hate. "Kill her!"

I was almost disappointed he'd lost his composure enough to want me to die so quickly, but on the other hand, his own death was even closer. He wouldn't get to enjoy any prolonged torture this time.

The guard looked back and forth between me and Jemma—a mistake he was about to pay for, because I didn't give him time to figure out which "her" he was supposed to kill.

I lunged at him, burying my shoulder in his stomach, and at the same time unsheathed his dagger. As he fought to regain his balance and attempted to grab me, I blindly slashed upward. A roar and the droplets of blood spraying over me told me I'd hit something, but as soon as I got a clear view of him, I struck again, adding a hole in his chest to the wide cut across his face. It might not be the most skillful attack, but I believed Sadb would have given me a nod of approval. I wasn't supposed to look pretty when I fought. I was supposed to be effective.

Before the guard's corpse hit the floor, I was already spinning around, ready to take on Muiredach. But he wasn't after me. When I turned to confront him, all he did was send me a hateful glare as soon as he got back to the table. With one of his torture tools in his unaffected hand, a large, cleaver-like blade, he struck down at his other arm, severing the curse from the rest of his body.

To my disappointment, instead of screaming in pain, he hissed with relief. He still stumbled backward, as his instinct must have urged him to get away from the curse. He wrapped a rag around his wound, activated a healing charm —I knew he kept those handy to revive his victims when they were too close to death—and watched his severed hand shrink and darken while my beautiful and deadly creation sapped all the magic and life from it.

I didn't wait for him to gather his thoughts. A quick dash and I was by the table, almost face to face with Muiredach.

He jerked and dropped the healing curse, grabbing one of the longer blades from his vast collection and raising his arm to swing.

I leaped backward. Once at a safe distance, I presented him the other curse I'd swiped from the table. Part of me regretted I didn't go for the kill, but I couldn't risk it. He'd made me believe he wasn't a fighter type, but he did heave me all the way up to the torture room after my staged escape attempt, and concealing his real strength would fit his deceptive nature.

Besides, even if he wasn't strong, the speed with which he went for the blade suggested good training, good instincts, or both. I would be a fool to ignore what I didn't know about him.

"And what are you going to do now?" He offered me a crooked smile. "How are you planning to escape?" He took a step forward, hugging his maimed arm to his chest, but he didn't relinquish his blade to pick up the discarded healing charm. He must have stopped the bleeding already, and no amount of magic would grow his hand back.

"I thought that I could activate the second curse and take you with me." I hoped this would suffice to keep him from attacking.

My words gave him pause, and he regarded me with sudden interest. "You don't want to die."

I moved my chin enough to indicate the husk on the floor that used to be his hand. "All things considered, it seems a better option than letting you capture me. Besides, I can't let you keep this curse."

Truth be told, I'd never seen past that point of my plan, having only a vague idea of sneaking out in the chaos that I'd anticipated to break out upon Muiredach's death. And that "somehow" definitely didn't take into consideration

Muiredach sacrificing his hand to survive. At least I hadn't wasted time planning something that would have failed, right?

"You gave me your word," he said.

"And I kept it to the letter. I made two curses for you, didn't I? I never promised that I wouldn't try to prevent you from keeping them."

I didn't care much about the accusations, but I needed time to figure out what I was going to do next. Jemma thrashed in her binds, and if I made use of the dagger to free her, there could be two of us against Muiredach, but with her treacherous past and personal dislike for me, I couldn't count on her taking my side. For all I knew, Muiredach would sway her back to his cause with a few well-worded lies. I'd seen how complacent she became upon his mere touch.

"Fair enough." Rage faded from his expression, a clear sign he'd regained his composure. A bad sign, because if he was thinking straight again, I would lose my meager advantage soon enough. "I should have watched you a little closer than I did, but you did well averting my attention and convincing me you were planning to escape... I didn't think you had enough wits to execute such a risky and elaborate scheme." He wasn't admitting to a mistake but analyzing, confirming that he was back to his cold and calculating self. "But if you're hoping for a miracle, you're going to be disappointed. I made sure that the Scáthanna received subtle leads over the last two weeks, so they're currently busy looking for you in places far from here."

"So what now?" I ignored his last remark, because it didn't make my situation any worse or better. If my teammates hadn't found me so far, I wasn't counting on them to show up this very moment anyway. "Are you going to convince me it could all still work out?"

"That sarcasm was unnecessary, though I admit, your schemes made it all that more difficult," he said. "If you decide to hand the curse over, I could be persuaded to not harm you in exchange... or cause you any pain."

His very existence caused me pain, but I doubted this would be included in the deal.

My thoughts were frantic, and no solution seemed good. I could attack Muiredach and try to kill him, but if he proved better than me, I'd be putting myself at his mercy unless I activated the curse. I couldn't even be certain I'd manage to take him with me. If I ran out, I had a whole building of hostile people to get through, and Muiredach would chase me. One wrong turn would have me cornered...

But to accept his deal meant that I would have to give him the curse. If I was lucky, he'd give it to Gobán, who perhaps would do me a favor and play for time, but in the end, he would have to admit he'd figured out its structure. It was much easier when the curse was complete, so I'd have days at best. Then Muiredach would be able to make any amount of them.

I had to be realistic about what would happen, too. This time I'd definitely be locked up and watched closely. I would be a prisoner with no means to stop him or try again.

My hands trembled slightly. I couldn't and wouldn't give Muiredach a powerful curse he could use to sow even more chaos in Dublin. It meant that I would never know if Riagán understood why I'd done what I'd done, and he wouldn't get to talk to me... It hurt more than everything else, but I had no other choice.

Muiredach narrowed his eyes. "Don't be a fool, Kaja!"

Since he'd experienced it firsthand, he knew it would take just a spark of magic to activate the curse.

I gave him a bitter smile. Someone like him would have a difficult time understanding loyalty, family, friendship, and—most of all—sacrifice. I was aware of the risk when I'd first agreed to be Cathal's bait, back when we were setting up an ambush hoping to catch Muiredach, and nothing had changed since then. The mission was more important than my own wellbeing. It wasn't even so different from the assignments I used to do for Trinity during the war. The stakes stayed the same, and only the enemies changed.

"I can't let you have this curse," I replied.

My heart was beating faster now in my desperation to find another way out.

Jemma was sitting on the floor motionless now, her wide eyes staring at me. She didn't understand either, but how could she? Blinded by love, or some feeling resemblant of it, she'd colluded with an enemy, putting everyone in danger.

I took a deep breath.

Before I activated the curse, a small-framed humanborn rushed into the room. I didn't recognize him, and he took in the scene before him with clear confusion, but then he looked straight at Muiredach.

"We're being attacked!" he shouted.

As if on cue, the whole building shook in response to what I guessed was a magic attack. Muiredach had it warded, but with enough magic thrown at it, any ward could collapse, and I doubted this place was a real fortress. It was more likely that he wanted to protect himself from detection and prevent any secrets from leaking out. Besides, Riagán once shot an arrow through Trinity's wards without destroying them, and I doubted Muiredach could match the protections of Albert's headquarters.

I smiled both at the memory of my cocky archer and the thought that, if I managed to stay alive a little longer, I would be getting my miracle after all.

"The Court? It's not possible." Muiredach's expression suggested he couldn't make any sense of the news. Another thing in his perfect plans had failed, and he wasn't taking it well.

The walls shook in violent waves, and I could tell the moment when the protections of Muiredach's headquarters finally gave way. Voices from the outside, silenced by the magic wards, flooded into my ears, and I stumbled backward, trying to control myself.

"Get guards in here!" Muiredach shouted at the humanborn.

He must have known that with the prospect of being rescued, I wouldn't activate the curse, and I would make an excellent hostage that he likely believed could buy him freedom.

The humanborn ran out, calling for guards, and soon enough, my guard entered. He had likely been waiting nearby to escort me back to the workshop, and I was lucky that he'd missed the commotion so far. With his bulky physique, I'd have had a hard time taking him down like I did Jemma's escort.

The mythborn guard scanned the room and fixed on me almost instantly—no wonder, as I was the only one there who looked threatening enough.

"I want her alive!" Muiredach barked.

I corrected the grip on my dagger. I couldn't help trying to listen in on what was going on outside, but I had to focus on my surroundings. My most immediate opponent approached carefully but with confidence, and I positioned myself to not lose sight of Muiredach. Two on one didn't look good for the "one" that I was. Sadb's training had focused on combining the use of curses and a weapon, so having only half of my arsenal deepened my disadvantage. I smirked at the thought that she'd still expect me to perform well, no matter the drawbacks. I was one of the Scáthanna, the mythborn's elite unit, and I couldn't disappoint the expectations put on me, even if the rest of the team wasn't around to witness my performance.

The floor trembled, and the sound of an explosion filled the room. With a powerful rumble, the far wall collapsed as a destructive curse sent the bricks flying. Light and wind rushed in through the jagged opening, and I held my breath at the sight of the outside world, my first in weeks, even as limited as it was.

Without any warning, an arrow whizzed in. Muiredach ducked, and so did I, but neither of us was the target. The archer went for someone looking like the biggest threat, and the guard gurgled from his pierced throat and collapsed, spitting blood. Considering the circumstances, that view was quite pleasant.

I glanced at the shaft. It wasn't Riagán's, but it looked familiar, and once I recognized it, I put things together.

"This is not the Court. It's Trinity," I said with a hint of amusement. "Looks like Jemma's going to get her rescue after all."

In a way, my situation hadn't improved much, at least not yet, and Muiredach could still capture me and use me as a bargaining chip, but to know that he was cornered lightened my mood.

I kept listening to the steady flow of orders as the Trinitians surrounded the building and breached the hastily erected defenses, making their way in. The one good thing about Albert's mistrust toward mythborn was that he kept his troops well trained and at the ready, in case "that treacherous Court" started the war again, so his people were much better organized than the mishmash of Muiredach's henchmen, who'd likely never had a proper drill. And why would they? I knew Muiredach well enough now to suspect that, in his pride, he'd never expected he could be found.

But as I listened to the reports passed to the superiors leading the operation, it became clear that the Snake's servants would hold for a while because of their sheer numbers and narrow corridors, and it would take my would-be rescuers time to reach the torture room.

Muiredach kept away from me, clearly buying time for more guards to get in, and I could only hope that everyone was too busy fighting Trinity or preparing defenses to make it all the way up here.

Then, among all the reports and orders and moans of the wounded and dying, among the battle cries and shrieks of pain that told me how fierce the fighting on the lower levels was, I heard the one voice I was hoping to hear.

"Find Kaja," Cathal ordered in his delightfully composed manner, and my heart sang with glee. My teammates were coming for me.

I smiled as I circled Muiredach at a distance, while he watched me with suspicion, since I was moving away from the only door and my escape route. I stopped where I hoped to be visible through the destroyed wall. If Orla was still out there, watching with another arrow ready, she could let others know.

The Trinitian bow mistress didn't disappoint me. As soon as I stepped into view, another arrow cut the air, its shrill sound like the most beautiful music. Back in the war, we'd used them as warnings or alerts, and it had to get everyone's attention.

Muiredach moved. My instincts kicked in at the abrupt motion, but he wasn't after me. As the shaft buried itself in the floor, he made a run for the door. He got out of the room before Orla had a chance to shoot again.

I didn't run after him. Without knowing the building, I was more likely to get lost or captured by his thugs. I fought to apply reason while my emotions demanded I chased him down.

A familiar, broad-shouldered silhouette appeared in the crumbled wall's opening. Faolan smiled as he landed on the floor battle-ready, making it look like he'd walked in rather than jumped up however many stories to get here. One day, I had to ask him for some serious lessons on using the jump charms, because he did look damn impressive.

I wished I could collapse on the floor, letting relief wash over me, but I wasn't a damsel in distress. If I didn't keep my chin up, Faolan would never let it go, and rightly so.

I walked over to him as he took in the torture room with his weapon still drawn, and his eyes became cold when they skimmed past the chain and the bloodied table. I had no doubt he thought of Cait.

"Muiredach escaped." I motioned at the door. Alone in the room, I was safe, and Orla would likely pin anyone who tried to enter anyway, so if he wanted to go on a hunt, I wouldn't blame him for leaving me.

He shook his head. "Others will get him. Who's that?" He pointed at Jemma, who was now fighting to get out of her binds.

"That's Jemma…"

"The traitor?" he asked.

As soon as I nodded, he lost any interest in her, while all I could think about was that Muiredach had truly kept his word and let Riagán go.

"She can wait, then," Faolan said. "I'll get you out of here first. Ready?"

Without delay, I walked over to him. He wrapped his arm around me, grinning, and held me tight. Then, with no effort, he stepped over the ledge, and his jump charm carried us softly through the air.

Wind hit my face, and it finally sank in... I was alive, and I was free.

CHAPTER ELEVEN

As soon as we got out, I recognized the area—about fifteen minutes on foot south of St. Patrick's Cathedral, if I estimated correctly. In a city where no single street or corner seemed perfectly straight, counting distance in blocks was useless. One block could have the length of three or five others.

The four- and five-story buildings around us all bore the marks of war, and since the area was mostly abandoned, no one had bothered with renovations, so the one that I had so eagerly vacated, with its boarded-up windows, didn't stand out from the others unless someone paid closer attention. With few people around, likely no one noticed that there were mythborn lurking in an area on the south side of the river, which was considered predominantly humanborn.

On the other hand, my own old neighborhood, the Liberties, also had a vibrant mythborn community. The division at the river line wasn't a hard rule, after all—more a natural split, since both humanborn and mythborn preferred the company of their own kind—and nobody was forbidden from choosing another place to live. If there was something that postwar Dublin didn't lack, it was houses and apartments. Not all of them were livable, of course, but the choice was still better than before the Magiclysm, when Ireland seemed to struggle with housing and renting markets all the time.

I looked around. The rubble-covered street teemed with Trinitians, suggesting Albert had mobilized a small army, and I spotted more than a few familiar faces. They passed me by without recognition, wrapped up in carrying out orders or helping the wounded being carried out of the building.

Despite the apparent chaos around us, the humanborn squads were as well organized as I remembered from the war, a testimony to Albert's efforts to keep his people prepared and trained. The only difference was that in the past, two mythborn—I was getting used to the fact that I'd be perceived as a mythborn now—walking through their lines would cause quite a stir and an instant bloodbath. Now, Faolan and I made our way through the humanborn ranks without being bothered, though I caught one or two disgruntled glances at his uniform.

On the other side of the street, Cathal stood beside Albert, two leaders sharing space and command as if they had worked together for years, and I couldn't help smiling. I had no doubt that my ceannasaí had asked the Trinitians for help to avoid raising Muiredach's suspicions. They knew that Jemma wasn't around to spy on Albert, so he could have announced some routine maneuvers while Muiredach's spies at the Court would have reported that the Scáthanna took his bait and were setting out to search another area.

A plan like that had a lot of moving parts, but I wasn't surprised that Cathal had pulled it off.

"Ceannasaí." I gave him a nod.

Albert arched his eyebrow at my formal behavior. When he was the one giving me orders, I was hardly official in my responses, even in public spaces. But he and I shared a very intimate past, and I was never exactly his subordinate, while ever since I'd met Cathal, he had always been my superior. Sure, we weren't always that formal with each other, and he even had a dry sense of humor, but during an official operation like this, I behaved like a member of his team should.

Cathal smiled. "Well done."

"Not yet." I shook my head. "Muiredach has lost his hand, but he managed to flee deeper into the building."

Until the one mythborn we itched to get was in our hands, nothing could be considered done, well or otherwise. After all, this was what I'd risked my life for.

"It's still quite a success." Albert inspected me in the same manner he'd used to look at the humanborn me when I returned from difficult assignments, in search of any injuries or signs of trauma. "Trinity and the Court working together again, this time openly, and a lair of terrorists neutralized."

I pressed my lips together, holding off a remark how it didn't matter if Muiredach got away. Being out of the loop for weeks, I had no idea how much Cathal had revealed to the Trinitians, and last time we spoke, Albert didn't consider Muiredach a serious threat.

Cathal smirked at me with satisfaction, as if my displeasure at the result of my mission was something he expected from his teammate. "You did well nevertheless," he said. "The information Riagán brought us proved invaluable. Did you have to fulfill any of Muiredach's demands?"

I appreciated he kept the topic general in Albert's presence, since I knew what he was really asking about. "I made the curses, but he doesn't have them. One got destroyed when I tried to kill him with it, and I have the other with me." I demonstrated the curse. "May I recommend destroying it as well?"

Back in my humanborn days, when I used my first-made curse to save Laoise's life, I told the Scáthanna that such a curse was too dangerous to be studied, and they didn't press me to tell them how to create it. This was a secret I shared with them, until Lorcan was forced to reveal it to Muiredach. But now, not only did he know, I suspected Gobán had a pretty good idea how to make one, so I could see the reason behind keeping the curse and letting some skilled and trusted craftsman study it. If we showed it to Connor, maybe he could find ways to counter its effect. On the other hand, it would also make him a target. I hadn't saved his life in the war and then made friends with him after I became a myth-touched only to put his life in danger. I already felt guilty enough about being the likely cause of his pain and difficulties in walking.

Cathal stretched his hand out. "I'll see to that."

I gave it to him without hesitation. "Any strong curse or charm will activate it," I said, painfully aware that Albert was right beside us, more curious than a kitten seeing a ball of wool for the first time. It wasn't a surprise, seeing as he'd never known about my little crafting hobby. Given a chance, I'd explain things to him later, but I'd keep the details of what the curse was to myself. Too many people already knew about it, and I didn't need Trinity launching a research to try to replicate it.

Cathal walked away, gesturing for Faolan to follow him, so I was left alone with Albert. I shifted uneasily at the thought that he might not have heard the bad news yet.

"You don't have to squirm," he said in quite a somber tone. "I already know."

"I'm sorry," I whispered. "Last time I saw her, she was fine, and they'll probably get her out soon."

Not that it was much comfort, considering she was a traitor and a spy. I didn't intend to mention Jemma's visits to Muiredach's bed on top of that. It seemed irrelevant to the situation, and Albert didn't need that final blow.

He gave me a short nod, as if he didn't care much anymore. Maybe he'd learned early enough to have already gotten over it, or had enough time to figure out how to hide his real emotions.

"I'm glad you're okay. When you disappeared from Trinity without a word, I got worried, but the mythborn didn't tell us anything specific until a few days ago." He gave me a lopsided smile, suggesting he was still uneasy about the whole situation. "It was quite a bomb to drop, Jemma's betrayal and your kidnapping delivered within the same conversation."

I sighed. I should have expected Cathal would keep Trinity in the dark for as long as possible. In a way, Muiredach was the Scáthanna's problem until I could tell my team about the extent of his operations.

"Don't blame them. We still haven't gotten all the spies the Snake has at the Court, and I'm sure Jemma wasn't the only one at Trinity."

Albert's expression made it clear he'd prefer to blame the mythborn for pretty much everything, from bad weather and bad news all the way to any misfortunes that befell this otherwise fine country. Thankfully, before I got to hear a response that could push us into an argument, a commotion in the street drew our attention.

A gray blur darted between the humanborn squads, startling everyone with his speed and focused face, and I smiled at Riagán making his way to me. He must have been on the lookout like Orla when the news got to him.

He hardly slowed down as he got close, and he almost slammed into me, closing me in his embrace. His arms, strong and possessive, made it clear that whatever he thought about my deal with Muiredach, it didn't matter. And with that, all the fear and the lies I'd had to tell in the past weeks didn't matter either.

I hadn't lost Riagán.

"I'm sorry. I had to improvise," I said softly. Later there would be time for lengthier explanations, but I had to say something now. "You weren't part of the plan."

"So I've heard," Riagán replied as he let me go. He glanced at Albert, who was staring at us, clearly uneasy, then took a step back and stretched his hand out. "Commander, it's a pleasure to meet you in person."

"Likewise." Albert kept his face straight, though I caught the side glance he threw me, as if he wanted to ask a question. Likely one regarding the rather expressive welcome Riagán gave me. "I can finally thank you for saving my life back when the Snake's agent made it into Trinity."

I appreciated that Albert didn't point out that, back then, the Scáthanna were hunting alone, and he wasn't privy to their secrets, while I was performing feats of intellectual acrobatics figuring out how much I could tell him without breaking the deal I'd made with Eithne and Cathal. At least now my allegiances were clear, and I didn't have to avoid revealing too much while answering Albert's questions. I could simply direct him to Cathal to get any information.

At the same time, I wasn't exactly comfortable having my ex-lover and my current one in the same space, even if my new relationship wasn't exactly at the "lover" stage yet. At least they both acted civil, and regardless of what Riagán had told me about the jealousy he used to feel, he didn't make a show. After the initial outburst of emotions, he kept away from me and acted as if we were just teammates. Not that I planned on keeping my feelings for Riagán secret from Albert, but there surely was a better time to talk about it than the middle of a military operation.

Cathal returned with Faolan, and soon some of Albert's officers joined us as well, bringing reports of the operation's success. I snickered, because many of them looked like they were trying really hard to be cool about the mythborn nearby, but their nervous glances at the Scáthanna's uniforms made it clear war habits died hard.

In the distance, a mythborn unit wearing Court emblems approached the perimeter guard, and after their leader talked to one of the humanborn lieutenants, they set up by the entrance to the building. Cathal gave them a nod from a distance, but he didn't rush away to speak with them, and I hoped that made it clear to everyone that the Scáthanna valued their humanborn allies.

The Trinitians exited, leading captives outside, and the Court mythborn shackled the prisoners in charm-enforced chains. Muiredach wasn't among them, and even though I still hoped to see his face, my gut was telling me that the sneaky bastard had managed to escape. There was some consolation in knowing that now he had one hand less with which to cause trouble and much fewer resources at his disposal, and both Riagán and I had seen his face.

When Sadb emerged dragging out Jemma, still bound and gagged, Albert tensed. Seeing his lover treated like a criminal must have hurt, and even though, in my opinion, the treacherous bitch didn't deserve any better, we owed Albert for Tadgh.

I turned to Cathal. "Ceannasaí, don't you think she

should be judged by the Trinitians? As a sign of goodwill similar to the one the commander offered us earlier when it came to Tadgh?" My cheeks burned with a blush that made it clear I'd abandoned my insubordinate ways along with my humanborn physique. On the other hand, I had no problem mouthing off to Eithne, or anyone else, for that matter, so it might be nothing more than the respect I had for Cathal.

He nodded and turned to Albert. "Commander, would you like to handle this case? As my team member says, we'd like to show that the goodwill goes both ways."

It didn't escape me that he didn't use my name. With so many Trinitians around, he likely didn't want to risk that someone would remember that there was gossip about Albert's private life, including his previous lover, whose name was supposedly Kaja...

I was sure that sooner or later myth-touched would not be a secret anymore, but such information had to be handled in a sensible way. There were Trinitians who'd take our mutual past as a sign that Albert was colluding with the Court, even though our relationship had ended long before Eithne finagled me into working for her. Timelines were a thing of no consequence to those who were desperate to prove their point.

"I'd appreciate that." The relief in Albert's voice was clear.

At least he could deal with Jemma within Trinity and avoid the humiliation of having his relationship with her discussed at length at the Court. If it were me, I'd make sure that Jemma was never put on trial. With her guilt undeniable anyway and a death sentence obvious, an "accident" that took her life before the trial happened would save Albert a lot of heartache. Besides, he didn't need his reputation tarnished because of something he had no control over.

"Ceannasaí." Faolan pointed somewhere over my shoulder, and we all looked that way.

Another group of mythborn entered the area. They wore muted green uniforms adorned with gold, but I didn't recognize the emblem on their chests. From a distance, I could hardly make out its shape—a closed fist or a mace, perhaps.

Cathal narrowed his eyes, and the corner of his mouth twitched downward, so whoever they were, they couldn't be bringing any good news.

"Commander, if I may..." Cathal led Albert to the side. Not too far, as if he didn't want to alarm his officers, but enough to make it clear the conversation didn't concern them. "I have a favor to ask. Would you mind being a host to two of my people? Kaja will need a safe haven for a while, and..." As Cathal looked at Faolan, Riagán tensed, and our ceannasaí nodded at him. "And Riagán will be accompanying her as a guard," he finished. "If you wouldn't mind ensuring no mythborn bother them until I'm ready to call for her, I'd appreciate it."

Albert was puzzled but nodded nevertheless. "Of course. I take it you'd like for them to depart immediately?"

"If you would be so kind." Cathal offered a smile, as if he was amused by the diplomatic dance they performed. "In return, I'm sure they both will be happy to fill you in on the past weeks' events as much as possible."

He threw me a quick glance that made it clear he knew I was eavesdropping. A slight nod suggested he was fine with us sharing at least *some* secrets with Albert, and he trusted me to decide how much I could tell the Trinitians, or at least their commander.

Albert and Cathal split, the former heading for his officers, and the latter for us. In another time, and maybe in another world, I could picture the two discussing military history over a glass of fine Irish whiskey, or even engaging in some strategic board game that was so complicated no one else would play with them. The daydream brought both a warm feeling of hope for a similar future and a spell of sadness, because many things could have been different if we hadn't waged that pointless war when mythborn first arrived after the Magiclysm.

While Albert gave instructions to one of his men, Cathal looked at Riagán. "Stay by her side and follow her lead. And if possible, you both stay in Trinity until I call for you. I'll send Sadb or Faolan, no one else, and no written orders."

"Yes, ceannasaí," Riagán replied without even a smirk, though that order put me in charge, once more proving that when it came to Cathal's decisions, the Scáthanna obeyed without questions.

Cathal turned to me. "Until Muiredach is captured, you're still making choices... and deals you think are best for the mission."

I nodded, reading between the lines. His words were giving me freedom to deal with any unexpected circumstances, and I appreciated that he'd considered that possibility.

He passed a bag to me. "Your uniform, a new weapon, and some curses, should you need them. Sadb had Connor make you the ones you used during training." He glanced at Albert. "Go as soon as you can, and I'll handle things here."

I immediately fished out the familiar shape of a curved blade, attaching the sheath to my belt, but the rest of my equipment would have to wait.

Cathal turned away without any parting words and headed straight for the newcomers. His stroll was one of confidence, but with no urgency, giving the impression he cared little about the mythborn he was about to talk to and even less about whether they had to wait for him, still held at the humanborn entry checkpoint.

Meanwhile, Albert got back to us with a lieutenant in tow, a lean woman with a serious, mature face. She carried herself like someone composed and used to both taking and giving orders. I didn't know her personally, but I'd bet she had actively fought in the war rather than being promoted to officer after it.

"Mary will escort you back to Trinity, and I'll meet you there as soon as we're done with the operation."

"Thank you, commander."

I watched his amusement at my formal response, but most of my former comrades would never recognize Kaja in me, so there was no reason to make them wonder why some random mythborn was acting all familiar with their leader. Not to mention that I didn't want to cause additional trouble for Albert. I wouldn't be surprised if some Trinitians still held on to their war grudges and were opposed to the idea of cooperation, so even if they didn't know my name and couldn't make *that* connection, too much friendliness between their commander and a member of an elite mythborn unit could become grist for their mill of hatred or a seed of doubt that would sprout into disobedience. With an organization as large as Trinity, there were bound to be people who didn't like Albert or his leadership style, but most at least respected and trusted him. I didn't want to destroy that by being inconsiderate.

Mary looked at us, and judging by her expression, she might be one of those disgruntled Trinitians. Or perhaps she simply hated mythborn on principle, and I couldn't blame her. A lot had happened during the war. As long as she could still do her job, her feelings were hers alone.

"Right," she said. "Follow me, please."

Despite that "please" tacked on at the end, she was barely polite, her voice having a distinct undertone of attitude ringing from each word.

"We'll go this way." Riagán pointed at the far end of the street, away from where Cathal was already talking to the green-dressed mythborn.

Mary didn't object, though she threw him a grimace. I didn't have a problem guessing what was going through her head. Burdened with a shitty assignment of escorting two former enemies, not only was she worried whether we were going to do something underhanded, but she also had to cater to what she likely considered Riagán's whim and wondered what else he'd make her do once we got out of Albert's sight. In her place, my mood would be sour too.

We headed down the street, and hardly anyone paid attention to our departure. I glanced at Riagán, but I knew we wouldn't talk much on our way to Trinity, not with Mary being able to hear every single word.

I must have let out a sigh, because as soon as we took the corner, he smiled and pulled me closer, matching his steps with mine. I took it as a promise and relaxed. With quite a long walk to Trinity, I could forget about everything for a little while and simply enjoy his company.

MARY SEEMED to know her way around the tangle of back streets, so we let her lead the way, keeping far enough behind to be courteous. She still looked over her shoulder regularly, and with the nasty glares she threw at Riagán, I was certain she wasn't checking if we were following.

Since I couldn't talk to Riagán about anything meaningful without Mary learning about it, I resorted to listening with my skill. If I wanted to, I could probably still pick up the voices from around Albert and Cathal, but it was a waste of time. They had everything under control over there.

Instead, I intended to catch conversations happening elsewhere. I couldn't count on Muiredach muttering even a single word, since he knew I could try finding him this way... I hoped that some of his lackeys, those who'd managed to escape or were still fighting, were more talkative. Even a mention of a location to regroup would be helpful.

Unfortunately, all I caught was worried exchanges between the few people living in the area who speculated about the military operation in their previously quiet backyard. My skill could be of so much use, except it seemed that my bad luck hardly ever allowed me to hear anything worthwhile.

"Muiredach! I don't care about Muiredach, and you shouldn't either," said a familiar voice. "He's the reason we're in this mess."

I immediately tuned in, because it sounded like Gobán was near.

"But his orders..." said a woman whose voice I didn't recognize.

"Look, you'll do what you want, but if I were you, I'd do my best to avoid Muiredach," Gobán continued. "It'd be easy in this chaos. Find a safe place, wait it out. Maybe disappear. Try to live a normal, quiet life."

I slipped out from Riagán's embrace. "I have to do something. Can you make sure our guide doesn't interfere?" I whispered. "It won't take long, and I'll be right around the corner."

Surprise flashed on his face, but he nodded immediately. While I rushed toward the alley from which I believed the conversation was coming, hoping to catch Gobán and his companion, Riagán caught up with Mary, asking her to stop for a moment. Since I was certain he'd make her wait, I didn't pay much attention to her and took the corner, entering the alley.

Midway down it, two familiar people stood. Both froze at the sight of me, but then Gobán stepped in front of the woman as if to protect her and keep me away from her. I recognized her—she was one of his workshop workers. Thankfully, not the one who had lost her lover, so I hoped things would go quietly and smoothly.

"Go!" Gobán urged the woman. "Remember what I told you."

She rushed off without a word, throwing a scared glance at me. I let her go. My business was with him, and it was all the better if we didn't have any witnesses.

"He managed to escape, didn't he?" he asked with a hint of resignation.

"He did." No reason to hide the truth. "But now he has one less hand to stir up trouble."

That earned me a glimpse of a smug smile, as if he was happy that I hadn't disappointed his faith in me. Then he looked at me with a serious expression, his eyes skimming past the blade at my side. "So, are you going to kill me or drag me back to the Court?"

"I'd rather not do anything drastic like that," I replied.

I was being honest. As much as I understood that, technically, Gobán was working for the enemy, he *had* helped me indirectly. He'd never demanded anything for the advice he'd given me, and later he'd risked a lot for me by lying to Muiredach. Gobán said we were even, because he'd also revealed my escape plan, but I knew that if he had told his boss the truth about how quickly he could finish my curses, I'd have been already dead when the Scáthanna arrived.

Yet I couldn't tell him that I felt like I still owed him, because I needed him to feel indebted to me for sparing his life.

"You want something from me," Gobán said without surprise. "The Court mythborn always want something."

I nodded, ignoring that he grouped me with the Court nobles. I deserved it. "I need someone found."

His eyes narrowed, and his molekind nose moved nervously. "I'm not going to help you find him. If I can help it, I never want to see him again."

"Not him. Someone else." I hesitated. Did this mean I was making a deal with the Snake's servant? Was Gobán still one anyway? The last weeks must have been enlightening to him. "Before Muiredach took me, there was another of the Scáthanna... His name was Lorcan. Muiredach is holding his wife and child. I don't know their names, anything about them, really," I admitted, "but if you ever learn of their whereabouts, this would be valuable information to me."

I didn't know if Cathal would approve, but I couldn't stand the thought that the two people Lorcan cared for so deeply were still in our enemy's hands. Even if they were safe, *away from the strife*, as Muiredach had put it, I could easily imagine how he'd manipulate them both, telling stories of how the evil Court and its cruel rules were responsible for Lorcan's death. I'd hate the idea that either member of Lorcan's family could be driven to revenge and deceived into doing something violent. It would be just like

Muiredach to pit them against us so that we would have to kill our dead teammate's family.

If I could avoid that, I would, and Gobán was my best chance of finding out what had happened to them or where they were.

"I'll see what I can do, but such information won't be easy to get," he replied cautiously.

"I understand." I looked over my shoulder, then back at him. "You better get going."

"Good luck," he said, and I knew he meant it sincerely, even if only in the context of catching Muiredach.

Then he took off.

I wondered whether he'd even make any effort to learn what happened to Lorcan's family, but in the end, it didn't matter. I had no other means of finding them anyway.

Riagán and Mary were waiting for me around the corner —one calm and patient, one visibly not.

"I apologize for the delay," I said in a formal manner. "I appreciate you waiting."

I doubted she cared about it, but a little courtesy couldn't hurt.

"Let's get going," she said, grumpily.

We resumed our walk, and Riagán shot me a glance with an unvoiced question.

"Let's just say that if I hope to get information in the future, I have to ask for it now," I replied vaguely, wondering how good Mary's hearing was and whether she was even paying attention to our conversation. "And this was someone I'm unlikely to see in a while."

The rest had to wait until we were alone. I didn't know what he'd think about dealing with the Snake's servant, but I'd bet he would care about what happened to Lorcan's family once I told him why he'd betrayed us.

"How is…" I paused, as I didn't want to say the name with Mary around. "Did Sadb and Faolan make it back in time? Is he all right?"

Thankfully, he caught who I was talking about. "Still recovering, badly wounded, but he'll live. Your quick decision to send them back made the difference."

I breathed a sigh of relief. Tadgh would live. At least something good had come out of all this mess.

Soon, we left the maze of narrow back streets and walked into the familiar area, with St. Patrick's Cathedral still standing proud and almost unscathed. It had taken a lot of effort during the war to protect it, but seeing a piece of history preserved made those sacrifices worth it.

Sadly, the small park beside the cathedral, or rather a gated square with a fountain, flowerbeds, and a few unimpressive trees, hadn't been that lucky, but after years of intensive restoration and rebuilding, it looked almost like it used to when I sat there with Ela.

The memory of my sister dimmed my mood, as it always did, but Riagán's presence brought hope for a brighter future that wasn't marred by nightmares of the past. Some of them would never go away, of that I was certain, but by his side I could have something beyond the ghosts of the war.

Of course, we had no time to stop and enjoy the park's tranquility, and it wasn't even Mary's eagerness to keep going. I wanted to get to Trinity in the hopes that she would leave us alone, and we could finally talk.

"We could race her to Trinity," Riagán whispered when Mary stopped to exchange information with a small Trinitian squad heading in the opposite direction. "I'd like to see the panic on her face when she realizes she's lost us."

"And be shot on sight as we run up to Trinity's gates?" I

whispered back. I could imagine how the guards would react to seeing two Scáthanna rushing toward them.

The look Riagán gave Mary made it clear he still considered the risk worth taking, and I smiled.

"It's not that far now. And then we get to talk."

"Then we should definitely race her," he teased. He clearly was waiting for that conversation as much as I was.

Soon enough, Mary parted with the Trinitians, and we resumed our journey. She avoided the main streets, leading us through pleasant but narrow alleys of what was once a vibrant commercial district of high-end shops and cozy eateries that were always full during lunchtime. With the rebuilding effort, the area had regained a lot of its prewar look, and if Mary had hoped for less attention in those back streets, she was in for a disappointment. Locals and tourists alike eyed us with curiosity, because a humanborn in a Trinitian uniform and two mythborn, one clearly militant, walking together was an unusual sight, especially as the "joint operation between Trinity and the Court" likely hadn't been announced beforehand, to avoid warning Muiredach.

To my relief, I found more curiosity than concern on their faces as we passed them by, and it made me hope for the day when mythborn and humanborn walking together would be as natural a sight as rain clouds in the sky. I smiled at the memory of my own neighborhood, the Liberties. The first seeds were being sown already, and with them, the dream of lasting peace grew stronger.

Of course, as soon as we reached Trinity, the wary faces of the guards reminded me of the work remaining. In a way, the Court was lucky that Albert, though distrustful, was willing to cooperate, because the veterans under his command were much less friendly. If not for Mary's presence getting us through the gate quickly, we'd likely be searched thoroughly and maybe even detained.

It was a small blessing that she wanted to get rid of us as quickly as possible, so she made the guards cooperate by complaining about the shitty assignment she got—yes, I did eavesdrop on her, because even my trust only went so far, and I wanted to be ready in case the guards decided to do something underhanded.

I'd never seen a more relieved person than Mary when she led us to a waiting room and left with no goodbye of any sort.

I didn't mind, since it meant that Riagán and I were finally alone.

CHAPTER TWELVE

Riagán took the room in with the curiosity of someone discovering a new civilization, but truth be told, there wasn't much to see. Only bare walls painted in some off-white color, worn wooden floor from prewar times, and a simple table in the middle with four chairs around it. These rooms weren't the guest quarters for welcome visitors, but places where Albert dealt with people he didn't like or didn't trust enough to let deeper into Trinity. I wouldn't be surprised if, according to Mary, we met both of the criteria.

I slumped into a chair, letting the stress of the last few days leave me.

Even if we hadn't caught Muiredach, and even if my curse had failed to kill him, there were bright sides to consider. I was free and unharmed, and the most important part: I hadn't had to make a deal I'd come to regret or sacrifice my life to avoid committing treason. Besides, the building seemed to be Muiredach's center of operations, and even if he had some other lairs across Dublin, losing the place and the workshop's contents must have dealt a serious blow to both his pride and his resources.

Of course, this led my mind back to more pressing matters, and I abandoned the thought of relaxing. Questions swarmed my head, and since I had no idea where to start, I picked the first that came to my mind.

"Those mythborn back in the street... Who were they?"

Riagán looked around, his eyes narrowed and searching, but he relaxed when I shook my head. He trusted that I knew Trinity and its procedures well enough to reassure him we weren't being spied on.

He said a word in a mythborn language and then added in English, "The Fist of Light. A rather pompous name for a bunch of annoying pricks." He grimaced, and his eyes dimmed as if he were recalling an unpleasant memory. "They are the ones who track the agents of the Snake, and they like to assume power to do so. It took the ceannasaí three days to get me out of their clutches, and they still made problems afterward. That's why we didn't manage to find you earlier."

"But you made it in time."

"Ceannasaí shouldn't have been so secretive about his plan."

As he sat down beside me, his displeasure emanated from his body like heat, and I couldn't blame him. I wouldn't be happy either if he'd agreed to a high-risk mission and wasn't allowed to tell me.

He sighed. "When you disappeared, he asked me about the brooch, but the charm didn't seem to get a good reading on you. Just like... with Cait. Back then we didn't know what happened. The Trinitians claimed you'd left with one of our own."

"Muiredach wore our uniform," I said. "He threatened to

stage an attack on Trinity if I didn't go with him willingly. The blame for that attack would go to the Scáthanna, and we would have war again, so even if Cathal hadn't given me the mission, I had to comply."

He huffed, and another grimace spoiled his face. "Mission! Telling you that you are to willingly give yourself up to an enemy who already killed three of our team is hardly giving you a *mission*." He grunted his displeasure, but when he looked at me, there was respect and appreciation in his eyes. "You took a huge risk with this one."

I wasn't about to disagree with that. "He would have gotten to me sooner or later anyway. At least this way we were prepared." Then I remembered all the things that went wrong, so I added, "Well, as prepared as we could be. So, how did he get you?"

He pulled me closer, and I shifted from my seat onto his lap, enjoying the gentle touch of his fingers brushing my arm.

"We were searching for you, but the reading was weak. Connor wasn't sure whether the brooch's magic had started to wane, or if you were someplace we couldn't reach you."

"The whole building was heavily warded," I said.

He nodded. "We needed something stronger. Something you were more attached to than a brooch you gave away to pay off the life debt to a mythborn you didn't even like back then." He adorned the words with a playful smirk, as if questioning whether he'd been truly so unlikable then. "So Cathal sent Sadb and me to your apartment while he and Faolan followed a lead before the trail went cold. It was a risk, but we didn't really expect him to do anything, since he already had you. Besides, Sadb herself can substitute for an army. I had her back in the ambush, but they separated us..." He trailed off and shook his head. "They swarmed her, many of them dying just to keep her away from me. Then they dropped enough stun and sleep curses to take me down. When I woke up, I got to meet Muiredach. You know what happened next."

He seemed uneasy talking about it, and I understood. Even if he already knew I'd allowed Muiredach to capture me, following Cathal's orders, witnessing me being treated fairly well and making deals with the Snake's agent couldn't have been easy to get over. Not to mention that, for all he knew, I might have crossed the line and actually betrayed the Scáthanna.

I wanted to lean against him, but instead I sat stiff, regretting that I'd gotten on his lap. It wasn't an easy conversation for either of us, and one that intimacy wouldn't help. "At least he kept his word," I whispered. "I feared that he'd lied to me, and kept you somewhere, alive only enough for the blood-bound charm to deceive me."

Riagán nodded. "He kept the deal to the letter. I even got all my gear back, including my bow and the keys to your apartment. I don't think he'd have parted with them so eagerly if he knew what they were."

"I'll be changing the locks anyway," I replied grimly.

There was no certainty that Muiredach didn't know what he had. The Scáthanna were aware that Riagán had keys to my apartment, and Lorcan might have been forced to share that information with Muiredach. I believed he'd tried to tell our enemy as little as he could, but without knowing what he had revealed, I had to assume it was more rather than less. Not to mention that it would be just like Muiredach to make his own copies and give the keys back to make me believe I was safe in my apartment.

Riagán arched his eyebrow at me, so I added, "Don't worry, you'll get a spare set again."

I wanted to tease him about it, but he deserved to have them even more now than when I first traded them for one of my life debts.

Riagán smiled with confidence, as if he hadn't expected anything else, and I wanted to tease him more and enjoy his bold response, but then he became serious. In an instant, the mood changed, and it told me we were approaching the difficult part of the conversation.

"And did you keep your word?" he asked.

I didn't hesitate. "I did. But he doesn't have the curses. I agreed to make them for him, not to let him keep them."

My last remark earned me another smirk, but the tension between us wasn't gone, as if Riagán was still deciding between trusting my word or trusting what he'd seen. In a way, this confirmed what Muiredach had said about Riagán's feelings toward me being so strong that he would be prone to manipulation. His memory had told him one thing, and his heart another.

He must have noticed a change in my expression, because he touched my chin in a gentle, hesitant manner. "When I first saw you with Muiredach, so willingly agreeing to his demands, I had doubts. Then you mentioned the brooch, and I understood you were playing for time. No matter what little I saw, I trust you wouldn't do anything that brought dishonor to your name or to the Scáthanna."

"You had every right to doubt me," I replied softly.

"Ceannasaí didn't." He looked away.

It dawned on me that his uneasiness wasn't coming from being unsure whether he should believe me. He felt ashamed that he'd ever questioned my loyalty.

"He didn't see me with Muiredach." I leaned closer and met his eyes when he turned his head to look at me again. "I understand how you must have felt, and I appreciate that you're still willing to trust me."

I almost lost my breath when he held me tighter. It was the hug of someone who was never going to let me go, no matter what.

"After what you did for us... Risking your life and putting your own reputation at stake... None of us will ever doubt you. If not for the risks you took, I'd likely be dead now," he said.

"One less debt I have to pay off," I offered in a light-hearted way.

He murmured as if displeased, but his face expressed amusement. Then he kissed me all of a sudden. His lips on mine and the scent of campfire smoke and pine enveloping me were like a grand prize I'd won by risking my life. Before he was done, I had to peel off to catch my breath.

"I've been wanting to do that for quite a while, but I thought we should get out of Albert's sight first." He chuckled, but without malice. "The look he gave me back in that street... I'm surprised he didn't try to detain me for even getting close to you."

I sighed. "Albert's just a bit overprotective sometimes."

Technically, it was true, but to be accurate, I should have used words like "a lot" and "all the time" instead.

"And he likely thinks that it was the Scáthanna's fault I was in danger," I added as an explanation.

Riagán arched his eyebrow. "I can understand if he's jealous. We somewhat switched roles, didn't we?"

I shrugged. "I don't know what he is," I replied honestly. "The last time we spoke, he seemed torn between who I was and who I am. Even if I don't feel like I've changed that much, I do look like a former enemy now. I guess I'll have to talk to him... about everything."

"We'll be here for a while. You'll surely get a chance."

I sighed at the thought of how such a conversation would go, and how many times Albert and I would end up in an argument in the course of it. I needed a change of subject, and I scrambled to pick up where we were before personal matters took over. *Right, Muiredach...* Another "pleasant" thing to discuss.

Yet recalling Riagán's story of the ambush sparked my curiosity. "So, if the brooch wasn't working, how did you find me?"

He smirked at the question but didn't call out my not-so-smooth attempt to avoid discussing Albert. "Connor made a new charm, a stronger one. As soon as the Fist let me go, we went back to your apartment to find something you were more attached to." He laughed when I tensed. "Don't worry, you'll get your precious earrings back."

I didn't even have to ask which earrings he was talking about. "Out of all the things there, you could have taken anything... *anything!*" I said, fighting to keep my frustration at bay.

He shrugged, unmoved. "We didn't have time to play guessing games. I knew that those earrings were more important to you than paying off a life debt." He looked me in the eye, his teasing expression gone. "I made sure Connor treated them like precious items, and you won't see the difference unless you look really close. He also said that since it was a set of two, he could make the charms resonate and empower each other."

Even if my emotions demanded I did something dramatic, I couldn't argue with the voice of reason. Riagán didn't know my apartment well enough to pick "the next best thing," and he hadn't had time for repeats if his choice turned out not strong enough.

Yet I still whispered in a hurt tone, "They're the only keepsake I have of my sister."

He shifted and held my shoulders as if ensuring I didn't look away. "I'd burn your whole apartment down without a second thought if it was the only way to get you back. I'd rather have you here, complaining about your earrings being a locating charm, than stare at them, thinking that you're gone."

The tone of his voice, determined and serious, made me drop any further complaints, even if I'd only meant to tease him. Those were the words of a mythborn who'd do anything to save me, and he deserved his efforts being recognized.

"You're right." I offered a smile, and there was nothing forced about it. "I'm lucky you noticed how much I like them. If you picked something else, you could be still looking for me."

"We might have been... The locating charm's readings weren't clear. We were receiving information that you might be held to the north, at Dublin's outskirts," Riagán said.

"Muiredach mentioned he was trying to mislead you," I replied. "He was very confident that you were nowhere near discovering where we were."

Riagán nodded and swallowed. "We had... unexpected help. One evening, Donovan came to visit Cathal. We thought he was trying to stir up trouble after that one time we messed up his operations. But Cathal and he talked for a long time..." He smirked. "You can imagine we missed your presence at that time quite a lot."

I couldn't help smiling. Once the Scáthanna discovered what my listening skill could get them, they'd been quite shameless in using me to eavesdrop on Cathal. Though, truth be told, I would be curious myself what Donovan had to say to our ceannasaí. Then it hit me. I had something to share about Donovan as well...

"When Donovan left," Riagán continued, "ceannasaí said that from now on we would focus only of the south side of Dublin."

I stared at him. "Donovan told you that?"

Riagán shrugged. "Whatever he said, it caused the ceannasaí to make that decision."

"Donovan knew exactly where I was," I said. "I saw him there, making deals with Muiredach's lackeys, and he recognized me." My thoughts were running in circles trying to figure out the motives of that mythborn. He'd suspected I was planning to fool Muiredach, yet instead of warning my captor, he went to Cathal. "I think... I think it was in his interest if we got rid of Muiredach. He was drawing too much attention, and he made personal enemies of us."

"That would make sense. Donovan likes to toe the line of what's right and wrong." Riagán clenched his fist, and I felt him tense. "He *knew* where you were, and yet gave us only vague suggestions."

"It's still better than warning Muiredach that I might be plotting something." I shivered when I thought of what would have happened if the Scáthanna and Trinitians hadn't arrived. I could be dead or tortured. The memory of what Muiredach did to Ann tied my stomach in a knot. "If he did..." I couldn't bring myself to finish.

Riagán pulled me to his chest, closing me in a tight embrace once more. "Tell me what happened after he took you," he asked. "It might help you to share, and it might make it easier to tell the same story to the ceannasaí later."

I nodded. The Scáthanna had to know, so I could start with Riagán and take advantage of being able to share feelings and thoughts that wouldn't be included in the official report. We also had time, since I didn't expect Albert back anytime soon. Military operations always seemed to drag, and he wasn't the type of a leader who left while his people were still risking their lives.

I leaned against Riagán, making myself comfortable, and started talking.

ALBERT RETURNED LATE AFTERNOON. I heard him from quite a distance from Trinity, so when his tired face appeared in the room's entrance, Riagán and I were more than ready to leave it.

He didn't react to the sight of our sitting together—I wasn't going to pretend there wasn't anything between Riagán and me—but I didn't expect him to. After all, he'd seen enough earlier.

"My apologies. I should have guessed what Mary would consider comfortable accommodations for two mythborn-looking guests." Albert didn't hide his dissatisfaction. "I take it no one offered you any food or drink either?"

"No one bothered us, and we appreciate such a display of trust," Riagán replied politely.

My expression was less polite, and Albert read the truth on my face.

"Come," he said. "We'll talk in my office."

We left the room together and followed him through the courtyard and into the main building. Albert stopped to talk to one of the Trinitians, asking that a meal for three be brought up as soon as possible, before leading us upstairs.

Riagán threw glances around, taking in the interior of the ex-college and current humanborn fortress, but as his eyes skimmed past objects and people, they didn't carry the innocent curiosity of a first-time visitor. If I had to guess, he was memorizing the route and taking note of any possible threats.

And threats, in a way, were plentiful. As we climbed the stairs, the veterans glared at us with open suspicion. They weren't hostile, but their tense bodies told me enough. Even though members of the Scáthanna had visited Trinity before, we weren't welcome here, even if we accompanied the commander himself.

I breathed out with relief when we reached our destination. With a gesture, Albert invited us into his office.

It looked like it always did. Even his desk, always covered with piles of documents, stood in the same spot, inviting another arrow to be shot from one of the buildings opposite Trinity. When it happened the first time, Riagán had saved Albert's life by shooting an assassin through what we'd thought was a heavily warded window. After that incident, both Orla and I hoped he'd move his office... or at least the desk. Of course, he hadn't back then, and I shouldn't have expected anything would change since my visit and disappearance. Maybe he'd at least posted guards on nearby rooftops. On the other hand, that wouldn't do him much good if the Scáthanna decided to take him out, and other enemies clearly had the means to get inside the buildings. They got Tadgh in his jail cell, so nothing would stop them from assassinating Albert anywhere on Trinity's grounds.

"Kaja? Tea as usual? Riagán, what will you drink?" A charm sparked, feeding the kettle with magic as Albert switched it on. The Magiclysm had made electricity impossible, but magic had replaced it seamlessly enough once we learned how to do it. "Food should be here in a few."

"Tea's fine," Riagán replied as we both sat down.

"Your ceannasaí didn't say how long you'd be staying, so

I assume it'll be at least for a couple of days?" Albert moved some papers to the side of the desk, making space for the mugs. Then he sat down. "I'd offer Kaja her old room, but it's in the veteran wing, and two mythborn guests there could cause... unwanted tensions. I also understand that you want to stick together, preferably in one room?"

I caught a hint of amusement in his words that suggested he'd wanted to mention one bed, not one room.

"I'm her personal guide, and our ceannasaí made it clear I shouldn't leave her side," Riagán said. "So please, see to her comfort and don't worry about me."

"I understand." Albert's expression became solemn. "I wish I could assure you both that Trinity is safe, but in light of recent events, Kaja's kidnapping and the discovery of a spy among us, I fear Trinity might not be as secure as I'd like to believe." He sighed. "We also didn't find anyone who fit Muiredach's description at the site, so he's still out there. If he got in here once, he might do it again."

I shook my head. While I wasn't going to ignore possible threats, Albert deserved the details of what happened. "Last time he used the commotion of the explosion, and he was wearing our uniform to mislead your people. If I wasn't alone back then, he wouldn't have gotten me. You should, though, scan Trinity for explosives. He claimed some people here carried them, and that they could be triggered remotely."

I doubted he'd detonate them and risk my death in a blast. I've gotten to know Muiredach well enough to be certain that by forcing him to cut his hand off and keeping the curses away from him, I'd made it *very* personal. And personal to him meant torture and slow death, stretched for as long as my body could endure, not a blitz attack that would kill me quickly.

That wasn't, of course, something I'd mention to our dear host, unless I wanted him to post half of Trinity's staff as my guards.

Albert sighed, spreading his arms. "We scan the grounds and visitors regularly. If he managed to get explosive curses inside, it has to be something our anti-curse devices don't pick up."

"He had accomplices here, so they might have let him in without scans or smuggled the curses themselves." I rubbed my chin. "There was a workshop at Muiredach's place... You could ask the Court if they're willing to share their findings so that you can adjust your scanners."

Doubt was clear on Albert's face, and he arched his eyebrow. I couldn't blame him. With the years of war and the years of distrust that followed, when the Court in general and Lady Eithne in particular played the human-born whenever it was beneficial to them and never bothered offering anything in exchange, Albert didn't expect much.

"If I may suggest something..." Riagán leaned forward. "Contact our ceannasaí about it instead of the lady. Today's operation made it clear that at times the Scáthanna need Trinity's aid, so ensuring your grounds are spy-free and secure is in our team's best interest."

"The Scáthanna are willing to part with their secrets?" Albert didn't bother concealing his sarcasm.

Riagán grinned, abandoning all pretense of formality. "Of course not. But certain arrangements could be made to ensure people at Trinity are safe."

"Fair enough. I'll take what I can."

I cherished the sincerity in Albert's voice. It sounded like a promise to take a step forward instead of digging deeper in the trenches of mutual distrust.

A knock on the door disturbed us, and with Albert's

permission, two Trinitians entered, a boy and a girl, both in their teens. They were carrying heavy trays filled with food. The smell of shepherd's pie hit my nostrils, waking all sorts of memories, most of them good and predating the war.

"I hope you don't mind humanborn food." Albert's method of desk cleaning consisted mostly of taking the piles of documents and dumping them elsewhere. The wobbling towers of paper around his office were silent testimony to his backlog of paperwork.

"It has a certain appeal," Riagán said.

He glanced at me with a smile, as if he was recalling that night when we were drinking to Cait's death, and I introduced my teammates to Polish vodka. When this was all over, I promised myself, I'd introduce him and the rest of the Scáthanna to pierogi, Polish dumplings, and piernik, our gingerbread cake... And many other foods that would make them appreciate humanborn cuisine a bit more.

Albert served the food, and we ate in silence. I kept avoiding his eyes, because in the past, we used to eat like this... just the two of us. But the old Kaja was gone, and the person who was sitting in front of Albert looked like a mythborn female. On top of that, she was involved with someone else.

"So..." Albert looked at us after we cleared our plates. "Care to fill me in on what was going on in the last few weeks? The Scáthanna were quick to ask Trinity for help today but not so eager to share any details."

I hesitated. I'd been out of the loop and had no idea what Cathal considered safe to share. He might have given me permission to make my own calls back when I first went to Trinity, and the glance he'd given me earlier today suggested he was fine with me being honest, but I still wasn't sure where my openness and honesty should end. As much as I trusted Albert, my loyalty was with my team, and I wasn't going to endanger any secrets the Scáthanna wanted safe.

Riagán stretched in his chair and offered a wolfish smile. "We do indeed prefer to keep our matters safe. Our ceannasaí trusts you, commander, but the same can't be said about the rest of Trinity's staff."

"Secrecy again." Albert cringed. "But fine. I won't discuss the details with my officers and staff. Especially as I still don't know how many of them have hidden agendas."

It must have stung to mention Jemma, even so indirectly. I bit my tongue. It wasn't my place to offer him any words of comfort. If the humanborn Kaja had stayed in Trinity, just like Albert had always wanted, he might have never gotten involved with Jemma. Not that I felt guilty about my choices, but since this was how life went, I wasn't in a position to ease whatever pain he might be feeling.

"The Scáthanna appreciate your understanding, commander," Riagán replied before I could figure out what to say.

"Albert. No need for formal titles within this office," Albert offered. "And I'd prefer a story, not a report. From what I understand, Muiredach was somewhat of a personal enemy to the Scáthanna, but it's clear he also had his moles in Trinity. Anything you can tell me of him will help me keep my people safe."

Riagán nodded. "Kaja will start, then, since she worked closely with our ceannasaí on this. I'll fill in whatever she is unaware of."

I took a deep breath. Telling Albert that I'd willingly become bait and allowed a sadistic mythborn to imprison me sounded like fertile ground for an argument or twenty. I could only hope that Riagán's presence would keep Albert from going all out, and that my unfamiliar, mythborn-like physique would make him forget I was the same Kaja he'd always been overprotective about.

With no way out and under two insisting glares, I started talking, telling the story once more. This time, though, I'd be sure to omit any details with argument-starting potential.

By Trinitian standards, the room Albert gave us was big. In practice, that meant one could walk to the opposite wall without having to push their way between the queen-size bed and the wardrobe. By the window stood a small desk with an uncomfortable wooden chair that made me wonder if it had been there since the time Trinity was still a college, not a humanborn fortress. And that was it, the full inventory of the room.

Riagán inspected it with a generous dose of discontent, and I couldn't blame him. Even our rooms back at the Court were bigger.

I became used to similar quarters throughout all my years in Dublin, as many apartments around the city center were tiny. Not rooms but walk-in closets, as my American friend would call them. If one wanted more space, one had to find accommodation further away, preferably in the districts with newer developments, but that meant frustrating commutes, so I'd chosen small living space over the time wasted in transit. Since I'd shared an apartment with my sister, we were comfortable spending time in the living room together rather than locking ourselves in tiny bedrooms.

"At least the window faces the inner yard," he said.

"We're three stories up." The last thing I expected was

anyone coming after us through the window. Faolan could probably jump that high, but he might not fit through the frame.

Riagán gave me a shameless grin. "I might be the best archer, but I'm not the only one there."

"I think Muiredach is going through the hassle of making it much more personal than having me shot from a distance. And he's not going to get you killed either, because you're perfect for making me suffer. He hardly could resist the thought the last time he had both of us."

His expression soured at that. "If we don't find him, you'll never be able to leave the Court's grounds alone."

"We'll get him."

Besides, even if I was stuck at the Court until the end of my days, it was still a better option than being tortured for weeks, if Muiredach decided to use healing charms liberally, or watching people I cared about die one by one. The latter could happen regardless, but that wasn't something I wanted to dwell on.

"Albert took the story quite well," I added to change the topic. "I think it's because you were there."

"I don't think so. He looked like he'd prefer I wasn't present."

I chuckled at how he had misinterpreted Albert's discontent. "Of course he'd prefer you gone. With you in the office, he couldn't escalate the conversation to a full-blown argument about how ridiculous the plan sounded, how incompetent our ceannasaí was to endanger his team member like that, and how little he thinks of me for agreeing to become what in his eyes amounts to a human sacrifice... Well, a myth-touched one. If he had any way of making you leave, I'd hear a full lecture about risking my life so foolishly."

Riagán stared at me, and the expression on his face

suggested he was having a hard time processing what I said. "You're of the Scáthanna, and you're our scout. He can't expect that we'd let you sit somewhere safe and smile and wave at the humanborn passing by." The slight arch of his eyebrow suggested he was trying to keep sarcasm at bay. "Besides, he sent you on many dangerous missions himself."

"Want to hear the whole list of reasons how that doesn't count?" I offered.

I remembered them all too well. After all, I'd raised the same argument countless times in the past and heard every single excuse and rationalization in response, from the simple "in the war, it was different" to the vague "but I always ensured you had the best chance" and anything in between.

Riagán smirked. "I'll pass. But I can understand now why you left Trinity." His smile shifted into a smug one. "Straight into the Scáthanna's nets."

I couldn't help laughing at that. "Took you years to set those nets."

"The lady's orders." He shrugged. "If it were up to me…"

"You'd sweep me off my feet as soon as I stepped out of Trinity's gate?" I finished for him.

"I'd wait till you got to the corner so that the Trinitians wouldn't see and come to your aid… Besides, I'd need time to get off the roof I was watching Trinity from." He stepped closer, greedily pulling me toward him. "We have some time before ceannasaí sends for us. I think we could use it more pleasantly than talking about the feats I didn't get to perform."

After what we'd been through, we deserved some peace and quiet, enjoying each other's company while we were both safe, so I didn't argue. When we kissed, my lips were as hungry for him as his were for me.

CHAPTER THIRTEEN

I was still in bed when Riagán collected the tray from the boy who knocked at the door, and I couldn't resist a chuckle. The sight of a half-dressed mythborn, with his skin looking like he'd been rolling in the mud, startled the young Trinitian, and he rushed off as soon as he made sure Riagán wasn't going to drop our breakfast. No pleasantries, not even a goodbye... Just a bewildered glare at Riagán's bare chest and a mad dash away from the room.

But as amused as I was, I made a mental note to speak to Albert about it. Not about the boy himself, who wasn't at fault, but about the fact that Trinitians weren't accustomed to seeing mythborn around. Nothing bred fear and hate like otherness we didn't understand, and if Albert was serious about peace, he could help his people adapt by making them more familiar with their neighbors.

Regret flashed in my mind at the thought that if we had done so right after the Magiclysm, maybe war could have been avoided. But we were just humans, terrified and alone, and mythborn were no less confused than we were. I could only hope that we had at least learned from the past.

"Nothing expresses trust like making sure your guests don't roam your home in search for food." Riagán set the tray on the table, watching me with an arched eyebrow as if asking whether I was going to get up.

With a sigh, I rose from the pillow. It seemed that I had some teaching to do, because apparently mythborn weren't familiar with the concept of a breakfast in bed.

"I thought it was hospitality." I scuffled out of the bed, throwing on a shirt, more out of habit than modesty. "Making sure your guests are well fed and don't have to make the effort of roaming and searching."

He bit into a sandwich. "We shall see about well fed." Chewing, he inspected the bread with a grimace. "It tastes foul even by humanborn standards. What did they put in it? Pickled grass or something?"

I didn't get to respond. Riagán froze, and the sandwich slid out of his hand. I was by his side before he dropped to his knees, a spasm shaking his body as if he was about to throw up, but his wheezing breath told me I needed something more than comforting words or jokes about delicate stomachs.

I rushed to the mostly unpacked bag Cathal had given me the previous day. I tossed the contents out onto the bed and grabbed the utility belt. The healing charms and antidote were there, and I didn't waste time pondering whether either would even work on something that must be an allergic reaction...

Then another thought struck me: poison.

Without delay, I got back to Riagán and forced his head upward as I uncorked the antidote. He tried to sit up, but his body was refusing to obey him. Half of the yellowish liquid trickled down his chin when I poured it into his mouth, but he swallowed the rest between desperate gasps. It didn't seem to have any effect, and my heart sank a little.

Riagán was trying to say something, but I didn't pay attention. Nothing was more urgent than saving his life. I held up the healing charm, steadying my breath and heartbeat. I needed focus. If it was poison that was killing him, the charm wouldn't neutralize it, but if I used it the way Lorcan had shown to me, maybe I could keep Riagán alive until his body and the antidote dealt with it.

Of course, my next thought was on how little practice I had controlling the flow of magic, but it was always easy to be wise in hindsight. Lessons like that seemed insignificant and easily postponed when one had to deal with the threat from Muiredach. I had to make do with what I knew and hope for the best.

It took a painfully long half an hour and five healing charms, mine and his, for Riagán's breath to become deeper and steadier, and as soon as I was certain he wasn't dying, I fished out another antidote from his belt. Once he drank it, I kept pouring in magic from the last charm.

I didn't hear anything outside, but I wasn't using my skill. I wanted my focus solely on the mythborn I was trying to save.

Riagán sat through the process patiently, his eyes fixed on me as if I were some sort of a miracle worker, and I'd be lying if I said I didn't like it.

"It seems you were wrong about Muiredach." His voice was still weak, but he spoke with a slight smile.

Yet my moment of hesitation before I responded was all he needed to become serious.

"You don't think it was Muiredach." The way he said it made it clear he'd gotten good at reading me. Not that I minded. "But Albert wouldn't risk you..."

I shook my head. "I'm certain he doesn't know about it," I almost whispered. Indeed, Albert would not risk my death even if he was ready to start another war with the mythborn. "Can you move into the corner behind the bed?"

I had to help him, but he made it. I threw my uniform on, more bothered with the access to my arsenal than looking proper, though I suspected wearing the Scáthanna's badge and their colors would make me look more formidable.

The curses were slotted in the utility belt and a few cleverly concealed pockets, and I smiled. Sadb had done a good job making sure I got most of my gear back, and it made me feel more confident about what I was about to do.

Then I unsheathed my blade and stood by the door, ready. I couldn't be sure, but I was counting on the perpetrators wanting to check if we were dead. If I caught them, the conversation with Albert could go much easier, and maybe we could figure out whether they were just mythborn-hating Trinitians or if they worked for Muiredach.

Standing motionless, I engaged my listening skill. It'd been over half an hour since the kid brought us the food, so whoever was trying to kill us had shown remarkable patience. I had to consider the idea they weren't even around, hoping that someone else would discover the bodies, but people who killed because of hate usually liked to see the effects of their work and witness the objects of their loathing perish.

Soon enough, I heard a whisper.

"Do you think they finally ate?" The woman's voice sounded vaguely familiar, but I couldn't place it, so it wasn't anyone I knew well. "I can't hear anything from their room."

"It's because they're already dead. Wolfsbane extract works fast," a man replied. "Let's check."

"And what are you going to say if they're still alive?" the woman asked. "That you came to finish them off?"

There was no answer, and I heard footsteps out in the corridor. They must have been closer than I thought.

After a moment of silence, a knock sounded on the door.

"Uhm," said the familiar voice outside. "The commander sent us to check if there's anything you need."

Neither of us replied, but Riagán shifted and reached for his combat knife. Even barely alive, he was readying for a fight.

After a painfully long wait, the door handle moved, and the man poked his head in. As his eyes landed on Riagán, he smiled with satisfaction, because my archer looked every bit dead in his motionlessness. I envied him both the nerve to keep his eyes still and his acting skills.

The Trinitian walked deeper into the room. "He's dead. And where is—"

He spotted me too late, because I was already squatting down, throwing a stun curse between his legs and into the corridor. The magic's explosion pushed him into the room, and as he flew toward the bed, Riagán was already scrambling up to take care of him. My instinct demanded I come to his aid, but I had to trust he'd manage, even in his poor state, because the man wasn't the only threat.

I jumped outside to deal with the woman.

She was fighting for balance after my curse had sent her against the opposite wall. I recognized Mary, our guide from the other day, in an instant, but Sadb's training ensured that while my brain worked through the mild shock of her betrayal, my fist delivered a quick blow to her temple. I didn't want her dead, so I used the hilt of my weapon rather than the blade. As she collapsed, I heaved her into the room, right before two Trinitian guards came into the corridor.

Their alert behavior told me that they must have heard the curse go off. I didn't want to speculate whether they happened to be making rounds nearby, were checking on the two guests they considered a threat, or were in cahoots with Mary and her companion, so as they approached, I stood battle-ready and didn't conceal it.

They immediately tensed, and I could guess what was going through their heads: would they take me down before Riagán showed up?

"Inform the commander that we've been attacked," I said in a neutral tone, hoping that things wouldn't get ugly. "The assailants are alive, but their attack can't go without consequences."

One of them narrowed his eyes. "Surrender your weapons, and we'll take you to the commander."

I sent him a nasty smile. "Tell Albert what I told you. He knows we aren't a threat." It wasn't even about upholding appearances. Relinquishing my weapon meant they could try something, and I hardly had the fighting skills they believed I had. That belief, reinforced by the uniform I wore, was something that kept them in check.

The suspicious guard glanced at his companion. "Report this to Officer Orla. I'll stay here."

I could read his hesitation as he gave the order. Alone with me in the corridor, he must have thought he stood no chance if I chose to kill him. I spread my arms—just enough to appear nonviolent without giving them an opening.

"I'll go back inside. It's best if my companion and I wait there."

The guard nodded, and I could swear he wanted to breathe out with relief, which told me he wasn't looking for a fight.

As the other man took off, I stepped back into the room

and closed the door. I didn't bother locking it, since anybody could kick it in or use a curse to shatter it to pieces, but I was not letting my guard down.

Mary remained unconscious on the floor, and the other attacker lay stretched across the bed, his face down. His lack of movement told me he was knocked out as well, as I couldn't see any blood. Riagán was sitting nearby with his blade at the ready.

"How are you feeling?" I asked. He still looked pale and weak, but if he'd managed to take the attacker down, it meant he was on the mend.

"I'll recover." He glanced at the mess. "I allowed myself to be careless."

I shook my head. "It's my fault. I feel at home here, even though I shouldn't anymore. You trusted my judgment against your own instincts."

"You didn't trust Albert more than our ceannasaí did."

I huffed. "Albert had nothing to do with it."

"They are his people, and we trusted he could keep them in check." Riagán shrugged. "But what's done is done. I only hope no bigger trouble comes out of it. In this state, I'm not fit to protect you, let alone fight my way through half of Trinity."

I chuckled. "We could just use a jumping charm. I'm sure we could manage... Faolan makes it look almost effortless."

"You don't even know how to use one yet, and given my state, I can't be sure I can stabilize us both," he replied with a hint of amusement that suggested he was picturing me trying to keep my balance in flight or during the landing.

"Orla should be here soon, and she will alert Albert to the situation too," I said.

With what had transpired, no matter how much I

trusted both of them, I refrained from reassurances that would put Riagán at ease. Despite the declared trust, which I hoped was mutual enough, things could go wrong, especially with other Trinitians involved, so it was better if he was watching out for any foul play.

Riagán gathered his things, and when he had all of his gear on, we tied up our would-be assassins, moving them into the corner that Riagán had once occupied.

After that, all that was left was the waiting.

THE NOISE outside suggested that Trinity took the two members of the Scáthanna with all the seriousness we—well, at least one of us—deserved. More and more voices joined the hushed discussions in the corridor, and I gave up on counting the participants or trying to recognize old friends.

Instead, I worried. Neither Orla nor Albert were there yet, and without them, someone could decide acting was better than waiting.

If it came to fighting, our chances were slim, so giving up made more sense, but I had to consider that some of the Trinitians would not care about taking us alive.

I glanced back at Riagán. He was watching our prisoners, who had since come to. They remained silent, as Riagán had promised to kill the first one who screamed or tried something underhanded. Mary kept shooting angry glares at both of us, as if we had seriously overstepped the boundaries of courteous behavior when we didn't die of poisoning.

Voices stirring outside made me pay attention again.

"It's not up for discussion," Albert said. "I'll talk to them."

"You might be walking into a trap, commander," someone replied. I didn't recognize her, but I could bet she was one of his overprotective officers.

"I'll be fine. I know she won't kill me."

The thought of Albert still trusting me created a warm, fuzzy feeling inside, but understandably did little to relieve the tension outside.

"But *he* might," Orla muttered.

"He doesn't have a reason anymore, does he?"

A strange note lingered in his words. I could guess that he still regretted how things had turned out between us, though in the end, if my life had taken different turns, I'd now be dead or a mindless monster roaming the streets of Dublin and killing innocents, because I doubted I'd have been offered the ritual that saved my life if I was still a Trinitian.

Outside, someone tried to speak again, but Albert cut in before I could even make out the first word. "Thankfully, we aren't running a democracy here. I'm going in, and meanwhile, you're free to discuss how you'd avenge my untimely death should it happen."

A flood of protests followed, which he must have decided to ignore, because then there was a knock.

"This is Albert. May I come in?"

I let him in and shut the door quickly, before some Trinitian decided to chance throwing a sleep curse in.

"Commander!" Mary called out. "They attacked us for no reason! We were just checking if everything was fine, and—"

I didn't listen. With a rather abrupt move that startled Albert, I snatched up the plate with the sandwich I never ate. "Let me offer you some food as an apology, then." I almost shoved the dish into her face, but after fighting to keep Riagán alive, I wasn't in the mood for subtlety or running in circles to prove the truth.

Mary's eyes widened and she turned her head away, even though I didn't try to force her to eat. I put the plate back on the table and looked at Albert. Her reaction should have told him enough.

He connected the dots. "Poison." His face hardened, and he headed for the door, poking his head outside. "I need someone to escort Mary Nolan and Philip Beatty to prison. They'll be charged with an attempted murder and conspiracy to reignite the war."

Murmurs rose in the corridor, but no one questioned Albert's order. Two guards walked into the room and, without delay, dragged our prisoners out.

"Orla." Albert waved her over, and as soon as she joined us, he closed the door again. "Anything you two can tell about this attack? If we have the Snake's net in Trinity…"

Riagán gave me a telling glance. If someone was to explain my theory to Albert, it wasn't going to be him.

I sighed. "I don't think it's the Snake's doing. Muiredach wouldn't want us dead, and that poison…" I glanced at the table. "Quick and nasty stuff."

"But you survived." The hint of doubt in Albert's voice suggested he wondered if I was exaggerating.

"If Kaja was hungrier, we wouldn't have." Riagán looked straight at Albert as if challenging him to question that statement, but he kept his tone neutral enough. "If you want to blame it on the Snake, we won't object. But you needn't worry about some bigger plots. It was just two disgruntled Trinitians. I don't even think the child knew what he was bringing us."

Orla inspected him with curiosity. "You don't seem too upset about almost dying here."

Riagán shrugged. "It's Trinity. We're the Scáthanna. I'd be suspicious if things went smoothly."

"We appreciate what you do," I added. "Without Trinity's help, I'd still be in Muiredach's hands, and trust me, it's not somewhere anyone wants to be."

Albert gave us both a nod. "I can promise you that Mary and Philip will answer for their actions. I'll arrange a change of quarters for you, perhaps in the officers' wing. They should be more levelheaded."

I arched an eyebrow. I remembered quite a few that disliked me even back when I was humanborn, because I didn't fit within Trinity ranks well, and I could imagine they'd be even less joyful about playing host to two of their former enemies. Not to mention that Mary was an officer as well.

"Maybe it would be best if we left as soon as possible," I said. "Our presence here makes your job all the more difficult."

From the look of his face, I could tell he would have none of it. "Nonsense. I won't be sending a message that one underhanded act is enough to make me go back on my word. Your presence here is part of the deal Trinity made with the Scáthanna, and we need what they offered in exchange. If anyone feels like complaining, I'll remind them of it."

"Your decision, commander," Riagán said.

Albert shot me a glance that told me at least *someone* wasn't trying to argue with him, and I should learn from that example. I rolled my eyes, since I only argued with him when he was being unreasonable—which, admittedly, was more often than not, at least from my perspective. From his, I was the unreasonable one. Thus the constant arguments.

Not that I'd mention it to him now, as it would lead to yet another fight.

Judging by the look on Albert's face, he was satisfied with my lack of verbal retaliation. Or, at least, he was sparing me a comment about it.

Orla, though, had no such reservations. "Mythborn Kaja seems much more amenable than the humanborn one, and with much less attitude," she said. "I could almost start to *like* her."

"Maybe you should try the ritual yourself, then." I doubted any amount of magic could heal Orla's natural bitchiness. If attitude was a superpower, I'd be a mere sidekick to her.

Albert cleared his throat, preventing Orla from delivering some nasty riposte. "Stay with them until I get their new quarters organized. I'll also send someone to collect the food for testing. Snake conspiracy or not, I want to know what's been used and where they might have gotten it." He looked at me and Riagán. "You'll eat with either Orla or me from now on."

Riagán nodded, and I said nothing. It would be inconvenient for both of them, but at the same time, it was a sure way to prevent any future attempts on our lives. There were a few Trinitians who wouldn't be broken up if Albert died, but they also weren't the ones who'd resort to underhanded means.

When Albert left, I passed the chair to Orla and took a spot on the bed, right beside Riagán.

"So, are you two together now?" she asked as he wrapped his arm around me. "Albert knows, I assume? It'd explain his mood lately." She made herself comfortable on the chair. "Though I'm curious. Does it have anything to do with a certain giant?"

I tensed as I remembered that time when she and Riagán met by accident, in my apartment. The stories we'd shared back then, though intended to be lighthearted, had led to me learning that Riagán saved my life back in the war. Even though we'd both kept it from Orla, she must have put together that there was something more behind those stories. I shifted uneasily, because she might also suspect that I'd had ties to the Scáthanna even during the war.

"This was when our paths crossed for the first time," Riagán replied before I could find the words, "but Kaja didn't even know it was me until... well, that day when you told the story. Not the best timing for it, so I appreciate you didn't pry back then."

She nodded with more compassion that I'd usually expect from her. Even though we didn't get along, every now and then she surprised me with tact. "Do I get the full story now?"

I'd be lying if I said I didn't feel uneasy about that. Telling the full story meant not only revealing that Riagán had saved my life but also admitting that I'd rescued an enemy back then.

At the same time, it hardly mattered anymore, even if war was to break out again. As a member of the Scáthanna, I'd be fighting against Trinity, and as much as the thought pained me, I'd made my choices, including the one to become one of the Shadows. I could only hope that when it came to the worst, I'd never be forced to deliver a fatal blow to a friend. I knew that—torn between my new family and old comrades—I might just choose death instead.

Under Orla's curious gaze, I pushed those thoughts away. Worrying about an uncertain future did no good. We could prevent the war and build bridges, bridges that would last for a long time, and stories were one way to do it.

"Sure, why not?" I said.

CHAPTER FOURTEEN

I wouldn't call breakfasts with Albert "awkward," at least not exactly, but they did have an air of oddity about them. I thought we didn't need them—it was enough if we collected the food from his office and ate somewhere else—but Albert insisted on hosting us, which led to quiet meals with mostly failed attempts at conversation. In a way, he reminded me of myself when I first met Riagán—frantically searching for any topic that was safe enough to discuss.

"Have you received any communication from our ceannasaí?" I asked before Albert could come up with yet another neutral topic none of us were even remotely interested in exploring.

Besides, after five days in Trinity, I was ready to leave. Even back when I was a humanborn, I couldn't find a place for myself within its walls, and looking like a mythborn only made things worse.

Of course, I yearned to do something to improve the relations between the former enemies, but I knew that wasn't going to happen so easily. The operation that Albert and Cathal had led together was a solid first step, though. Our presence in Trinity could be another—as long as someone didn't use it to reignite hostilities, so it would be better if we left soon. Every passing day was likely stretching the veterans' tolerance thin, and one incident would erase all those incident-free days. On the other hand, the poisoning attempt had already happened.

"No, nothing yet," Albert replied with a hint of amusement. "I should have expected you'd be dying to get out of here as soon as possible."

I gave him a sour glare and focused on my breakfast. The sooner we ate, the sooner we could get out of here. Riagán shot me a glance suggesting that he found the situation entertaining, and I was ready to swear I'd use all my contacts and information networks to learn if he'd ever had any girlfriends. I would then arrange a sit-down with all of them at once, so he could learn to be more compassionate about awkward circumstances.

He leaned back, the slight smile never leaving his lips, as if he was confident that he would survive any retaliation I could come up with.

Albert cleared his throat, and I immediately remembered where we were. Even if Riagán and I weren't openly flirting, our glances and smiles must have shown a bit too much. Not exactly something I wanted Albert to suffer.

"Maybe you should give Riagán a tour today," he said in a casual way, but I read slight uneasiness in his tone. If I was to make a guess, he still cared about me, the old Kaja he searched for when I caught him inspecting my face every now and then. "The library should be impressive enough even to a mythborn accustomed to magic."

The Trinity Library. Years ago, it was a place anyone could visit, but the Magiclysm and the war had changed things. When Trinity became a humanborn fortress, access to its grounds became limited, and no mythborn could dream of seeing the historic library. Even tourists had a hard time nowadays, because Albert had put complex security measures in place to ensure no people with malicious intent sneaked into Trinity grounds under the guise of sightseeing.

Riagán hesitated, and I could swear he was about to refuse. Perhaps he wanted to spend more time with me, or less with Albert and his people. Being stuck in Trinity affected him too.

"That's a good idea," I replied. "Trinitians should see us around in non-military circumstances."

Albert nodded. "I'll see if Orla's free. She can accompany you both so that no one gets any funny ideas."

I'd rather not consider what Orla thought about babysitting Riagán and me yet again.

When we'd told her the story of how I saved a mythborn during the war and how, unbeknown to me at the time, Riagán saved us both, she reacted with her usual dry demeanor. What was surprising was that she had also spared me any scathing comments, even though she had every right to call me a traitor—but it didn't mean she had suddenly started looking forward to spending more time with either of us.

Yet Orla was still a better choice than any other Trinitian. Even if her remarks were aligned with her general bitchy nature, at least she was willing to have something resembling a conversation. I preferred her attitude to being followed all day by someone who remained silent and brooding, making their assignment seem like the worst possible torture. Come to think of it, to many it might be actual torture to guard their enemies, the mythborn that they had fought in the war.

I nodded to Albert, showing my appreciation of choosing her. No matter how much Orla disliked the mythborn, she'd be the last one to do anything underhanded, even if she'd truly had enough of us both.

"I will also send a message to the Court, asking if Ceannasaí Cathal has any additional instructions," Albert added with a smirk. "If he knows you well enough, he'll read between the lines."

I refrained from a dramatic sigh. I didn't want to explain to Albert how I went from being stuck at the Court to being stuck at Muiredach's evil den and then to being stuck at Trinity... all while Muiredach was still out there, likely concocting another dangerous plot. Yet I had no choice, and a message to Cathal wouldn't change much.

Before I'd agreed to the risky plan Cathal proposed, he'd warned me that if I had to cooperate with Muiredach, I'd be seen as a traitor by many mythborn, and he'd need time to sort it out. Then Riagán had told me enough about the Fist of Light for me to not expect miracles and swift resolutions, no matter how much Cathal tried. I just hoped we wouldn't be stuck in Trinity for months, because that would test the patience of many more people than just me and Riagán.

Albert was looking at me with an expression that suggested he was waiting for me to say something, but I would not share those thoughts with him. If he learned that mythborn were after me, that would be it—his safeguard measure to prevent me from being imprisoned, put on trial, and sentenced would be to ensure I never left Trinity.

Thankfully, a knock on the door saved me from making up another discussion topic, because after so many meals my mind was drawing blanks, unless I wanted to inquire of Trinity's stance on dinosaurs or some other absurdity.

"We've got a problem," Orla said as soon as she walked

in. She paused, noticing me and Riagán, but when I was about to get up, she waved her hand. "It's about Jemma, so I suppose they can hear it."

"What now?" Albert asked tiredly, with clear disregard that he was about to discuss what was, in fact, Trinity-only business with two of the Scáthanna present.

Even if he was to ignore me on account of my knowing many of Trinity's secrets already, Riagán was another matter, and though he could offer some courtesy in keeping secrets, he wasn't obliged to do so.

"She making a lot of noise about how she shouldn't be imprisoned," Orla said. "She says that the accusations against her are false, made by the mythborn to sow discord in Trinity. She's arguing that during the operation everyone could see she was being held against her will. That they found her in a torture room, bound."

Albert sighed, and I felt a mixture of compassion and guilt. It seemed that my suggestion to hand Jemma over to the Trinitians was causing him trouble instead of making things easier.

"I take it that there's more?"

"Remember Samuel?" Orla grimaced. "It seems that he found an opportunity to return to his old practice. He's advising her on what to say and what demands to make."

"Lawyers!" Albert scoffed. "Next time any magical cataclysm or a war breaks out, remind me not to let just anyone to Trinity. Lawyers should be permanently banned."

I stayed silent, hoping it was Albert's frustration talking, because even though I personally shared the general sentiment about lawyers and getting them involved in anything, there were many good ones out there too. They did their jobs and helped people, so they didn't deserve unfair treatment.

This Samuel likely saw an innocent woman accused by the evil mythborn who didn't have anyone to ensure her fair treatment... That thought gave me pause.

What if Jemma *was* innocent? Muiredach could have made me see what he wanted me to see, but I'd also witnessed how obedient and docile she was. A mixture of drugs and his magic could have made her helpless against his manipulations.

I didn't allow myself to go down the compassion route. I'd spent enough time as Muiredach's prisoner to eavesdrop on her stark demands for my death. A woman who had been coerced wouldn't have asked for anything, except perhaps for her freedom or the lives of her loved ones if they were threatened.

"If we don't do something about it, things could get ugly," Orla said when silence lingered. "Samuel has started asking for some solid proof."

Albert looked at me. "Anything you can give us?"

I shook my head. "I witnessed her in situations that made it clear she was working with Muiredach, but it's her word against mine, and we both know how much the word of someone who looks like a mythborn counts. Besides, she could counter that she saw me cooperating as well, and that would make the situation even worse."

While both Albert and Orla knew the details of Cathal's plan already, no one else in Trinity did, and I wanted to keep it that way in case this information reached Muiredach.

"How well do either of you know this Samuel?" I asked.

"He's been with Trinity since the war," Albert said. "You don't think..."

"I don't know." I shrugged. "It would be so like Muiredach to stir trouble in Trinity in the hopes that I'd be forced to leave, but it could have been anyone that planted the idea in Samuel's head. Maybe Jemma asked for him if she's aware of his background."

Albert rubbed his temples. "I'd hate to have to release her."

Thankfully, he didn't notice Riagán's quick smirk. I could imagine that Riagán had a clear plan when it came to Jemma's release, and our gracious hosts wouldn't approve of a sneaky arrow in the dark, but to me, it seemed like a better choice than allowing her to become Muiredach's accomplice once more.

"I'll deal with it," Albert said when no one offered any solution. He looked at Orla. "Meanwhile, if you could take them to the library today... maybe show them around a bit. Trinity having guests from the Court shouldn't be a hush-hush thing that people gossip about."

"People will gossip either way," Orla replied dryly. She eyed our plates. "If you're done with the food, I might as well take you now. The sooner we're done, the less likely someone will want to stir up trouble."

I gave her a nod, though I was ready to spring to my feet and leave the very moment she offered. As much as I liked Albert and considered him a friend, I could only take his company in limited doses, otherwise we ended up in an argument.

"Your company is always a pleasure," I replied, adding a grin.

Orla rolled her eyes, but I caught a flicker of amusement in them, as if she had expected no less from me.

I NEVER WAS much of a reader, but back when I first saw Trinity College's library, I was sufficiently impressed. The

Long Room, with its floor-to-ceiling bookshelves, was an endless paradise for any bookworm. Even now, as I strolled through it with Riagán by my side and Orla behind us, I took in its grandeur with appreciation. Many priceless treasures had perished during the war, when defeating the mythborn seemed more important than preserving history, but Trinitians had done their best to keep the library and its contents safe, and it still drew tourists from all over the world.

Riagán looked around with an expression of polite curiosity, but I failed to see the spark in his eye that would indicate a deeply rooted love of books. No, he definitely wasn't a reader either, but it seemed he at least appreciated the collection for its historic value.

"So, am I the first mythborn to see it?" he asked.

"Second," Orla replied from behind. "Until recently, we *did* have a resident mythborn here."

I could swear there was an unspoken accusation behind her words, about how Tadgh had yet to return to Trinity. I would be surprised to learn that Orla cared about him, but it could be that she wanted him back on principle. After all, Tadgh was a part of Trinity.

Riagán let out a somewhat theatrical sigh. "And second of the Scáthanna as well."

I nudged him, amused. "Stop complaining or you might be the first dead mythborn here."

My remark wasn't all that private, but Orla showed no reaction to it. She still kept a step or two behind us, as if making sure everyone saw she wasn't friends with us but simply doing her job. I doubted she would go as far as semi-publicly complaining about Albert assigning her to body-guard duty all the time, but the distancing already grated on my nerves. Those few steps closer and several conversations would show Trinitians that mythborn could be allies or at least something other than objects of hate.

I was clearly asking for too much.

We made our way through the library. As impressive as it was, there was only so much to be amazed by unless you were actually going to browse the books and make a reading list for yourself. Even for a non-reader like me, this much was clear: libraries weren't to be admired—libraries were to be used. I could imagine books hated sitting still on the bookshelves. They wanted to be in people's hands... and in their minds.

It didn't escape me we were on display too. Over the past few days, Trinitians might have gotten used to our presence enough not to stare every time we were around, but the Long Room was full of tourists as well. They couldn't recognize us as Scáthanna members, but to them, any mythborn constituted an attraction worth viewing. Maybe in the evening, when they went out to Temple Bar to experience the authentic feel of Irish pubs, they'd get enough of such a sight, but for now, we were as good as it got.

"Cathal would enjoy this place," Riagán said with quiet somberness.

I caught the meaning. Things between humanborn and mythborn would have to get much, much better for Cathal to even consider visiting Trinity. It was one thing to risk that Riagán or I would get captured, and another to potentially hand our leader over to the enemy.

"One day..." I whispered. I hoped.

"If you've had enough looking at bookshelves, we can go downstairs," Orla said. "The museum is scheduled to reopen soon."

"Including *the* book?" I asked.

She nodded.

This was a surprise. Ever since the Magiclysm came, the museum had been closed for viewing, and even though—thanks to the efforts of scholarly Trinitians, many of them former students and lecturers—Albert had agreed to keep the Long Room open to the public, the museum and the Book of Kells remained off-limits, except for select Trinitians.

I couldn't blame him. With the war looming over us, especially in the first years of peace, he didn't want to put money into reopening the museum, including sufficient security and preservation of the exhibits. That he intended to finally let people see the book again meant he trusted the peace would last, because otherwise any additional funds would go straight to the war preparedness budget.

I pulled Riagán's arm. "Come. Second mythborn or not, it's worth seeing. It's a piece of Irish history."

He was eager to go, if for no other reason than to change our surroundings. I guessed he was getting tired of watching the rows of bookshelves and books he could do nothing with.

Orla led the way, and I allowed myself a moment of a daydream.

I pictured the day when it would be safe enough for Riagán and me to just stroll across Dublin. I could show him all of my favorite spots from the past and tell him stories of how it used to be before the Magiclysm. Then we could discover new places we both liked, perhaps some hidden gems that survived the hostilities, or the new ones created in response to the reality we were all living in.

As we walked into the museum, Riagán wasn't the only one who stopped in awe. There was little, except for the few exhibits, that looked similar to me. I didn't know whom

Albert had entrusted with renovations, but they'd converted it, and not in the way I'd have expected.

Instead of a bright and modern space full of digital displays and other technological marvels, the museum was now a place out of legends. The clever use of props, prints, and light charms made it easy to believe I had stepped onto the Emerald Isle as it was in the past. It didn't reflect any particular historical period, from what I could tell, instead capturing the heart of the old Ireland—one that even before the war was nothing but a glimpse preserved in historic buildings, artifacts, and culture.

I couldn't see everything, as the space was divided into smaller ones, perhaps like a labyrinth between trees and hills, but I could swear that one nook evoked the mood of Connemara, with its green hills on a drizzly, misty morning, complete with an ancient stone wall. A wave of nostalgia immediately hit me, as the west of Eireland, *of Ireland*, was always the most magical to me.

Beside me, Riagán took a step forward, fascination on his face... and a shadow of something else, melancholy or longing, perhaps. As if he'd touched something he thought was long lost.

As I stood near the entrance, unwilling to disturb him, Orla stopped nearby, and I caught her smirk as she said, "I was beginning to wonder if we had anything to impress a mythborn."

I thought of that one time when I showed video games to Riagán, and the other when the whole team was watching me with fascination as I performed a children's trick with an invisible message written in lemon juice, and I smiled.

"Sometimes it just takes something unexpected." I glanced at her. "Tadgh wasn't impressed? I thought he'd appreciate it."

She gave me a side-eye to clearly communicate that Tadgh—being a Trinitian, even if recently accused of treason—didn't count as a mythborn.

In the meantime, Riagán had made it to the book display.

I wasn't sure how much he or any other mythborn knew of the Book of Kells, one of the most precious, if not *the* most precious, treasure of Eireland. Sometimes I wondered whether the choice to make Trinity into a humanborn fortress early in the war came from the deep-rooted need to protect the book that was kept on its grounds. Though more likely it was Trinity's central location and a vast complex of buildings with various spaces that could be adapted to war needs easily enough that sealed the decision, I still hoped the romantic angle played its part.

The book looked exactly how I remembered it when Albert was showing me around Trinity first time I came here, except that the glass protecting the book now looked reinforced with magic as well. It only showed two pages of the book, but Riagán stood there for a long time. Whatever was his reason, I felt it would be rude to interrupt him, so I waited, and with me, Orla.

"I might have been wrong," she said all of a sudden, still watching Riagán.

If words could make one jump in surprise, Orla's confession definitely came close. Though she'd never pretended she was perfect, and had enough confidence to own up to her mistakes, she also wasn't one to make admissions unprompted... well, at least not to me. After all, we definitely weren't friends.

I didn't sense any trap, but I remained silent, letting her decide whether she was going to elaborate. It took a moment of silence, as if she were testing or teasing me with the previous remark.

Finally, with her eyes still on Riagán as if we weren't having a conversation, she added, "I still don't like you, but it's possible that you becoming a myth-touched is exactly what Trinity needs."

It took me a moment to understand what she meant, and that she was referring to the conversation we had several weeks ago, before Muiredach took me.

If I got the meaning of her words right, she thought that even though I looked like a mythborn now, within I was still the Kaja she and Albert knew, and one thing was certain: I would still be willing to visit them. And with me, eventually other mythborn would come, and over time their presence on the grounds of the humanborn-only fortress could become something normal. On the other hand, if I had stayed in Trinity, and that was assuming that I didn't die of the affliction, I'd have been just another humanborn with very little trust currency among the mythborn. Even if I returned to live here as a myth-touched, I'd be just another "resident mythborn" like Tadgh—tolerated but not exactly bridging the gap.

"I'll do my best," I replied.

And just like that, our personal moment was over. I almost expected Orla to throw in some jaded comment, but all that followed was silence as we waited for Riagán to finish his extended inspection of the book.

For non-friends, we understood each other quite well, and it was good enough.

CHAPTER FIFTEEN

To my surprise, Riagán didn't show much interest in the other parts of the exhibition, so even though he'd spent quite a while looking at the book, the visit didn't take as long as I'd expected. I'd also seen most if not all of the exhibits already during my time at Trinity, so the only novelty to me was the arrangement of the space. As magical, figuratively and literally, as it was, it couldn't hold my attention for long when my mind was circling back to Muiredach and fears of what would come next. The longer we were stuck at Trinity, the more time he had to plan his payback.

As we exited the museum, Riagán tensed all of a sudden, coming to a stop, and only then did I notice a Trinitian girl approaching Orla. I stopped as well, allowing them a private conversation... or rather letting them believe they were going to have one.

In any other circumstances, I'd be courteous enough to not eavesdrop, but the poisoning attempt had made it very clear to me that I had to abandon foolish sentiments. Our safety was more important. Besides, Orla or anyone else in Trinity would never know.

"What is it?" Orla asked.

"The commander requests your immediate... immediate..." The girl paused, clearly struggling with the formal language and tone. "The commander said you have to come as soon as you can," she finished in a more casual manner.

"What is it about?"

The girl shrugged. "The commander wouldn't say. He's waiting for you in the prison section."

Orla's expression changed, calmness replaced by concern and suspicion. "Thank you," she said, but she was already looking at us. "Albert needs to see me," she said as soon as the girl was gone. "I'll arrange for someone else to be an escort for you..." She looked around, but the closest Trinitians were at the gate.

Riagán knew I'd be listening in to the conversation, so he shot me a glance as if checking if I'd caught more than Orla was sharing. I didn't expect her to do anything underhanded, but at the same time, she could be unaware of any plots. The girl's message could be a ruse to draw Orla away from us. I hesitated. She was still scanning the yard in search for suitable replacement, so I shook my head and added a slight shrug, letting him know I wasn't sure.

"You don't need to concern yourself with our safety," Riagán said to Orla, "or the safety of anyone else, for that matter," he added playfully. "We'll spend some time alone, in a place no one will likely bother us."

As Orla looked at him with doubt, he shot her a shameless smile and pointed upward.

"We'll be on the roof."

He didn't give either of us time to fully process his response.

When he put his arm around me, pulling me close, I had less than a second to hold on to him—and then we were off, in that breathtaking rapid ascension that only a jump charm gave.

Within moments, we were on top of the roof, and Riagán set us down with enough skill for us both to keep our footing, though it was hardly a graceful landing like the ones I've seen him perform before.

"Faolan makes carrying others look much easier than it is," Riagán said. "At least no one was around to witness that less-than-perfect performance."

"There will be enough eyes on us once we go back down."

"We'll wait till nightfall, then," he replied confidently.

"Or use stairs..."

I was certain there was a stairway somewhere on the roof, because I remembered Albert had been planning to make use of the space back when I was still at Trinity. Judging by our empty and very roof-like surroundings, he never got around to it or changed his mind.

"So, why up here?" I asked.

Riagán grinned. "So that I can be the first mythborn to have a picnic with my beloved on top of the humanborn stronghold."

His amused tone reassured me that he wasn't upset about being second-mythborn "everything" in Trinity, so I allowed myself to tease him. "In human culture, a picnic is usually associated with blankets and baskets full of food."

"I had to make some concessions, this being an enemy territory, after all." He spread his arms in mock apology.

"One poisoning attempt is enough," I muttered in agreement, playful mood abandoning me.

Riagán, on the other hand, wasn't going to ruin the moment. He gave me a warm smile. "We can repeat it later at the roof of the Court." There was a seductive promise in his words. "Fine food, veenya, a blanket, and nothing but a full moon over us."

I leaned closer, pulled in by the vision, even though the more skeptical part of me wondered what Cathal and Eithne would say about such an idea... On the other hand, there could hardly be any consequences, seeing as they couldn't kick us out of the Scáthanna. Though I could see us being assigned to some humiliating duty, like assisting the Keeper of Flowers or Master of Crafts—even the mere thought of those two mythborn made me cringe.

"For now, though, we'll have to settle for the relative solitude of this roof," Riagán added with quite a theatrical sigh.

I didn't fall for the lighthearted remarks. He'd chosen the roof because it was still Trinity, but as far away from it and its denizens as we could get. Being alone in our room wasn't the same, with its closed space and people always walking by. It also, personally, reminded me of being Muiredach's prisoner, and even though I hadn't shared those thoughts with Riagán—not willing to complain, given our circumstances—he'd likely noticed my frustration growing with each day.

"Thank you," I said. "For being so thoughtful."

Contrary to most of the roofs on Trinity grounds, which were slanted, this one had a flat space in the middle, so we could walk around a bit. With Trinity buildings the same height as any other in the neighborhood, there wasn't much of a skyline to see, but it still offered a different perspective, and we sat down by a group of chimneys and vents with Dame Street to our side.

Since we were four stories above it, I could see quite far down the street, letting my mind wander. It'd been a long time since I walked down it toward Trinity, unaware that the simple assignment Albert was about to give me was going to be the first step of my life changing in ways I would have never imagined. Back then, I was dying and somewhat resigned to my fate, but now I had a new life, and I was going to cling to it desperately.

Riagán was sitting beside me, silent but calm and relaxed. He leaned his head on my shoulder, and with his eyes half-closed he looked like he was enjoying the mild though sunless weather. The ever-present breeze played with his gray hair, and by just watching him, I found myself calming and relaxing as well.

I smiled. Only he would think about a food-less picnic on top of Trinity.

"So what was so special about the book?" I asked. "You spent more time with it than anything else, and I doubt it was to give our ceannasaí an accurate account of it."

"It reminded me of the story of a similar book," he said. "It was long time ago, but back then, we'd already been in the other world for a long time, slowly forgetting about all that was here. I'm told we still had peace then, and the land was lush and beautiful."

I couldn't help imagining that world as a reflection of Ireland, perhaps just more vibrant with magic and not so cloudy. But I'd heard enough of centuries of fighting the Snake's servants to know it wasn't like that anymore. Just like the human hand had scarred the Earth, the mythborn's never-ending warfare had done the same to their home.

"One day, they say, we had unexpected guests. A handful of humans entered our world, though we never figured out how they managed to cross, with most magic gone from their lands. They brought an invitation for us to return."

A moment of silence followed, and I didn't rush him.

"We refused, of course. We had our new home, one we

didn't have to share with them. Many were convinced that they didn't want us back—just the magic we'd bring. The humans left soon after, but before they returned to their world, they gave us an offering—a beautifully illustrated book that, if tales are to be believed, looked much like the one here. It was to be a symbol of friendship between our peoples and a reminder that we would be always welcomed back."

He fell silent, and I appreciated he didn't point out that when the mythborn finally returned to this world, it wasn't a warm or even neutral welcome that awaited them. Even though so much time had passed between the promise and their arrival that humans had no record of it, not even in a half-forgotten legend, as far as I knew, the mythborn had taken care to pass the story across countless generations.

"What happened to the book?" I asked.

He sighed. "I don't know. Tales said it got lost during one of the sieges, but there's no telling whether the Snake's servants seized it or a group of mythborn managed to spirit it away and kept it safe in some secret place. Since it didn't reappear when we came here, I doubt it exists anymore. Maybe it never did." He shifted to look at me, and a smile softened his regretful expression. "But that's why I got so curious about your book. It's something not only our ceannasaí would like to see, but many mythborn scholars."

"I'm sure Albert will be willing to arrange something as long as they don't come in droves," I said. "And if he's reluctant, the Court has things to offer that would convince him."

"Crowds of mythborn swarming Trinity and trying to be polite about it." Riagán smiled again. "Now that would be a sight to see."

I chuckled, because if we could make fun of it without being concerned about shattering the peace, it meant that there was hope things would change, and at some point, war wouldn't be looming over our every thought and action like a hawk waiting to strike. But for that to happen, people like Muiredach had to be captured first.

Before I could ponder how many other Muiredachs were out there, Riagán shifted and leaned over me. His face was in front of mine, our noses almost touching, and all I could see was his smiling face and silver-shining eyes.

"I thought picnics were supposed to be fun," he said with playful disapproval, "and I have a strong suspicion that you're letting your thoughts ruin the mood. Perhaps we should return to our room, so I can remedy that."

His lips were so close to mine, all I had to do was lean forward... But even if we were alone on the roof, it didn't mean no one could see us, whether from the windows of other buildings or even further away in the street. Two members of the Scáthanna making out in public, and worse, while being guests and Court representatives at Trinity, wasn't exactly what one would call good publicity. Riagán must know it too if he'd suggested going back to the room.

"I like it up here," I replied. "It has the lowest number of Trinitians per square meter available. Maybe we should stay here a little longer."

Riagán didn't get to reply, as an arrow shot up from the courtyard straight into the sky. With reluctance, I moved away from him and stood up, convinced that Orla hadn't bothered looking for a stairway leading to this roof.

"We could pretend we didn't notice it," Riagán offered half jokingly, but he got up as well.

"She's the only one willing to talk to us." I was already making my way to the edge of the roof's flat surface. I wasn't willing to risk going down the slanted part, but thankfully Orla stood far enough from the building for me to see her.

With a measured move of her head, she indicated that we should get down. No wonder—I didn't picture her having a shouting conversation with people four stories above her.

"So much for waiting till nightfall," I teased Riagán. I doubted anyone would realize our landing wasn't perfect, considering that they would get to watch us make a jump from the roof.

"Then I'll have to do better this time." He took a step back and offered me a perfect deep bow that suggested he got a lot of practice around the Court. "Will you allow me to carry you, my dear?"

My eyebrow arched at such a formal question, I nodded. Instead of pulling me to his side, he lifted me up as if I weighed nothing and held me in his arms.

"That should help with balance," he said. "But you might want to put your arms around my neck... just in case."

I obliged, refraining from a remark that if he lost balance with us in this position, we'd both land on our faces.

And he jumped.

Having had some involuntary practice with Faolan in various situations, I was used to the sudden rush of air and magic, but was still happy I didn't have to make those jumps on my own. One day, I was sure Cathal would put me through some training—until then, I preferred to rely on others to do the heavy lifting, literally.

Riagán landed near Orla, this time almost perfectly balanced. I still felt the slight wobble as he bent one knee, but I doubted anyone noticed, as he concealed it by helping me stand on my own.

Orla waited with a stony expression and a slightly arched eyebrow, as if asking whether we were done showing off, and Riagán gave her a dashing smile.

"Do you have need of us?" His voice carried just enough amusement to suggest his playful mood wasn't going to be ruined by the dry reception to his feat.

"Albert does," she replied. "It's about Jemma."

In an instant, Riagán's expression changed, and he nodded with all due seriousness.

"Lead the way," he said.

Orla glanced at me when I nodded as well. We both knew I was so familiar with Trinity that I didn't need a guide to get anywhere on its grounds, but whether I liked it or not, I was a guest only, and a member of the Scáthanna now, so my days of roaming the ground free were over.

She gave me a slow nod back and led the way.

LIKE TADGH BEFORE HER, Jemma was held in the smaller of the two prisons. From afar, I scouted two guards posted at the entrance instead of the usual one, which suggested that the attack on Tadgh had made Albert tighten security around the building. Since there was a middle-aged man arguing with the guards, I guessed they were actually doing their job and weren't letting just anyone in.

As we approached, the man glanced in our direction, and once recognition flashed on his face, he abandoned the guards and turned to us.

"It's their doing, isn't it?"

Orla's lips twitched downward, but this was the only sign of an emotional reaction. "During the operation in Warrenmount, three Scáthanna members had access to her before our forces even made it to the building," she said. "If they wanted her dead, she would have never made it here."

"Yet here they are," he fired back. "You can't deny their involvement with my client."

"She wasn't your *client*, Samuel," Orla replied coldly. "She was a prisoner accused of conspiring with terrorists, and it was the Scáthanna's courtesy that allowed us to hold her here instead of the Court, like the rest of prisoners."

Riagán and I exchanged glances. That "was" didn't escape either of us. Jemma was likely dead, and judging by the name Orla had used, we were facing her wannabe defense lawyer.

"She was still entitled to legal counsel!" Samuel almost shouted, which didn't sound all that professional.

"And she received it from you, didn't she?" Albert's tired voice came from the doorway just before he stepped outside. "Now that very counsel makes you a suspect in her death, so no, you won't be permitted anywhere near the body until you're cleared."

The lawyer swallowed hard. "Commander..."

Albert lifted his hand. "I'll have no more of your accusations, especially directed toward our guests. Escorted at all times, they are the only ones who were actually incapable of any kind of foul play here, and they have knowledge about the terrorists that might help the investigation. If I were you, I'd stop throwing accusations and make yourself scarce. The longer you stay here, the more it looks like you're trying to get in there to remove evidence."

This had the intended effect, as the man mumbled some apologies, much less articulate than his earlier demands, and made himself scarce exactly like Albert requested. As he departed, he also spared no glance, let alone courtesy, to Riagán or me.

"Let no one else in," Albert instructed the guards as he waved us in.

We made it down the narrow corridor, and I couldn't help thinking of my previous visit to the prison. I knew another attack was unlikely, but memories, still fresh enough, tugged on my instincts. Riagán looked at me with concern, so I gave him a weak smile and shook my head— no reason to get him anxious because my own mind was messing with me.

Jemma's cell was midway down the corridor, and Albert stopped by the open door, inviting us to have a look inside.

She was lying on the bed, dead. No blood or visible signs of struggle, but her body rested in an odd position that excluded any possibility of her being asleep or unconscious, all twisted and tense. Her eyes stared motionlessly some-where at the opposite wall or ceiling—it was hard to tell with the unnatural angle of her head.

Riagán raised his eyebrow in what looked like a wordless appreciation of efficient problem solving, and I turned my questioning gaze to Albert. He had said he would deal with her, but this wasn't his style.

"I found her like that, " Albert said. "I spent the last few hours trying to figure out who had access to her this morning and who were the previous guards on duty."

"I'd recommend checking yesterday evening as well," Riagán said. "She's likely been dead for a while." His expres-sion was grim. "I've seen similar bodies, and I know of a curse that can cause them to look like this. It's commonly used by those who serve the Snake."

Albert looked at Orla, and she gave him a nod and left.

"There was something more," he said as he produced a scrap of paper from his pocket. "She was holding this in her hand."

The note contained only one sentence: *You're welcome.* There was no signature, nothing else on the paper distinct enough to help us identify the author, but I knew who it was.

I closed my fists. "Muiredach's claiming he did us a favor."

Aside from the lawyer's complaints, Jemma's death had indeed made it easier for everyone. Albert wouldn't have to suffer the humiliation of everyone in Trinity learning that he'd had a traitor for a lover, and I wouldn't be dragged into a trial as a witness when it came to light that I was also Muiredach's prisoner, which would make everyone question my allegiances and likely damage relations with the Court.

But her death was also in Muiredach's best interests, because Jemma likely knew at least some of his secrets, like his other hideouts, and I'd bet she would have been willing to trade this knowledge in exchange for her freedom or a lighter sentence. With that lawyer helping her, she could have wriggled out of the worst while putting the remainder of Muiredach's operations at risk.

I had to consider another motive as well. If Jemma had started throwing accusations at me, I could've been stuck at Trinity indefinitely, partaking in the trial as a witness or even another accused. That in turn meant I could be out of his reach for a long time, and I doubted he wanted to wait for his revenge.

"Some favor." Albert crumpled the note, making it clear no one else would see it. "Now I'll have to deal with the mess it caused, including hushing that overzealous lawyer of hers. As soon as he secures his alibi, he'll be back pestering me."

"We best leave you to it, then," I said. "Don't worry, I know the way back to our quarters," I added, because his expression suggested he was about to assign an escort to us.

We left the prison undisturbed, and when we got out of

the guards' earshot, Riagán asked, "Do you believe Albert had nothing to do with her death?"

"Yes. Why?" I couldn't blame him for asking, since he didn't know Albert as well as I did.

"If this was truly Muiredach's doing, he was unbelievably quick about it." Doubt still lingered in his voice. "It was only this morning that Orla brought the matter up with Albert."

"But the lawyer was probably making noise earlier, and I'm sure Muiredach has spies in here, just like in the Court, and Jemma was a liability to him. Besides, I'm certain he's nearby, even though he's too smart to give me any proof." I looked at him, dead serious. "I made it personal to him, and I think his desire for revenge overshadows his usual caution."

Riagán looked at me with a mix of curiosity and concern. "You have something in mind."

"It'll have to wait till we hear from the ceannasaí," I replied. "But if Muiredach is indeed so focused on revenge, it might be our best chance to get him. It's going to be risky, but I want us to be safe and free to go where we want, not endlessly stuck in places that aren't even truly safe with him still out there."

Especially, given that Muiredach's patience could run out at some point, and he'd decide that having Riagán assassinated was revenge enough. I almost shivered at the thought. He'd likely have him killed to either make me suffer or try to draw me out in pursuit of my own revenge—probably both.

Riagán pulled me closer, and we walked holding each other tightly. Several Trinitians threw glances of curiosity at us, and a few even smiled at the sight, as if seeing former enemies showing affection eased the bitterness they might feel toward the mythborn.

"It can't be riskier than what you already did," Riagán said. "And you succeeded once already."

It wasn't riskier, because if my plan succeeded, I'd never become Muiredach's captive. On the other hand, it was, since now I wouldn't be able to make a deal that would keep me safe and unharmed should my plan fail.

I said nothing, certain that Riagán knew it all already. I walked beside him, appreciating the silence that spoke of the confidence he had in me.

CHAPTER SIXTEEN

Sadb was standing in Trinity's courtyard, alone, and all the humanborn gave her a wide berth as they passed by. She didn't look threatening, at least not in any obvious manner, but she was far from relaxed, and people must have instinctively sensed she wasn't to be messed with. Anyone who thought the lonely member of the Scáthanna an easy mark was in for a nasty surprise.

She didn't relax when we approached, shadowed by Orla as usual. By now, I thought Orla was getting used to being around us, because she graced Riagán's often-teasing remarks with responses. I still remembered the time when both of them sat at the table in my apartment talking casually about archery, and I wished she could have spent more time with Riagán in less formal circumstances, away from Trinity's militant atmosphere. Riagán was by no means a representative of all the mythborn when it came to personality, but if she could warm up to him, it would be a step away from her general dislike of mythborn.

"I thought Faolan would accompany you," I said to Sadb

when we got close enough. No matter how good she was, Cathal had said we weren't to go anywhere alone.

Sadb shook her head. "It's bad enough that the Trinitians are already in a position to seize two of our members."

"Three," Orla corrected her casually.

Nothing in Sadb's posture changed, but when she looked at Orla, I could swear the air filled with an unspoken challenge. Silence hung heavy between them. They glared at each other for the longest time, and then the Trinitian bow mistress gave Sadb a nod.

"Two," she corrected her previous statement, yet there was nothing apologetic or submissive about it. It made me wonder whether Orla was truly as confident as she seemed or didn't care how dangerous the mythborn warrioress might be.

The corner of Sadb's lips lifted ever so slightly while she looked Orla up and down. Yet it didn't resemble a victor's smile, more an evaluation of someone who'd proven they might be worth more than they appeared. She might have chosen to not antagonize Orla, given we were in the middle of Trinity, or she recognized a fellow soul in her.

The sudden realization that Sadb and Orla were very much alike was a dreadful feeling, even if I got along with at least one of them.

"You beat our archer in a contest yet?" Sadb asked by way of changing the topic.

"We're both smart enough to avoid such a challenge," Orla replied with a smirk. "Too much pressure with the whole of Trinity watching, and no outcome would bring anything good."

Both mythborn standing beside us looked slightly puzzled, but I understood. If she lost, it would damage people's morale. If she won, some Trinitians could get too cocky for their own good. And after the poisoning attempt, no one needed encouragement to make the situation more volatile.

Sadb narrowed her eyes, looking straight at me. "Something happened." The tone of her voice made it clear I was to reveal the whole story to her.

I tensed. She was even less amicably inclined toward Trinitians than Riagán, so her reaction wouldn't be good. Yet not telling her would be worse.

"Some of our disgruntled veterans tried to poison our guests," Orla said before I could put the words together in some it-isn't-as-bad-as-it-sounds manner.

The grimace on Sadb's face was ugly, and she graced all of us with it equally. "And no one bothered to inform the ceannasaí about it?" Then she stared straight at Orla. "Albert promised a safe haven."

Orla shrugged, unmoved by the veiled accusation. "As safe as it can be. Many still see your kind as enemies, and we can't do much about changing their mindsets, except for making gestures like hosting two of your team as guests."

"And you?" Sadb asked coldly. "Do you see us as enemies?"

It shouldn't be a challenge, but I had a strong feeling it was. Beside me, Riagán tensed, but at the same time he put his hand on mine as if telling me not to interfere.

"Former enemies," Orla replied casually, as if the sudden shift in the atmosphere escaped her. It was more likely that she chose to ignore it. "And I trust you about as much as you trust me. But they"—she indicated Riagán and me—"are our guests, and by Albert's order, I'm to protect them. So you needn't worry I'll look the other way if someone tries to slaughter your teammates."

Sadb snorted. "I'd like to see anyone try."

The glance Orla gave me was doubtful. She knew me and my fighting skills, so she had reason to question Sadb's statement. Then her expression shifted into a cunning smile as she said, "They'd see a mythborn wearing the uniform of an elite squad. Before they realize she isn't as skilled as the rest of you, she'd likely manage to take down one or two."

I smirked when Sadb's amused expression told me that her count was at least three. But she was my trainer, so she had the best idea of what I was capable of. In a way, this was the highest unspoken praise I could have gotten from Sadb: the trust in my ability to fight. Of course, the very moment she got me back in the training room, drilling routines and practicing moves, I'd hear the full list of what I was still lacking, but clearly, the Scáthanna didn't belittle their own in the presence of outsiders.

"So how much longer will I be babysitting these two?" Orla asked. "Or are they moving in here for good?"

Sadb smiled. "I'm here about that."

I looked around. Trinity's courtyard was hardly the place to conduct any Scáthanna business, especially things I wanted to discuss away from any spies. People had given us some space, but many were still within earshot as they passed, and the guards arguing with some man at the gate were getting noisier, which suggested we couldn't count on a hushed exchange to help maintain secrecy.

On the other hand, I couldn't picture Sadb agreeing to talk somewhere more private if it meant going deeper into Trinity's grounds or being cornered in a room with one exit. I didn't blame her. As she'd said herself, Trinitians could already capture two of the Scáthanna.

"It's going to be hard to talk in private here." Riagán's words echoed my own thoughts.

At least the commotion at the gate had died out. The

guards let the man in, and for a brief moment, it seemed like he was headed in our direction, but instead, he stopped at a distance, still in the middle of the courtyard. There was uncertainty in his moves, and the expression on his face that seemed odd. Most visitors either had an idea where they were going or received an escort.

I was considering flagging him to Orla, because he could be drugged, or worse, when the man's face brightened at a woman approaching. All good, then.

I was about to turn my attention away, but the woman just passed the man instead of stopping. It looked like she bumped into him but kept going with not even a word of apology. Odd...

I immediately knew it was too late to do anything when the man froze in a spot, his face a mix of pain and shock while his body began to change. His scream carried through the courtyard, drawing everyone's attention. I'd seen this process several times already, and it always terrified me, especially back when the fear of going through the same transformation constantly lingered in my thoughts.

Even now, free of my personal terror, I still fought the panic of realizing that a humanborn was changing right in front of us.

Orla cursed under her breath. I could swear that Sadb did as well, but the warrioress was too quick to regain her composure to be sure.

Already unsheathing her sword, Sadb looked at Riagán and me. "You two stay out of the fray. Riagán, you don't leave Kaja's side no matter what." Her expression was serious and suggested she was expecting a diversion to follow. Then she turned to Orla. "Get your best team here. I'll hold it off."

Orla didn't offer her usual attitude. She never did when the situation was serious and required action. Perhaps that was why even though we didn't exactly get along, I didn't hate her. She nodded and took off.

"That's not good..." Riagán said as Sadb turned toward the changing humanborn. He already had his bow out, arrow nocked, but refrained from loosing it.

It took me only a second to realize what he was talking about. The Afflicted usually gained mass beyond their human form, as if magic swelled within and expanded their limbs and tissues, but this man was already growing way beyond what anyone with experience would consider "usual."

His body was twice the size of a human, covered with bulges that pulsated with glowing liquid. Then his skin split in multiple spots, revealing round eyes that rolled at a sickening speed.

If the sight made Sadb hesitate, I didn't notice. She launched at the creature with her sword ready.

"Is that even an Afflicted?" I asked.

"We've seen one like this only once," Riagán replied. "I hope the Trinitians are good enough, because Sadb's going to need help."

The creature was slower than Sadb but fast and powerful enough to pose serious problems. While Riagán and I stood still, forced to be spectators, Sadb was moving constantly. She didn't square off with her opponent like she did with me during my training, and I realized just how far I had to go. She danced around the hulking figure and used her blade to force it into defensive maneuvers, like she was waiting for an opening to appear. But the Afflicted's size provided longer reach, slightly longer than Sadb's, and it didn't seem to mind batting her blade aside at the cost of red gashes on its arms.

Most people had cleared the courtyard, with only few

still rushing along its edges, as if wherever they were going was important enough to risk getting close to the battle, and the guards closed the gate, though I doubted it would keep the creature inside if it decided to go on a spree through the city.

"We have to do something about those eyes," I said as it became clear the creature had no blind spot for Sadb to exploit.

Riagán hesitated.

I understood. Not only had Sadb told us to stay out of it, but she'd also given him the task of protecting me. "Look, we can move away a bit more. I'll stay by your side and within view. All you'd have to do is shoot some eyes from a distance." I looked at him somberly. "We can't lose her."

"Kaja..." Riagán started, then paused, in search of words.

But I didn't afford him the time. "Even if something happens, I'll be fine." Of course, it all depended on what that something was and how one defined being fine. "If it comes to the worst, I'll make another deal... Do anything to give you time to find me. You did it once, and I'm certain he doesn't know how..." I was unwilling to even mention the locating charm in public. I couldn't risk Muiredach learning of it. "But without Sadb, we're all worse off."

He nodded. "Eyes it is, then," he said and loosed the first arrow.

I didn't bother to check whether it hit, instead searching for a good spot for us to stand—the furthest spot within range.

"There." I pointed closer to the nearby building's wall.

There was a side entrance that would allow us to retreat if we caught his attention, but it also meant I had to keep an eye out during the commotion. Even if Muiredach's henchmen weren't around, some Trinitian opportunist could decide that a chance to get rid of us with a curse to the back was worth risking Albert's displeasure.

Riagán glanced back then returned to shooting, letting me guide him as he walked backward. Three arrows in three eyes by the time we made the wall, but the Afflicted's skin kept splitting, sprouting more.

His expression was a mix of focus and concern.

Another shaft with lighter fletching dove deep into the Afflicted's shoulder from somewhere else. Orla had returned, bow out and arrows flying as she approached. She didn't stay away like we did, instead cutting the distance and drawing the monster's attention. Her expression was a mask of calm and concentration, a clear indicator she wasn't one of those showoffs who waded into danger with disregard for plans and caution.

I wouldn't expect any adversary to stand long against two expert archers and Sadb pressing steel, but the Afflicted was quicker than its size suggested.

Orla knew where to shoot and was quick to seize its attention, but when it tried to turn and charge her, another eye met with an arrow, and Sabd lunged, forcing it to stop and defend.

The more I looked at them, the more it felt like the initially chaotic engagement had shifted into a viable strategy. Orla steadily added arrows to the Afflicted's arm and side. Riagán loosed fewer arrows, but each took out another eye. He was obviously working on one side of the target to create a blind spot. And Sadb was able to land several blows with full force.

Yet nothing seemed to make the Afflicted stop or even slow down. New eyes sprouted from its skin, each more distorted than the last, as if magic was trying to fill every cut and wound with them. Its legs were already coated in crimson, and drops of blood were flung everywhere as it lunged and swung at its opponents.

Sadb and Orla seemed to have just figured out their timing, passing the target's attention back and forth between them instead of just attacking as much as possible, when a voice called out, "Out of the way!"

Soon enough, a group of Trinitians came into view. They were in full gear, and several carried heavy chains and long spears. The cavalry, or rather Trinity's Anti-Afflicted Unit, was coming to the rescue.

They didn't slow down at the sight of the Afflicted they were dealing with, and I wasn't sure whether I should admire their confidence and courage or sigh at the stupidity of charging in without assessing the situation.

As soon as they got close, both Orla and Sadb disengaged, giving the squad space to work. Neither showed signs of exhaustion, but I'd bet they were tired enough to take a break... Well, at least Orla was, because I believed Sadb could likely go for a couple more rounds.

Riagán finally took two steps back, instead of his previous steady two steps forward each shot, lowered his bow, and satisfied his itch to survey his surroundings again. I knew, because I felt it too. He dropped back into a defensive position.

I'd seen the TAAU in action before, and from what I could tell, they weren't altering their strategy to account for the size of their opponent.

In an all-too-practiced approach, three armored infantry got in close to the target with their shields, while the chain bearers moved up behind and try to wrap heavy chains around the Afflicted. One of the chains cut the air as the Trinitian swung it in preparation, and one of those tiny voices we all have in our heads squeaked to me... The chain was too short.

I couldn't say their execution of the drill they'd likely practiced on some dummy somewhere wasn't nigh on perfect. It was just the wrong drill on the wrong target. Two of the vanguard crouched as the chain swung right over their heads, striking the Afflicted in its ribs under its raised arm. The barrel-chested opponent ignored it as the chain failed to wrap around the full two and a half times necessary for the maneuver to succeed.

I was pretty sure they knew the risks of their formation and tactics, but I was also certain the chain bearer wasn't ready to be snatched up by the chain and hammered into a wall... For my myth-touched senses, the whole sequence of events didn't even happen that fast, but I was also only an observer. In the heat of battle, everything depended on split-second decisions.

While the spearmen were encircling their quarry, finding their range, the Afflicted's massive forearm dropped onto one of the shield bearers and smashed him into the ground. The vanguard hit the dirt exactly when the chain bearer yanked the chain with all he had, in what I guessed was an attempt to pull the target off balance. The chain unwound from the Afflicted's chest, ripping some of the eyes open, but the Afflicted grabbed hold of it and, with apparent ease, snatched the chain bearer off his feet and drove its fist into his guts to send him flying.

As he hit the wall and then the ground, I couldn't help wondering whether having policies and procedures for everything was that good of a thing when people without imagination and initiative followed them. On the other hand, without all those rules that Albert had carefully implemented over the years, Trinity would likely be just a bunch of disorganized humanborn.

"Aim for the head!" Sadb shouted.

She was back in, fighting. I couldn't blame her. She'd given the TAAU enough time to show that they had everything under control... until it became clear they didn't.

Orla was shooting too. By now neither she nor Sadb seemed concerned by what the others were doing. The officer leading the TAAU called out something I didn't catch in the general commotion of the battle, but he had to be confirming Sadb's words, because the three other chain bearers swung high.

Beside me, Riagán kept his bow at the ready but didn't shoot. The way he was watching the monster suggested he was looking for weak spots or patterns in its frantic jerks and swipes while conserving his arrows.

To the side, a woman stood, way too close to be safe. She seemed reluctant, shifting her weight from one leg to another, as if her body was responding to her indecision. She looked vaguely familiar, too...

It took me a moment to recognize the woman who'd passed by the man right before he transformed. Perhaps she was trying to find the safest way to get back inside, but there was more than one door in the area that didn't require her to be anywhere near the fight. Even those who had to risk going from building to building did so along the walls, not by cutting through the middle of an ongoing battle. Did she have no self-preservation instincts?

Then she lifted her arm and I froze. Throwing a curse at an Afflicted was always a gamble, because many of them simply shrugged off any magic, but in a pinch, I'd used them myself effectively enough. Yet it was never a good idea to toss one when there were other people around that could get caught within range.

"Riagán!" I pointed at her.

He understood immediately.

She was already throwing when he loosed his arrow. It cut through the air, and with the precision that made him nearly a legend, it... missed.

Right, even the mythborn had their limits when it came to impossible feats.

As I was finishing that thought, another of his arrows flew, this time hitting the curse. Upon contact, the curse activated, and flames exploded in the air. The arrow pushed the source of the fiery tongues away before they could reach the fighters and the Afflicted.

I wanted to breathe out with relief, but the woman still stood there, staring at us with a bewildered expression. Did she have anything else to throw? Would she? As soon as Riagán's attention was on her, she turned and ran.

It was tempting to give chase, but I knew better. With Muiredach's penchant for elaborate ruses, I might be playing right into his hand.

Riagán hesitated, then turned back to watching the fight. As much as I'd prefer he'd shot the woman, it was possible that she wasn't involved with Muiredach and the curse thrown was just a poor judgment on her part. Dead, she could become a diplomatic nightmare. Wounded but alive... probably even worse.

Sadb and Orla were still fighting while the TAAU members worked on getting the Afflicted immobilized. Two of them managed to wrap heavy chains around its neck but had a hard time keeping their opponent in place. Half of the spear bearers had already lost their spears, now broken and sticking out of the Afflicted's body, so they were helping their compatriots hold on to their chains. The officer leading them was shouting something about needing more people.

Another woman successfully threw her chain. She was tall and bulky, the type who could put a weightlifter to shame, but even she wavered when the Afflicted pulled and twisted. It looked like an animated training dummy after hours of use, arrows and spear shafts jutting from every side, but was no less deadly than before the fight had started.

Sadb was right in the mix, but had to account for the TAAU members, which left her trying to maneuver amongst a formation of which she wasn't a part. Orla was free to skirt the fray and land arrows, many of which gave the TAAU the moments they needed to jam in another spear or duck a wild swing.

I had a feeling that before any reinforcements arrived, the Afflicted would break free from the binds and wreak havoc.

"There has to be something we can do," I whispered in desperation.

Riagán wasn't shooting anymore, and his hand hovered around the hilt of his short sword. "No," he said, and I knew he was responding to my urge to go and help the fighters.

I clenched my jaw. I wasn't a warrior, and strong was probably the worst word to describe me, but I still could hold the chain with the others. In situations like this, victory didn't boil down to one powerful person, and every human-born—or myth-touched—counted.

"I'm sorry," he added, his voice but a whisper.

I understood that he wanted to help too, but Sadb's order and concern for what could happen if he ignored it held him in place.

I sighed. My life had been much easier when I could do what I wanted, when I wanted, with cherished disregard of any authority, namely Albert, telling me what to do. But back then I was also alone, with only a few friends, dying of the very affliction that had claimed this poor man's body and mind. Being part of the team came with restrictions, and I would not throw away that companionship and trust just because I felt like doing something other than what I was told.

With no other ideas on how to turn the tide, I scanned the surroundings in case some other humanborn came up with another not-so-brilliant idea to jeopardize the losing fight even more.

The man looked inconspicuous enough poking out from around a building's corner—like someone who wanted to observe the fight without putting himself at too much risk. Except that his eyes weren't on the battle. Instead, he stared straight at me, and didn't turn his head away when I caught him.

I wanted to run toward him. I didn't. It wasn't even Sadb's order that kept me in place, but the clear understanding that, just like the woman throwing the curse, the man could be but a tiny cog in an elaborate trap, and running after him could mean stepping right into it. So all I did was stare back at him, memorizing his face while trying to pay attention to everything else that was going on.

The Afflicted attempted to dash forward, struggling against the chains holding it. Sooner or later, it would realize that it would be enough to jerk backward to make its captors lose their balance, but thankfully it was slow on the uptake, giving us a little more time to figure out something... anything.

Its massive hand with fat fingers more suited for

smashing than gripping hit the ground, and even at this distance, I felt the tremble. The time we had was slipping away from us.

Sadb ran by Orla so close it almost looked like she was trying to lure the Afflicted that way. She said something to the Trinitian bow mistress, but in all the commotion, I'd never thought of using my skill, so it escaped me. Orla nodded, rapidly firing arrows. They reached their target, popping more eyes, but otherwise had no effect.

The Afflicted had regained its footing, but only barely. Most of the TAAU were pulling the chains, trying to bring it to ground, while two shield bearers kept slamming their shields into its legs, and it was becoming clearer that without more people, they wouldn't succeed.

The man watching me still stood in the same spot, and I had a feeling he was waiting for me to do something.

Meanwhile, Sadb was circling the battle without engaging, headed toward us. She slowed only enough to say, "On my mark, throw and shoot your stun curses," and then dashed back toward the fray.

I pondered her request. With magic having a lessened effect on the Afflicted, and considering this one's large mass, accumulated stun curses could at best stagger it for a few seconds. I doubted she wanted to give that time to the Trinitians to reinforce their hold on the Afflicted, so she had to have something in mind. Needless to say, I couldn't conjure anything that could be effective while taking fewer than a few heartbeats to execute. But I trusted Sadb, so I fished out my three stun curses.

"Aim for the body," Riagán said. "I'll take care of the head."

I nodded. Since the Afflicted was constantly moving, even with its restricted range, it would be easy for me to miss the head. With his bow, Riagán had much better precision and therefore a higher chance of success.

The Afflicted finally roared and jerked violently. The Trinitians held tight, and one of the remaining spear bearers, a tall woman, lunged forward, aiming the tip low. The creature swung wide, hitting the woman square in the head. The poor attacker flew straight into the Trinitians holding the chain that was stopping the target from moving left, just as the chain on the other side prevented it from moving right.

They didn't exactly fall down like dominoes, planted too heavily in the ground as they were, but the impact knocked one of them down and drove the line sideways toward the Afflicted's rear, leaving the right side unchecked.

And that did cause a domino effect, since their opponent had realized it had more freedom of movement. So it jerked again, this time pulling the Trinitians off their feet.

My blood turned to ice. I knew that within seconds, the carnage would start.

Sadb had already made it to the far side of everything, and she shouted, "Now!" as she turned to face the Afflicted and charged.

I threw my curses without hesitation. Beside me, Riagán shot his arrows, and I was guessing Orla did the same, as her shafts hit from the other side.

The curses all activated in quick succession, and the Afflicted paused. The Trinitians took those moments to get their bearings and stumble away, though they were likely aware that with the Afflicted loose, none of them would reach a safe distance in time.

Sadb charged, and I watched in awe, trying to figure out what the head-on attack was supposed to accomplish.

Then she jumped, higher than anyone was supposed to be able to.

"I seriously need someone to teach me how to use the jumping charm," I said as Sadb flew through the air. Everyone on the team seemed to know how to use them and perform stunning feats, except me.

Riagán smirked. "We'll have to be somewhere much more private for that. You don't want to be seen while learning." It sounded like he spoke from experience, and I promised myself to ask Faolan or Sadb whether they'd witnessed it.

Sabd twisted in the air as she sailed right above the Afflicted and plummeted, her blade held tip down with both hands.

I froze for a moment, fearing the Afflicted would overcome the stun curses before she hit, but then her sword shot straight into its skull all the way to the hilt, and she slammed into it before falling back to the ground—on her feet, no less.

The Afflicted collapsed instantly without a sound, those ever-moving eyes frozen, and Sadb approached casually and pulled out her weapon.

I looked back at the familiar corner, but the man watching me was gone, and suddenly I knew exactly what he'd been waiting to see.

As SOON AS the battle was over, Sadb headed to us, cleaning her sword on the way and letting the Trinitians handle the aftermath.

"Is it always this exciting over here?" she asked me with

a hint of lightheartedness, as if she hadn't just risked her life to protect her former enemies.

"Never," I replied.

Sure, incidents happened in Trinity, but an Afflicted was a first, and I had a storm of thoughts in my head as I tried to put together my speculations. Everything seemed to make sense when considered alone, but together I had trouble pinpointing what Muiredach's plan might be.

Sadb matched my serious expression but didn't push. There was too much commotion around, and too many people who could catch a word or ten not meant for them.

And Orla was definitely one of the people I didn't want hearing what I wanted to discuss. She stopped a few steps away, and I could swear there was an air of restrained respect around her. I'd never thought I'd see someone able to make Orla rein in her usual attitude, but then, it didn't surprise me it was Sadb who'd left an impression on the Trinitian bow mistress.

To my surprise, Sadb gave her a short nod, no sneer or smugness in her expression, as if fighting together had made them into something more than former enemies... Even if it was only for a day.

I broke the silence first. "Can we use one of the meeting rooms? We have to talk, and it seems that Trinity has every-thing under control."

Orla waved her hand. "I'll tell everyone to not disturb you, but once you're done, I'm sure Albert would appreciate some kind of update." A shade of smirk crossed her face, as if she suspected we weren't going to share everything.

Without delay, I led Riagán and Sadb to the meeting rooms in the nearby building. It seemed like yesterday I was sitting in one of them, alone with Eithne after the meeting with Albert had concluded, and I was telling her I knew the

Court kept secrets. At the same time, with all that had happened, it was lifetimes ago... But it had set things in motion, in a way, even if Eithne and Cathal already had their plans for me, because that moment had put me on the collision trajectory with those plans.

As Sadb entered, she took the room in with the attention of a strategist, suggesting she expected to have to fight her way out of here or make a last stand. I couldn't tell whether the slight downward dip of the corner of her lips came from her assessment of the defensive value of the room or its rather spartan furnishing, but her reaction was so different to Riagán's not so long ago when he took everything Trinity in with curiosity and almost childlike excitement.

Satisfied with her inspection or not, Sadb sat at the table, moving one of the chairs to face the entrance, and Riagán leaned against the wall by the door. I hid my disappointment. We had just fought side by side with Trinitians, but these two still chose to treat them with mistrust. At the same time, I couldn't blame them, especially Riagán. He'd almost died in a place that was supposed to be safe.

I sat at the table.

"You know, if we head back, we could do this in much more pleasant surroundings, and with ceannasaí present," Sadb said.

Riagán narrowed his eyes. "That was awfully quick of the Fist to stop making problems."

"They were making a lot of fuss," Sadb said with a nod, "and ceannasaí was starting to lose patience, but then the lady intervened. She said that the Snake's spies crawl all over the Court and the city, and they're praised for their deeds while we treat anyone who's willing to risk their lives to gather information for us like traitors."

I didn't hide my surprise. Eithne didn't seem like

someone who would vouch for me if it brought no gain, and staying on Cathal's good side seemed too minor an advantage. Unless, of course, she'd meant what she said. Even if she didn't care that much about me or the Scáthanna, supporting me now would create a precedent for later, when she truly needed it.

Sadb smirked. "The lady has her moments." She looked around. "So, what's so important that can't wait until we get back?"

I took a deep breath—time to untangle the ball of guesses and speculation I had. "I think Muiredach is around."

"You think he's behind that poisoning?" Sadb asked.

"No, that was some Trinitians' idea of hospitality. Albert has dealt with it. But Jemma was conveniently murdered before she could reveal any secrets..." I lifted my hand. "No, it isn't Albert's doing. He's too righteous to resort to underhanded methods. Besides, the note left with the body, *you're welcome*, is very much in Muiredach's style."

"The murder happened quickly, too," Riagán added. "He wouldn't be able to react that fast if he was holed up somewhere far away."

She looked between us. "So, as long as you're here, you think Muiredach will be around?"

She was catching on quickly. We might not know where exactly he was, but as long as we knew where his focus was, it allowed us to plan something. But we had to act fast, before he did something or withdrew.

"I think this Afflicted was his doing too," I said. "I saw a woman bump into that man, and she could have triggered the change. Later she was attempting to throw curses to disturb the fight. It all felt like an attempt to cause maximum chaos."

Sadb didn't look convinced. "But what would he gain from it?"

I shrugged. "I'm not sure. Throwing Trinity in chaos could give him better access, or maybe he was hoping that we would leave when it got too dangerous. There's also the matter of the curse." I didn't have to say which curse. "During the fight, a man was watching me as if he was waiting for me to do something. Muiredach could have been checking if I still had the curse and was willing to use it. If I had, not only would he have a true test of its power, but it could also cause all sorts of political problems."

We kept the curse's existence secret for a reason, and if Albert learned that I—and through me, the Court—had something so powerful, it could cause all sorts of tensions. Not to mention that I'd never regain his trust if he knew that I'd created such a curse long before I became a myth-touched.

"And since you didn't use it, he can speculate that you still have it," Sadb finished. "Or somebody does."

I swallowed as I nodded, because I desperately hoped that Cathal *did* have it destroyed as promised.

Sadb stretched back on her chair. "Either way, we could have this conversation back at the Court. Judging by the relieved looks on your faces when I first arrived, neither of you is particularly interested in staying here any longer."

I hesitated. Going back to the Court meant the safety of the full team being around and Cathal's calm strategizing instead of Albert's emotion-driven decisions, but if we did go back...

I shook my head. "Not yet," I said. "Tell me, does anyone else know that I've been cleared of suspicion?"

She shook her head. "The Fist would rather pretend you

don't exist and this never happened than admit openly that they made a concession."

"Do you think they would be willing to participate in a ruse if we offered to hand Muiredach over to them?"

That got her interest. "You're thinking of another trap, aren't you? But why here? Why not do it someplace where we have allies and better control?"

"I think that at the moment Muiredach is still enraged and in pain," I said with caution. I didn't have enough insight into his mind, but from what I'd learned about him, it made sense. "He wants revenge. We could use it to draw him out, to make him make mistakes in his rush. If I return to the Court, he might take a step back, disappear and plot. Then he'll strike when we aren't prepared, and we'll be back where we started."

From his spot at the door, Riagán gave me a concerned look. He already knew I would be putting myself in danger once more, but I had no doubt he also knew that if we didn't get Muiredach, I'd be in danger all the time, and sooner or later, something would happen. I had to see it through. With a solemn expression, he gave me a nod.

"You have something particular in mind." Sadb didn't even make it a question.

"I have an idea of what might work. Ceannasaí will have to agree to it, and we'll need the Fist's help as well."

A small twitch of her mouth suggested that it could be a problem, so I could only hope that the prospect of getting their hands on Muiredach would be enough for the Fist to agree. Without their cooperation, our enemy might not take the bait. Even if he was in pain and obsessed with revenge, Muiredach was no fool. I needed something believable enough to lure him out.

"Very well," Sadb said. "Tell me what you need, and I'll let ceannasaí know."

A hint of excitement traveled through my body. No matter the risk, we had a chance of capturing Muiredach. I smiled at Sadb. "First, before I forget, I'll need your flare."

CHAPTER SEVENTEEN

The three days that followed dragged like a college lecture on... almost anything, really. But contrary to the obligatory college courses from my youth, I was more anxious than bored. Even though Sadb had warned me that making the Fist agree to cooperate could take days at best, I worried about other things. She seemed confident enough making the trip from Trinity to the Court on her own, and I knew she could take on a small army. Yet I worried that Muiredach had found some way to get to her.

Riagán was unsettled as well, though his trust in Sadb's capabilities never wavered. His discomfort had more to do with being surrounded by his former enemies. Despite Albert's remarks about peace and threatening disciplinary actions, some veterans were still open about their hate toward the mythborn in general, the Scáthanna more specifically, and one famous archer in particular. He was polite and ignored the obvious taunts, but I could feel how the whole situation grated on his nerves, and even if he was too professional to snap, I cared too much to watch him be tormented like that.

Of course, I got my fair share of taunts as well, since nobody except for Albert and Orla knew who I really was. Even though I had a better understanding of how the Trinitians felt about hosting two mythborn from the Scáthanna than Riagán, my composure was wavering as well, though for different reasons. Trinity or not, friends or foes—I was feeling trapped. For months now, I'd had none of my freedom. First Eithne's manipulations kept me at the Court, then I was training with Sadb, and when I finally got proficient enough to become part of the team, I was stuck at the Court again because of Muiredach's plots. I almost grimaced at the thought that then I was Muiredach's unwilling guest, because those memories still gave me shivers, and I preferred not to ponder how close my brush with death had been.

Now, I was supposedly free but stuck again. I couldn't leave Trinity's walls, and there were enemies lurking within them, too.

To say I'd had enough of the constant confinement was putting it mildly.

As we were sitting in front of Albert's desk, in his messy office that was always filled with more documents that one person could possibly handle in their lifetime, the commander was looking at us with curiosity. Something in our behavior must've hinted at our weariness.

"I received a letter from Ceannasaí Cathal," he said. "Nothing out of the ordinary, and oddly, no mention of plans for you two... Except for the request to pass you this." He handed a single sheet of paper to Riagán.

I held my breath as he unfolded it. It wasn't secured in any other way, but the contents wouldn't tell much to anyone trying to glean our secrets, because it would only contain one of the two code words.

Riagán looked up from the paper and nodded to me before turning to Albert. "On behalf of Ceannasaí Cathal, I'd like to request Trinity's aid in setting up a trap for Muiredach," he said in a formal manner. "Trinity, of course, will be compensated for its participation, but this would have to be discussed after the operation is concluded. For the trap to be successful and for the safety of everyone, our ceannasaí would prefer not to discuss the details until then."

I sat silent, letting him speak. Even if the Scáthanna didn't have ranks, he'd been with the team longer, so he should be the one to negotiate on Cathal's behalf. But more important, if I didn't engage, maybe Albert would agree before realizing that our plan put me in danger.

"I take it you already know the details." Albert shot me a suspicious glance. "What will you need?"

"We would appreciate if you mentioned in passing to your officers, or anyone listening, really, that the Scáthanna will be finally departing Trinity this evening," Riagán said. "The more, the better, as we're hoping for Muiredach's spies to learn about it. I will also need a female Trinitian to accompany me through the main gate, cloaked and pretending to be Kaja. I can assure you that no harm will come to her and she'll never be in danger."

Albert's head snapped to the side, and he looked at me sternly. "And where will *you* be?"

"Setting the trap with the rest of the team." I thought this was a good response that didn't go into the details of my role in said trap.

His expression told me that it wasn't *that* good—or perhaps he knew me and my evasions all too well. He looked at Riagán. "I can't agree to that." He spread his arms in an apologetic gesture, but the tone of his voice said otherwise. He wasn't even a bit sorry for refusing us.

To my surprise, Riagán nodded in a very agreeable way. "I understand, commander. It wouldn't be fair to endanger your people at our request. Trinity has already done so much for the Scáthanna."

I sensed a trap coming, and so must have Albert, because he narrowed his eyes.

"I'm glad that's settled, then." He didn't cease watching Riagán, as if looking for a reason for such unexpected compliance. "I'll be happy to provide an escort back to the Court for you both, or you're welcome to wait here for your companions to arrive."

"We'll be leaving tonight, without any escort," Riagán replied calmly, but the slight arch of his eyebrow suggested he was enjoying this exchange, or maybe the prospect of getting under Albert's skin. His personal reasons to do so aside, Albert was still a former enemy and the leader of Trinity. "Your decision doesn't change our orders, commander."

The glare Albert gave him resembled the one he usually reserved for me. "You're putting both of you in danger. I understand that you want that mythborn captured, but we'll find him soon enough, and Trinity will be aiding the search for as long as necessary. To risk your lives just to speed it up is foolish. I expected more from the Scáthanna's leader."

I wished I could see him say that to Cathal's face. As much as I admired Albert's charisma and strategic skills, he was prone to emotions, and my gut was telling me that he'd lose a pissing match to Cathal, who always seemed the epitome of composure. Even back when Cathal was convinced I was the Snake's spy, he never showed any sign of anger.

"You could help and make our chances much better," I threw casually.

The betrayed expression on Albert's face suggested that I should have stayed quiet, but we didn't have time for arguments. Contrary to his conviction that capturing Muiredach was only a matter of time, I was certain that if we allowed that conniving mythborn to plot, he'd end up besting us once more.

Besides, I had no doubt that this whole conversation was nothing more but fussing about my safety.

Albert cringed. "I can see now why you joined them." The unspoken suggestion that the Scáthanna were as reckless as I was hung in the air.

I gave him my best defiant stare. I wasn't about to let this shift into a personal discussion about my life choices and—in some instances—the lack thereof, which Albert was conveniently forgetting.

He must have gotten the message, because he let out a heavy sigh. "Fine, have it your way. In appreciation for the Scáthanna helping with the Afflicted several days ago, Trinity will aid you in your plan."

"We appreciate it, commander," Riagán replied.

Albert held his hand up. "But since you're on my grounds, you're going to do it my way. It also means no secrets or trying to go behind my back. And if you refuse, I'll have you both held here until your ceannasaí comes to collect you."

Beside me, Riagán tensed. Had it been anyone else issuing those veiled threats, they would quickly learn that the Scáthanna were not easily "held," and things would end in blood.

I touched his shoulder, unsure what to say to defuse the situation, but when he looked at me, I caught a playful flicker in his eye, as if my presence alone was enough for him to get back to his usual self.

"I can see why you left," he said with just a hint of amusement.

I swallowed my snort, because it wouldn't help the situation. Petty jabs wouldn't either, but I thought Albert deserved this one for being difficult. Now it was time to play nice again.

"Deal," I said before Albert could react to the remark. "But sharing the operation's details doesn't mean the Scáthanna owe you any other information. We will trust you with our 'secrets,' as you call them, and you will trust that we've told you everything that's relevant."

Albert grimaced but nodded. He knew he'd won as much as he could. "Very well. I'll get Orla to join us, and then you can explain to me what exactly you are planning."

As he headed for the door, Riagán and I glanced at each other. Orla wasn't part of the deal, but at the same time, we were supposed to let Albert make decisions. Besides, we still needed someone to accompany Riagán through the main gate, which meant letting at least one more person in on the plan. And if there was one Trinitian I trusted to never listen to the Snake's whispers, it was the Irish bow mistress. Hopefully, she wouldn't be too appalled by the idea of pretending to be me.

I let out a quiet sigh. Back when I'd presented my plan to Sadb, it seemed solid. I thought that I had covered all the possibilities and prepared for any outcome, for any counter Muiredach might come up with... But I'd forgotten that our supposed allies, in this case represented by one stubborn leader of Trinity, could still derail the whole thing.

Suddenly, the success of my plan seemed much less certain.

~

IN THE FALLING DUSK, Dublin looked darker than the hour would suggest. Before the war, countless city lights would make the evenings warmer and more welcoming. Without them, the buildings across the street of Trinity's side entrance looked almost sinister. Anyone could lurk within, and dark windows, their glass long broken, could hide any number of threats. Even if I knew that Muiredach wouldn't want to kill me right away, I remembered all too well the last time he got me, with a sleep curse knocking us both out.

I resisted the urge to close my fingers on the flare I got from Sadb. If a powerful enough sleep curse hit me, it would do me no good, and I doubted Muiredach would settle for half-measures if he decided to have me kidnapped in this manner. But I'd made it personal for him, and I had to hope that he'd rather come for me in person, gloating again about having seen through our plan and trap.

I chased those thoughts away. Soon, it would be time to move, and I couldn't have my wits affected by fears and speculations.

Even though I couldn't see him, I knew Riagán was standing by the main entrance with Orla by his side, cloaked and with her face concealed by a deep hood. We were of similar height, but that aside, no one would ever believe she was me if it wasn't dark.

I almost jumped when I heard Albert's voice behind me. "I thought that your archer would insist on staying with you. After that display of emotions during the operation in Warrenmount, I expected him to insist he had to accompany you. I'm surprised he wasn't more... invested."

He didn't have to say anything else. The suggestion that Riagán didn't care about me enough was more than present in the subtly mocking undertone of his voice.

"He's selling our deception," I replied with a half-truth.

He was also there so that if the plan went sideways, Muiredach wouldn't capture us both. I alone could try to make deals or lie to my captor and hope to survive long enough, but if he also had Riagán...

I didn't even want to finish that thought.

I eyed Albert with suspicion as he approached. "Why are you here?" It was dim here with the darkness falling, but I could see he wore more than his usual gear.

"You didn't seriously think I'd really let you go alone, did you?"

For a few long seconds, I was speechless. It was so foolish of me to believe that I'd won the argument we had in the morning when Albert insisted I should have an escort, and I tried to find a way to convince him it was a bad idea—from making the trap less likely to spring, through having my companion killed in said trap, and all the way to giving some Trinitians a perfect opportunity to kill me and blame it on Muiredach.

I should have known that an hour of argument after which Albert had given up didn't mean that he had finally agreed with my points.

"Then send someone with me." It pained me to say so after all the convincing that I was better off alone. "A *one*-person escort, and someone who Trinity can afford to lose." Compromises. I hated them, all the more when it came to dealing with Albert. I didn't even know why we did it to each other, those little concessions that satisfied neither of us. As if we always had to find some sort of a middle ground.

Albert didn't move.

I grimaced. With everything prepared, I had no time to argue with him, even if I was foolish enough to believe that a public fight would make him change his mind. The only other choices I could see were to either abort or keep going with the plan and hope that Albert's decision wouldn't be our undoing.

I clenched my teeth and closed my fists. There was no time to discuss it with anyone, to send word to Cathal...

I took a slow, deep breath. I had to stop thinking like Kaja and start to think like a member of the Scáthanna.

Albert knew what he was risking, and I wasn't his mother or superior to tell him what he should and shouldn't do. Besides, we had to take our chances. I couldn't claim to know Muiredach all that well, but everything I'd learned about him suggested that if we didn't catch him now, he'd gain the upper hand again, hiding, plotting, and striking when we weren't prepared. I couldn't live in fear of that happening.

Albert was still looking at me, but I ignored him, because even an annoyed "fine" seemed like too much of a concession or giving credit to his bad decision. Instead, I focused on my listening skill.

From the conversations around the main gate, I knew that Riagán and Orla were just leaving. Soon enough, I picked up her voice.

"You're enjoying yourself way too much." Orla's displeasure carried even within her careful whisper.

"And you aren't enjoying yourself *enough*." I could hear Riagán smile through his voice. "At least lean on me comfortably, because now your body's saying that you'd do anything to get away from me." Silence followed. "Now, that's better. Don't worry, it's only a few steps more. Ceannasaí and the others should be waiting by the corner."

The grumble Orla gave in response made it clear that even those few steps were far too many for her to suffer. I couldn't blame her. Not only did she have to pretend to be me, likely an insult in and of itself, but also Riagán was insisting on her being more convincing in that role, and on top of that, she was walking alone toward Trinity's sworn-enemies-turned-maybe-allies.

Then a mythborn called out, "Kaja Modrzewska, you're under arrest for betraying the mythborn and conspiring with the Snake!"

I couldn't hear anyone else, but I hoped that the Fist of Light had brought enough people along to make it look impressive... and to ensure that later, if we caught Muiredach and his lackeys, there would be enough of them to thwart any escape attempts.

"Keep your hands to yourself." Orla's response could freeze the air, suggesting the mythborn had pulled her hood down.

"A humanborn!" I was sure I caught some thinly veiled disgust in that mythborn's voice. "Ceannasaí Cathal, explain all this!"

I didn't know whether it was superb acting on his part or if he'd truly expected Riagán's companion to be Kaja—for all I knew, Cathal had made a request to the Fist without sharing details of the plan. After all, Muiredach had spies everywhere.

Cathal was talking in that always-composed manner of his, explaining that he wished to personally thank Orla for saving one of his team in the recent joint operation. I tuned out and glanced at Albert.

"Time to go." As I said it, the faint hope for him having changed his mind flickered and died the moment his expression became sharp and focused.

I pulled my hood over my head to make it look like I was trying to sneak out of Trinity while Cathal distracted the Fist of Light. My heart rattled from adrenaline overdose. So many things could go wrong, and with every step, my clever plan seemed to have more and more holes. But, as I reminded myself, in the end it didn't matter whether Muiredach knew that we were setting a trap for him. All that mattered was that he believed he could outsmart and outplay us.

Of course, cold sweat ran down my spine when I thought that he potentially *actually* could.

We walked outside the gate. The guards gave as little as a nod to their commander, as if his strolling out into the dark with a cloaked woman was a commonplace occurrence and nothing to be concerned about.

As I stepped onto the street, I wished I could share their lack of concern.

CHAPTER EIGHTEEN

The street we crossed was bustling with commerce before the war, and it still had more visitors than most other parts of Dublin. So close to Trinity, which embodied as much safety as one could get in a destroyed city, humanborn businesses thrived and drew both local and tourist customers. The lanterns in front of the small cafés glimmered invitingly, but instead of falling for their charm and the prospect of traversing a well-lit area, I led the way toward the back alleys. Even if there weren't many passersby around, I didn't want to risk that Muiredach was desperate enough to go after me in the main streets.

"When this is all over, you should consider coming back to Trinity for good," Albert said when we delved into a darker and narrower street.

Our shadows shifted when the sources of charmed light disappeared around the corner, and then they melted with the darkness in front of us. It wasn't pitch black, but I still pulled out a small light charm and pinned it to the side of my shoulder. It wobbled to the rhythm of my steps, causing the darkness to scatter like a bunch of scared spiders. Its unsteadiness probably made the possible threats less visible, but I didn't care. The two of us could handle some random thugs, and I doubted Muiredach wanted to sneak up on me.

As we walked, Albert was still looking at me, making it clear I couldn't just pretend I hadn't heard his remark.

"Albert..." The surreality of his offer aside, he could have picked a better time to discuss it.

"I know you're taking orders from Cathal now, but it seems the Scáthanna have need for our cooperation and support, so having a trusted liaison in Trinity makes sense. And Trinity itself... You always wanted to close the gap between the humanborn and mythborn, and this might be the best way to do it, don't you think?" He stopped and looked at me. "You could have your archer visit or stay with us too. If Tadgh returns as well, that would make three resident mythborn in Trinity."

It all sounded nice in theory, but there was the question of why my ex-lover wanted me around, and on top of that was inviting my current kind-of-lover while both of us were wearing the uniforms that embodied everything Trinitians hated about mythborn.

I grimaced. This *really* wasn't the time for such a discussion.

"She's not a mythborn. She's only a myth-touched." Muiredach walked into the wobbling ring of light.

He looked composed, but his handless arm kept jerking ever so slightly, and the circles under his eyes suggested he wasn't sleeping well. Considering the not-so-distant-past events and his oh-so-charming personality, his current state was a pleasant sight.

"You sound like the mythborn from the Court." For someone who, all that time, had tried to convince me that he was beyond petty differences, he'd changed his tune quickly—as soon as things didn't go his way.

"I'm much less fond of you now." Muiredach cringed and rubbed his mutilated forearm. "I tend to dislike people who deceive me."

Albert stepped forward, but I stopped him with a gesture. Muiredach might be posing as vulnerable, but playing everyone was his second nature, so I expected he was neither alone nor an easy target. Instead of reacting in a brash way, as he likely expected us to, we had to wait for him to show at least some of his cards.

"I see you're going to risk your other hand for a chance at revenge." I was playing for time. I could fire my flare and get the others to join, but Muiredach would likely flee as soon as I did, and I didn't want to risk chasing him into the dark, because that could be his scheme. I had to stick to the plan I'd laid out to Sadb and Riagán, giving the Scáthanna a chance to get to us.

"Revenge would be both entertaining and satisfactory, but you owe me a curse, Kaja. You'll make it for me." His lips curled in an unpleasant smile. "Willingly, just like the last time. And if you don't try to deceive me again, I might consider forgetting about all the ways you've inconvenienced me so far. I still believe that we could work together and that your true talents are going to waste at the Court."

It struck me right there and then. Gobán had mentioned it during one of our conversations, but at that time, it didn't make sense: Muiredach wasn't only after the curses I could make. Undoubtedly, he considered them useful and wouldn't mind having them, but they weren't the goal—they were the means. He wanted something else, something I could only give him willingly, and the deal with making the curses was a way to convince me that he could be reasonable and I could bargain with him, that we could work together. Because there was no other way he could make me use my listening skill for his own gain. No torture or blackmail would guarantee that I told the truth about what I heard, and if he couldn't trust me, he also couldn't risk sending me out to listen to anyone he wanted spied on.

I almost burst out laughing at the thought that to get what he wanted he had to do one thing he was incapable of achieving, and that was making me believe in his cause. After all the murder, torture, and cruelty by his hand I'd witnessed, there was no convincing me that the Snake was good and benevolent and wanted peace.

"I see you put it together." Muiredach watched me with a smug smile. "So now you understand that I won't give up on being your host... but for the same reason, should you choose to be less of an inconvenience to me, you'll be spared any mistreatment." He sneaked into that friendly, alluring tone he'd used with me before. "So let's not make a mess here, shall we? You'll leave with me, and your companion will return unharmed to..." His voice trailed off and he stared at Albert intently. "Why, I don't believe we've met before, commander. I'm surprised to see you here, to say the least."

The glance he gave me was a mix of disbelief and amusement. No wonder—after all the effort to keep Riagán away so that he couldn't capture us both, I was walking as bait into a trap with another man that I cared deeply about. I had no doubt he knew that, since Jemma was his informant and lover.

I stared back with a bland expression. He didn't have to know Albert's presence wasn't part of my plan, and he definitely didn't have to witness the argument-filled side of my complicated relationship with Trinity's leader.

Before I could stop him, Albert took a step forward. I didn't catch the meaning of his stern words as he spoke, because at the same moment, Muiredach lifted his hand in an odd gesture, and at that, an arrow cut through the air.

We both reacted, trained by the war, but while I ducked to the side, Albert jumped in front of me like the caring fool he was. The sound of the shaft entering his body wasn't loud, but to me, it was like an explosion. It felt as if every single cell in my body froze in terror, and I hoped, I *desperately* hoped, that Albert wasn't dead.

Then I forced myself to look at him.

Albert was still standing, his expression marred with pain, but it looked like the arrow had missed his vital organs.

"I'm fine." He huffed... and went down on one knee.

I stared wide-eyed at the shaft sticking out of his shoulder, and more so at the slimy, lava-like mass moving from it to his body. In the charm's light, it looked dark, but I knew it was blue. I'd seen it once before, when a mythborn leader was assassinated during an operation in the Botanical Gardens—a memory I wasn't keen on revisiting for many reasons, starting with the risky attempt at saving the life of said leader and ending with one of the Scáthanna, Cait, being kidnapped.

Before the feelings of terror and helplessness could take over, a magical flare brightened the sky in the distance. Its colors, my colors, reminded me that I still had a dangerous game to play. If I focused instead of succumbing to emotion, I might just win it and save Albert.

"I hope you don't mind that I took the liberty of using your flare." Muiredach's posture changed, and once again he looked like someone who had complete control over the situation. "This way your bothersome teammates will be busy elsewhere while we negotiate the terms of the commander's survival." He made an encouraging gesture. "Go on, check on him."

Albert tried to make a dismissive gesture, but the pain twisting his face was telling. Keeping our adversary in the corner of my eye, in case he tried something, I helped Albert sit down. The lava-like creature was already sprawled across his chest more than I expected.

Muiredach didn't make a move toward us and didn't signal anyone either, though we were a good target for a curse. Instead, he produced a vial from his pocket. "One drop of this could kill the larbharóin before it causes too much damage, but I'm afraid you don't have much time. Humanborn have much less magic within, and they die much quicker, so if you want to save the commander's life, you shouldn't ponder my offer for too long."

I sent him a nasty grin. "I'd hate to disappoint you again."

"It's a good deal, Kaja," he said. "Your cooperation for his life... and my forgiveness for what you've done so far." He grimaced in an uncontrolled manner that suggested he was still emotional about losing his hand.

Yet I believed he was willing to forget about it if he could get me to work for him. I suspected making me turn and betray my friends and companions could mean a greater victory to him than having me broken through torture. Though I had no doubt he'd also take out his ill feelings on someone else, another innocent victim made to suffer because of me.

I didn't bother replying. Before I tried to buy us more time, I had to ensure that Albert lived. I tossed a stun curse in Muiredach's general direction, not to hurt him but to keep him from getting close to us. As expected, he leaped backward, away from the curse's range, and he watched me with narrowed eyes as if trying to figure out what I'd wanted to accomplish, since it clearly wasn't an attack. I hoped that not knowing would make him cautious and give me time for what I had to do.

I pulled out a healing charm.

The creature was spread out so much, I doubted I'd be able to pull it away like I did back in the Botanical Gardens. Nevertheless, I activated the charm, because failing to save Albert's life wasn't an option, no matter how willing that stubborn, overprotective Brit was to sacrifice himself. The war had taught me that not all life was precious and some was actually better exterminated, but I wasn't a fan of wasting said life. Especially since Albert's life was precious *to me*, and his death wouldn't resolve anything, just bring more problems along, like hostilities between Trinity and the Court or even a new war. Problems I selfishly didn't want to deal with in the future.

Of course, if Albert knew what I had in mind, he'd object, but thankfully we didn't have time for explanations and the argument to follow.

As soon as I moved the charm close to the larbharóin, the creature stirred and pulled away from Albert's flesh. His clothes and skin on that patch were gone, and the muscles underneath looked corroded by acid. But he was conscious and still sitting up. Not bad compared to Aengus, but the mythborn commander had also suffered a serious wound to the chest.

The larbharóin wrapped itself around my hand and the healing charm I clutched, bringing pain that blurred my vision. I clenched my teeth to prevent a moan from escaping. I had no doubt Muiredach could read my reaction and likely took pleasure from it, but it didn't mean I would act like a wuss.

Nevertheless, I had little time myself, because as soon as the charm's magic waned, the creature would feed on me more ferociously. But there was a plan set in motion, and I had to trust my team would do their part. Even though my listening skill required some focus, I couldn't help using it in hope I'd hear familiar voices in the distance.

"Kaja..." Albert stared at me with eyes as round as two full moons.

In moments like this, I'd prefer he didn't remember who I was and didn't see past my mythborn-like appearance, so that he would instinctively resort to his long-nurtured dislike for his former enemies rather than the caring he had for humanborn Kaja, because he'd be less prone to doing something stupid.

"Stay back, please," I whispered. "I got this." Then I stood up and turned to Muiredach. "How's that for a counteroffer?"

He was watching the larbharóin with a calculating expression. "It's quite fitting, isn't it? A hand for a hand. But you'll lose much more if you don't kill it soon."

I didn't reply. Somewhere in the dark, I caught muffled sounds that could have been stifled screams or shouts, and that made my heart beat faster. With so many things that could go wrong, and with some actually having gone wrong, those glimpses of what was happening in the darkness gave me hope that the most important parts of my plan had gone right.

Muiredach cringed at my silence. "I didn't think you were so keen on self-sacrifice. But do you think I'll let you die? I was hoping you'd be wise enough to make a deal with me and come willingly, but I anticipated you might be too stubborn for your own good. If you'd rather be persuaded elsewhere, I can work with that, but it also means I have no use for the human-born." He pointed at Albert with his stumpy limb. "You'll be my prisoner again, and he'll die because of your obstinacy."

"I don't think so," Cathal said from behind him.

The first thing to emerge from the darkness, to accompany those cold words, was Cathal's blade. It rested on Muiredach's shoulder, deceptive in its casualness, and my ceannasaí stepped out from the shadow, never moving his weapon away from our enemy's neck.

"Your henchmen are all dead, so don't bother calling for them," he added.

I grinned. The pain of having my forearm slowly consumed—or perhaps dissolved—was growing, but Muiredach's dumbfounded expression worked better than any painkiller would.

"They knew which route I'd be taking, and they knew that if I needed help, I'd call for it using Sadb's flare," I said. "I didn't forget you got a hold of my gear." It was satisfying to have countered his deception.

Muiredach's face twisted with disbelief and anger when he realized that, once more, I had played him. He must have thought himself so cunning, setting a trap for me while pretending to fall for our trap... but with his mind clouded by emotions, he'd failed to consider that we would adequately prepare for him.

Then, all of his composure regained, he lifted his arms in a mocking surrender. "Beaten." He glanced at Cathal. "Are you going to exact revenge for your people, ceannasaí, or are your orders to take me alive, and you'll have to settle for the mere satisfaction of having won?"

Muiredach might be mocking Cathal for his

subservience to the Court, but his taunts missed the mark. He might as well try to aggravate a rock.

Cathal whistled, and within heartbeats, Riagán joined us. His eyes locked on my hand, but his tense face showed little emotion.

"Kaja, the vial," Albert urged.

"Oh yes, the vial." Muiredach grinned like a madman.

Now that he couldn't use it to convince me to agree to his terms, I expected him to drop the vial in an overly dramatic gesture. To my mild disappointment, he didn't. Instead, he twisted his head to look at Cathal again.

"Ceannasaí, I believe Kaja is in need of my help. I think we agree she has so much potential that it would be a shame to see her die here, so if you would be so kind..." He made a motion as if he was ready to hand it over.

"The Scáthanna don't make deals with the Snake," Cathal replied.

Muiredach shook his head like a father amused with a naïve child. "Really, ceannasaí? Are you going to pretend she hasn't made one already?"

"She didn't." Cathal looked at me. "Go on, tell him."

This was my reward for all the risks taken. "I was following orders. My ceannasaí told me that, should an opportunity arise, I was to let you believe you'd captured me." I looked him in the eye. "I was to stay alive no matter what and buy the rest of the Scáthanna as much time as possible. I was also told that I was to do anything that would prolong my own life, including making deals and agreeing to your demands as I saw fit for the mission's success." I allowed myself a smile. "We knew that, sooner or later, I'd have to give you what you wanted. I couldn't risk dragging it out too long, but if I agreed too quickly, you'd have been suspicious. I should thank you, since you provided me with a very good reason to agree to your demands."

Muiredach's eyes darted toward Riagán, and I watched his expression change as it dawned on him why I'd agreed to his terms without a second thought. Even if I actually was desperate to save Riagán, doing so also gave me the opportunity I needed to see to my own wellbeing and survival. I'd said yes to Muiredach's demands, ensured Riagán lived, and got two weeks of safety while I was working on the curses.

A bitter smile crept up Muiredach's face. "Masterfully done."

"That's enough." Albert's voice was unwavering, contrary to his body, which refused to obey him as he tried to stand up. "Ceannasaí, if you really want to stick to formalities, confiscate the vial and give it to Kaja yourself. She needs it now."

After he'd experienced the larbharóin on his own flesh, there would be no convincing him that I was fine... well, fine-ish.

Still, before Cathal could reply, I shook my head. "No. He has to know I never needed nor will I ever need anything from him."

"And what, you're going to die for it?" Albert blurted out. "For fuck's sake, Kaja! Don't throw your life away for some bloody bollocks those mythborn put in your head." He turned to Riagán, half angered, half demanding. "You supposedly care," he added.

Riagán stared back at him, making it clear that he wouldn't have any of Albert's accusations. "It's her decision, commander."

I could swear Albert was about to face-palm. To him, it must have felt like arguing with yet another Kaja—or a whole team of Kajas, for that matter, though ones with much less willingness to compromise and whom he couldn't emotionally blackmail.

"It's not a decision. It's her damn stubbornness!" He looked between Cathal, Riagán, and me, as if trying to figure out which of us was most likely to listen.

Muiredach smiled. "They could try fire instead, but it's a very painful and risky process." A slight move of his hand invited Albert to get the vial himself.

Cathal reacted quickly. "We'll take the vial, even if Kaja has no need for it. The Fist will undoubtedly be interested in what's inside and whether it indeed cures anything." Then he looked at me. "Kaja? What's your plan?"

What I had wasn't exactly a plan, but I hoped that the solution that had allowed me to save Aengus's life would prove once more to be helpful. "I'll need at least two healing charms. More if you have them. Fixed to something, so they can't be moved, but within reach."

Without delay, Riagán collected Cathal's charms, while our ceannasaí tied up Muiredach with the thin anti-Afflicted rope. Using an arrow, Riagán pinned the charms to a nearby window frame, and I nodded.

"Activate them, please, and then move away." I wasn't sure whether it would work, but one thing Albert had right: I was stubborn enough to try, even if it meant risking my hand.

The magic from the other charms poured out steadily and strong, since no one controlled its flow. When I walked toward it, the larbharóin stirred. Bit by bit, it peeled off my flesh, each motion sending waves of pain up my arm, and as I got closer to the charms, I limited the flow of magic in the one I was holding.

Come on, stupid creature. Go and feed on bigger magic.

As if it could hear my thoughts, the larbharóin slid off

my limb and wrapped itself around the charms. With its stinging presence gone, I stumbled backward. Uncontrolled, the healing charms wouldn't last long, and I didn't want to be within the creature's reach when it realized its magic food was gone.

As soon as I cleared the distance, Riagán tossed an incendiary curse, and the blue lava jerked like a squished spider. Unmoved, Riagán threw another one. Flames consumed the creature, slowly charring its body, and the erratic moves of the jelly-like mass grew slower and slower.

I flexed my fingers with caution, checking the damage. My hand didn't look pretty, but all the muscles and tendons were accounted for, so I wasn't about to think how long it was going to take to heal and how painful the process would be. I was still in a much better state than Albert.

It all didn't matter. The most important thing was that the plan had worked, Muiredach had fallen into our trap, and we were finally safe.

CHAPTER NINETEEN

I was still cherishing the relief that flooded my mind when the sound of many footsteps brought me back to reality. Sadb and Faolan emerged from the darkness, leading a group of the Fist of Light mythborn. Some carried long staffs with light charms attached on top that lit the area in an instant, making them look like a mystical procession, but their outfits were on the practical side. They all wore chain mail covered with muted green tabards adorned with emblems of a stylized fist. Their weapons of choice seemed to be maces and morning stars, and I had no doubt they could use them as effectively as Sadb used her sword. It didn't escape me that every single one of them had that dead-serious expression that suggested any lightheartedness around was a crime as big as aiding a Snake servant.

Yet, to my surprise, their leader approached Cathal casually, his body language suggesting he wasn't about to boss everyone around.

"Ceannasaí, was the operation successful?" he asked.

"It was. Here's your prisoner." Cathal gestured at Muiredach. "I'll also need medical assistance for one of mine and for a Trinitian who was aiding her during this mission."

It didn't escape me that he didn't mention Albert's name or his position within Trinity, and I gave him a nod as a sign of appreciation. There was no telling what the members of the Fist thought of Trinity, and just like some Trinitians saw an opportunity to kill Riagán and me, some mythborn could consider getting rid of Albert a heroic deed, worthy of any consequences. It was much less likely that they would risk insubordination to kill one random Trinitian.

At the mythborn's gesture, the Fist of Light's members spread out.

Four of them approached Muiredach as Cathal stepped away, forced him to kneel, and put charm-heavy shackles on his legs. They then put a collar on his neck—a contraption that seemed to have no lock of any sort, but as soon as it snapped together, Muiredach froze, the light fading from his eyes. Only the corner of his mouth still creased upward, in a mocking smile that made me think it would have been better if we'd killed him.

I didn't have time to ponder it, because another member of the Fist of Light headed for me and Albert.

Riagán already stood beside me, his posture suggesting he was ready to defend me from any threat, and he tensed as a mythborn female stopped in front of me.

"Kaja, yes?"

She had a pleasant voice that didn't match the unyielding expression on her square-jawed face. Her silky azure hair flowed behind her in a high ponytail. It made me think of Cait, but where Cait was playful in her behavior and perhaps slightly tomboyish in her choice of attire, this mythborn seemed businesslike.

When I nodded, she added, "The Fist will have questions for you in the future, and we would appreciate your cooperation." Her smile was barely there, but it felt like an effort she was making to reassure me I wasn't about to be arrested.

She was probably doing her best when it came to being friendly, so I wasn't about to give her attitude—if for no other reason than to not risk the Fist changing their mind about letting me off the hook. "I'll be happy to help however I can," I replied.

She seemed satisfied with my response and lost some of her cold demeanor, but Riagán still eyed her with obvious suspicion. I couldn't blame him. He'd told me enough of how the Fist had treated him after Muiredach released him. They might have not crossed any hard lines, but they weren't gentle with him either.

I also couldn't help wondering whether the Fist had agreed to Cathal and Eithne's demands only because they must have realized that if they didn't, I could be staying in Trinity indefinitely, forever out of their reach. I glanced toward the edge of the charm-lit area, where four mythborn carried immobilized Muiredach away. Compared to him, I was unimportant, and if they let me be, they could always find me in the Scáthanna's quarters.

As the mythborn female walked away, the Fist's medics swarmed us.

"I'd prefer my own team," Albert said, "but if I show up at Trinity like that, I might cause too much of a commotion."

The commotion happened regardless, because a group of Trinitians appeared at the end of the alley, and they stopped abruptly at the sight of a large group of mythborn and wounded Albert. Thankfully, it was Orla who was leading them, so I could hope for no bloodshed.

Albert sighed and let out a series of quick whistles.

I recognized the code, telling Orla and the others that everything was fine and there was no danger. "You might consider changing your signals," I said.

He looked at me and smiled. "I might. But maybe we'll teach them to our allies instead. I'm sure someone in the Scáthanna can actually whistle."

I chuckled at the subtle jab. I had never learned the art of whistling, and back when I still had ties with Trinity, I carried a wooden whistle with me to send signals.

A mythborn, his youthful face unnaturally serious, was taking care of my hand and forearm as we spoke. To my surprise, he didn't rely solely on healing charms. Instead, he produced a vial and a brush from his pouch. He used the brush to spread a translucent fluid across my skinless limb. Whatever it was, it had to have pain-numbing properties, because I couldn't feel the bristles' touch.

Beside me, several other mythborn worked on Albert's spread-out wound, and they didn't bother with brushes, pouring the liquid straight from the vials.

Only when my hand was as good as drowned in their concoction did the mythborn hold out a healing charm. Watching my skin regrow on fast forward was mesmerizing, but the show ended sooner than I'd expected. The Fist sure had some powerful magic at their disposal, and I made a mental note to pester Connor about it. Back when I was his apprentice, he'd never taught me anything related to healing charms, but at some point, he had to cave in.

"Your skin will tingle for a couple of days and might feel sensitive. Don't scratch it and wear a soft glove over it." With those words, the mythborn departed.

"Not even a goodbye?" I couldn't resist.

Riagán smirked. "They aren't the friendliest of the mythborn, but it's no wonder. Today they patch you up, tomorrow their teammates have to kill you. It's also the reason why nobody likes them." He didn't seem concerned that two of the Fist's medics were well within earshot, still working on Albert's wound.

Orla approached us, but thankfully, she'd left the rest of her team behind. They kept to themselves, watching the mythborn around them, and the Fist kept their distance as well, as if they wanted to make sure no incident was provoked.

"I don't recall *this* being part of the plan," she said to Albert.

The smile he gave her was almost apologetic... almost. "We needed some firsthand knowledge about who we were dealing with, so I made that call. Things took a slightly unexpected turn, but everything else went well."

Orla's only response was a quick head shake expressing her disbelief. I wondered whether later, in the privacy of Albert's office, she'd give him a piece of her mind about Trinity's leader running off alone into the dark, knowing that a trap was being set up. I doubted she'd succeed getting through to him. Albert might call me stubborn, but he wasn't much better. If he got something into his head, there was no changing his mind, especially when it was anything related to me.

Riagán tugged at the sleeve of my healthy arm. "Come, let's see if there's anything left to do here."

The Fist's medics finished working on Albert's wounds, but it didn't escape me that even after their healing charms, he still needed bandages. At least he looked pain-free and stood up on his own.

"Before you go," he said, "a word with you, Riagán."

Riagán shot me a surprised glance but nodded to him. I made an "I'll wait over there" gesture and walked several steps away. Not that it made any difference, because I was about to shamelessly eavesdrop anyway.

Orla exchanged goodbyes with Riagán, waved at me in a manner that could be considered almost friendly, and walked back to the other Trinitians.

"Commander?" Riagán asked when they were alone.

"I owe you an apology for what I suggested earlier."

"No need. I know you care about Kaja."

Albert huffed at that, amused, but when he spoke again, he was serious. "I'm somewhat aware of my shortcomings in... certain personal matters, but I never thought it would be a mythborn who'd make them so painfully apparent. She trusts you, and I hope you're going to always be by her side."

"I'll do my best."

I glanced at them like someone checking if they'd finished their conversation would, but I couldn't read their faces. They exchanged nods like good acquaintances, and Riagán walked over to me.

"You were listening." It wasn't a question.

I flashed a grin. What good was a skill like mine if I didn't put it to use? Besides, the Scáthanna had no problem making me eavesdrop on our own boss when he spoke to Eithne, and what they were particularly interested in was our leaders' private lives, so I figured all was fair in that regard.

Riagán smirked, and we headed for Cathal, who said, "I'll wrap up here, and you can take Faolan and head back to the Court. Get some rest, and we'll talk in the morning."

To my surprise, Riagán didn't respond. Instead, he shifted in his place, hesitating. "Ceannasaí, with Muiredach's capture, there shouldn't be any serious threat, so we don't need Faolan," he said. "And Kaja... Don't you think that after all this she deserves something more than just 'some rest'? We both had plenty of it while waiting in Trinity."

Cathal glanced at me. "Very well. Noon. Don't be late."

Riagán led me away before I got a chance to ask what they were talking about. We passed between the members of the Fist of Light unbothered and approached the dark part of the street, but my light charm still worked, promising to light the way enough for us to not trip.

Away from others, he pulled out something from one of his pouches and handed it to me. I stared at the familiar set of spare keys to my apartment. I'd given them to Riagán a lifetime ago as part of a deal we'd made back then. I knew he'd used them on occasion, though always with good reason, like taking care of my place while I was stuck at the Court and, most recently, to find something suitable for a locating charm.

I couldn't understand why he would give them back to me.

"I know you left yours at the Court, along with everything else that you didn't want to fall into Muiredach's hands," he said softly. "Ceannasaí told me." In his voice, I still caught the traces of discontent that Cathal hadn't told him about my risky mission, but it felt more like a sign of caring than annoyance.

I turned the keys in my hands, finally understanding both his intentions and the odd conversation with Cathal moments ago. Tonight, I wouldn't go back to the Court.

"Let's go home," he said, making it clear that he'd consider it home as well, should I allow it.

I smiled at him. Back when I gave him the keys, I'd made it clear that it wasn't an invitation for him to move in or... anything else, really. But much had changed since then. We'd saved each other's lives, we'd suffered the loss of our companions together, and we'd almost lost each other too. After all those years of living alone and with the shadow of death forever hanging over me, it would be nice to have an apartment that was full of warmth and perhaps a real home instead of just a place I lived in. A real home—with Riagán in it, if only for one night.

"Let's go," I replied.

Home, with Riagán. I liked the sound of it.

ABOUT THE AUTHOR

Joanna Maciejewska is a Polish-born resident of the United States. Her fiction appeared in Polish magazines (Nowa Fantastyka, Science Fiction, Fantasy i Horror, and others) and anthologies (by Fabryka Słów, Replika, Solaris, and other publishers).

You can find the full list of her publications and more about her at:
http://authorjm.com

and connect with her via social media:

facebook.com/AuthorJMac
x.com/AuthorJMac
instagram.com/authorjmac
indiepocalypse.social/@AuthorJMac
threads.net/@authorjmac
goodreads.com/authorjmac
bookbub.com/authors/joanna-maciejewska